THE DEPTH OF THEIR SCARS

Book One in The Depth Series

E. Lynn

TABLE OF CONTENTS

I would like to dedicate this book to my husband. Over the last 3,148 days (yes, I counted… Just kidding, I used a calculator), you have helped me become a more confident and self-assured woman. Over the last 103 months and 12 days, you helped me to grow and heal from the scars of my own. Without your love and support, I never would have been brave enough to allow anyone to read my writing. Even if only a year ago, I was having mini heart attacks each time you tried to read my notes.

I love you, and I hope one day I will allow you to read this—maybe in another 8 years, 7 months, and 12 days.

CHAPTER ONE

JACKIE

As Jackie twirled the phone cord around her fingers, a smile spread across her lips.

"Jaqueline, I need to know if you're going to come. Florence will need to know how many people to set the table for."

Her mother's harsh tone pulled Jackie out of her fond recollections of the housekeeper. "Sorry, I'm not sure I'll be able to make it. I need to pack for my trip to California. I'm leaving Friday afternoon," she rambled. Her mind raced as she searched for a reasonable excuse. Any excuse.

"Today is only Wednesday. Surely, you can pack tomorrow night and Friday morning."

That had been Jackie's plan all along. Realizing she did not have a viable excuse, she accepted the offer for dinner. Her mother had always been able to make things happen.

"Good. Dinner will be ready at six o'clock. Will it be only you attending?"

Jackie rolled her eyes in instant regret for accepting the dinner offer. "Yes. Just myself. Now, I'm sorry, Mother, but I really must be going. I have another call. I'll see you at six."

With that concluded, Jackie hung up. She felt slightly guilty for the lie, but she didn't want to get into the discussion of her marital status while at work. The topic was overworked and overvalued by her mother.

She did not need a husband. She'd been at the same job for the last nine years. She'd only been in this office for five years, but in that time, she'd made it her second home. Everything in it had been placed with careful consideration. All the pieces of decor fit together perfectly. She'd selected what would be added to the space when she'd moved to this office. It was hers.

The floors were original to the building. They'd been scuffed up and scratched over the years. Jackie had purchased an area rug made to look old and worn, its navy blue dulled by white distressed details. On days she had several appointments, it ended up looking more like a beach towel because of its differing colors. The dark oak desk, an antique that gave the place a look of the past, had come with the office. She'd gotten a set of four mahogany armchairs. One she'd given to Marjorie, two sat opposite her desk, and the final one was what she used daily. The delicate details on the arms and back of the chairs added class. The cushions were a heathered gray, and an accent pillow complemented each chair.

The space was neither masculine nor feminine. Anyone could feel comfortable there, which was most likely why people felt compelled to be open with Jackie. Often, during her initial meetings, people would tell her about details they would not normally share with someone they'd just met. She enjoyed meeting people as they looked for the job that would help them get back on their feet. She was the bridge between the candidates and the employers. She was in constant communication with both. She notified the various other departments that helped the candidates meet bare-minimum requirements for entry-level positions. Some people who came in needed help studying and obtaining their GED, while others needed nothing more than to be taught the basics of Excel. No matter what the reason, people came to her door for help, and she did all she could, which, in turn, led them to give her far more information than she needed to simply assess their skill sets.

Then again, this could have been the result of Jackie's kind and gentle personality, because it had been occurring since she was young. She was a good listener—too good at times. She wished she could tell people they were oversharing, but she was afraid to come across as rude.

She could feel the hope pooling in her stomach as she thought of the chance to help create another office for promoting acceptance. The chance at a new beginning. Starting today, she would prove she was capable of taking on new challenges. She knew she could run a new location. She would be happy to move where no one knew her past, far from her parents and their influence.

Determined, she began to sift through her emails. She'd only gotten through half a dozen when there was a gentle knock on her office door.

"New partnership applications!" Margie exclaimed. "Your idea to advertise for employment partners from anywhere in the state has caused an influx in emails, phone calls, and paper mail. Everyone loves the thought of all the positive PR they can get from working with us."

Margie could hardly contain her excitement. She took as much pride in the business as Jackie did, making their working relationship flawless. They each cared about the well-being of all who entered their doors until long after they'd left.

"Shall we?" Jackie asked, indicating the large stack of files in Margie's arms. She happily unloaded them onto Jackie's desk, sending a stapler clattering to the floor. The two laughed and made space on the desk for the stack.

They sorted through the folders, separating the businesses by types of work. They had retailers, construction companies, restaurants, and a law firm looking for someone to help with their filing, with the option for tuition assistance. Jackie wanted to weep after seeing all the interest they were getting. The letters of interest from the companies were so endearing. Most companies would be willing to train the right candidates.

"I don't think we could have asked for a better outcome. This is the most partner applications I've seen since I came here. Mr. Dominic will be so happy to see what you've compiled from these companies."

"Well, I didn't do this all on my own," Margie said.

Too modest to take the credit, Jackie just blushed and thanked Margie for everything she had done. For the rest of the morning, they worked tirelessly.

"Oh my! We worked straight through lunch," Margie finally said.

"I am so sorry. You should have said something." Jackie checked her watch, seeing that it was already half past two. She looked apologetically over at the other woman, who smiled back.

"Not to worry. I lost track of time myself. How about I run out to the sandwich shop and get us both a little something?" Margie offered.

"That would be fantastic."

The older woman smiled as she put down her last folder. Once she was happy with how the files were arranged, Margie left for the sandwich shop.

Jackie pushed her auburn hair from her forehead—it never seemed to stay where it was supposed to. Looking out her window, she could see Margie making her way across the street. Their office was located on a dead-end street in the middle of town. The building had previously been a multifamily residence, but five years earlier, it had been converted into an office building when Hands, Hearts, and Homes had expanded. She'd helped with the move from the company's previous office space and accepted a new position afterward.

Mr. Dominic had created the company a year after his wife passed. She had always volunteered at the local homeless shelter. He felt this was the most appropriate way to honor his wife's memory. The company helped people get back on their feet, whether that meant finding a job, learning to better manage their finances, or purchasing a home.

Margie's return brought Jackie's attention back from the window. Excited to see what Margie had brought back, she turned to face her. The sweltering heat had made Margie's face flush, even though she had only been outside for a few minutes.

"Thank you! This looks delicious!" Jackie exclaimed, not realizing how hungry she truly was until she smelled the herb-roasted turkey panini. Saliva pooled in her mouth as she thought about the homemade potato chips that accompanied each order.

"You're welcome. I'm going to eat mine at my desk. I need to catch up on calls and emails." Calls coming into their office went to Margie's phone and were then transferred to Jackie if need be.

Margie left the room and closed the door with a small metallic click. Once she was alone, Jackie hungrily devoured her sandwich and chips in a manner that would not have made her mother remotely proud. She could almost see the disgusted curl of her mother's upper lip. Oh, how she hated having dinner with her parents. She wondered why her mother had been so insistent on her going over tonight.

Upon checking the time again, she noted that it was quarter past three. If she wanted to go home and shower before dinner with her parents, she needed to wrap things up. It would take approximately an hour to get there from her apartment, and she knew better than to arrive in work attire. She replied to as many emails as possible in the forty-five minutes she had remaining. Some were job openings from their partners, some were spam, and one looked like it was from an employment partner who was unhappy with one of the individuals who Jackie's company had recommended for hiring.

With a sigh, Jackie opened the email. As she read, her brows furrowed over her hazel eyes. The employer claimed she had falsely vouched for someone who was a lazy, incompetent employee. They went on to talk about how her knack for reading people must be getting faulty and was not up to its full potential and even suggested she consider submitting her resignation. They were certain this was not the first time she'd encouraged an employer to hire a subpar candidate, considering they were all homeless and lazy leaches. The employer let her know they would be contacting Mr. Dominic about her misguided, uneducated appraisal of this candidate.

Her blood boiled through her veins, mostly from the insults directed at the people she worked with, whom she'd helped get back on their feet. Some needed a little help to get things moving, but her company always screened people and coached them to get them to a point at which they were confident in their abilities to take on a job.

But she was also angry because she'd never been accused of purposely recommending someone with an inadequate work ethic. Her mind was racing. *What business is this? Who is the candidate?* She checked the email address. It did not belong to a business—it looked like a personal email. The email wasn't even a person's name but was something a teenager would come up with.

"Sixty-nine all night? Brilliant email address." Irritated with the whole situation, she deleted the email without a response.

While she cleaned up her desk, Jackie tried to figure out if this was someone's idea of a joke. Dread sank into her gut. *This could be someone trying to scare me out of my position or intimidate me to keep from applying for the new position.*

Still fuming about the accusations, Jackie almost jumped out of her chair when she found Darrin standing in the doorway. She hadn't heard the door open. She wondered how long he'd been standing there.

"Mr. Dominic," she choked out, knocking her thighs on the underside of the desk as she stood. A curse begged to be released.

"Ms. Martinez, Mr. Dominic is my father," he clarified, eyeing her up and down. She wore a matching blazer and pencil skirt, as usual. But the blazer sat draped over the back of her chair.

"Sorry, yes. Darrin, what can I do for you?"

"Did you review the building listings?"

"I did." She tried to slow her breathing. "A few times, actually."

His scrutinizing eyes all over her body were exactly what she didn't need at the moment. *Did Darrin already see the email? Is he waiting to see if I'll admit to it?* She smoothed the hem of her blouse, hoping to keep his attention from drifting to her chest. She hated feeling men's eyes on her breasts. She usually kept her jacket on.

He flashed his handsome smile. "Good. I hope the showings go well. Good night, Ms. Martinez." He disappeared just as he'd appeared—silently.

Heart pounding, she braced herself on the edge of her desk, allowing her head to hang between her shoulders. Her auburn hair created a curtain around her eyes.

"You wanted me to let you know when it was four o'clock." Margie eyed Jackie's face critically. "Are you all right?"

Taking a moment to take a deep breath, Jackie met her eyes, "Yes, I'm fine. Is it four o'clock already?" Jackie couldn't hide her irritation.

"Y-Yes, it is," Margie stuttered, her smile faltering.

Jackie felt a flush covering her face. She could smile through anything, but her cheeks would give her away each time.

"I just finished with an email. I'll shut everything down in here and head right out. Since you didn't get to take your lunch today, please feel free to head out early." To conclude the conversation, Jackie closed her laptop with a decisive snap. It was highly unusual for her to behave so irritably.

Margie withdrew from her office, wishing her a good night. Jackie had only let Margie see her so upset one other time, more than a year ago, when Margie had told her Harmon Westerly was calling. Jackie had felt her expression fade from shock to anger and finally to exasperation. Margie hadn't pressed her for information. Jackie did not speak of her personal matters.

Hastily, Jackie packed up the remainder of the files, her anger heightened when one spilled. Bending down, she unceremoniously shoved the papers back into the file. She packed her laptop into its case and swung the large black strap over her shoulder then grabbed her purse from the small shelf behind her desk in one fluid motion. On her way out, she bade good night to Margie and Stanley, the cleaning man, who leaned against the edge of Margie's desk.

The New Mexico heat almost took her breath away when she stepped out of the air-conditioned office. It could be seen radiating above the asphalt, like wafts of steam above boiling water. The intolerable heat—not to mention the knowledge that she would soon be eating dinner with her narrow-minded mother—did little for her mood.

With an irritated huff, she made her way across the packed parking lot. The steady click of her heels carried her across the distance. Sliding into her sweltering car, she felt like the turkey going into the oven to bake on Thanksgiving. She rolled down the windows to release some of the pent-up, unbearable heat.

Jackie weaved her way through the streets of town without having to think too much about what she was doing. When the car's air-conditioner finally began working, pumping out cool, comforting air, she put the windows up. These streets had been her home for the last nine years. All the curves were burned into her mind, as were the words of that demeaning email.

She cursed herself for thinking back to that asinine letter. *How could that have come from a business? It was not very professional in its writing.* She agonized over her predicament, wondering if she should recover the email and show it to Charles Dominic herself. That would look better than ignoring it. *What if it was already sent to him, and my shot at the promotion is already blasted to hell?* Perhaps the IT department could help her find the sender.

Shaking the thoughts out of her mind like a dog shaking off the excess water after a bath, she exited her car and made her way up the front walk. She lived in a large, well-maintained apartment building with five units, each one modern and comfortable.

Taking a deep breath, Jackie could smell the moist soil, fragrant roses, and fresh-cut grass. Looking around at the lawn, she could tell the sprinklers must have just shut off. She smiled and let herself enjoy the beauty of her home.

Inside, she was greeted by the cool air of the central air-conditioning. After dropping her keys and purse onto the table in the entryway, she removed her black heels and let them fall onto the carpet with a dull thud. The apartment was the perfect size for her—one bedroom, one bathroom, and a large, wide-open living, dining, and kitchen space. She'd been living alone for well over ten years. Truth be told, she enjoyed it. No one asked her what time she would be getting done with work or where she was off to. It could be lonely, but her resolve was strong, and she would not give in to the loneliness.

She padded into the kitchen and placed her work bag on the small table. Putting on a pot of coffee, she felt determined to push the email out of her mind. While the coffee brewed, she headed down the hall to her room and selected a nice summer dress for dinner. She entered the bathroom, removed her work clothes, and turned on the shower.

Leaning over the small sink, she washed the makeup from her face. She closely scrutinized it for evidence of the struggles she'd survived. But there were no worry lines or signs of stress. The steam filling the small bathroom fogged the mirror. Jackie pushed away from the counter and stepped into the scalding spray. Even on the summer's hottest days, she couldn't resist a hot shower. She washed all the worries of the workday from herself, or tried to.

She was reluctant to leave the calm of the shower. Each bead of water worked to relieve the stressors that plagued her. But knowing how much her mother hated tardiness, she exited the shower, put on the light floral sundress, and fixed her hair for dinner. After taking one last look in the mirror, she extinguished the lights, giving a small sigh.

Jackie poured herself a cup of coffee and collected her purse and keys from the table. Then she slid on a pair of flats. She left the entry light on as she locked up her apartment, leaving the comfort of her self-imposed isolation.

Chapter Two

DARRIN

DARRIN DROPPED INTO HIS chair. He couldn't shake the feeling something was off with Jackie Martinez. Or perhaps she was always pale.

Leaning back in the chair, he wondered if she would be a good fit for the California location. *How can she run an entire location if she gets flustered over me visiting her office?*

In his gut, he knew something didn't add up. He both liked and hated being able to read people. It rarely failed him. Something was off, and he needed to make sure she wasn't going to cost him and his father everything. After all, this company had been created in his mother's memory. He would not allow it to be tarnished.

An idea catapulted him out of his chair. After knocking briefly on his father's door, Darrin found him still sitting at his desk. His white hair was cut short, but that was one of the only signs of his age.

"Dad, how set are you on being the one to be going to California? I want to take this opportunity on," he said, settling in across from his father, resting his right ankle on his left knee.

"Why the sudden interest?" Charles asked.

"I want to be part of the selection process." *And I want to watch Ms. Martinez work.*

He waited. Charles leaned back in his chair, mimicking Darrin's position. Darrin had a feeling his father wanted Jackie for the promotion and didn't want to start the meeting with words of suspicion. And he doubted his father would concede to the switch.

"You want to go with Ms. Martinez in my place?" Charles asked.

"Yes. If I'm going to be taking over for you at the end of this year, I need to make sure everything is going to be done to my standards."

Charles scrutinized him. Darrin was careful to keep his icy blue eyes locked on his father's.

"All right," Charles said after what felt like hours. "I'll let the realtor know you will be attending instead."

Heading back to his office, Darrin loosened his tie. He felt confident he'd be able to get a better read on Jackie while they were away. He would find a way to make sure she wasn't going to be doing anything detrimental to the company. She didn't seem the type to take advantage of others, but criminals weren't always what they seemed. That was likely why he kept hearing how surprised people were about embezzlement scandals. But he would not be that easy to fool.

Pausing, he asked his assistant to contact the hotel to change the booking from Charles's name to his. "Donna, why don't you head home after that. It's late—you don't need to stay just because I do."

She never complained, but he knew she had children and a husband at home. He didn't want to be responsible for her husband burning down their house. He'd overheard her telling others in the office about how he'd burned the grilled cheese one night. Who knew what other damage he would do.

Darrin knew of the rumors that coursed through the halls about him. They flew from one mouth to another without anyone considering their validity. He was the boss everyone feared. No one thought he cared about their personal lives or feelings. Unlike his father, he wasn't good with employees, making them feel at ease, although he'd once been better at that. Darrin didn't care for the rumors, but they kept people in line in his presence.

When he left, he was surprised to find that his car was the only one in the parking lot. Checking his phone, he cursed when he noticed the time. Getting to dinner on time would be damn near impossible.

He tried to have dinner with Mia at least once a month. She was always good to bounce ideas off. Her opinion was one he could count on no matter what.

He planned to ask her about Jackie's confused reaction to him earlier. *Is Jackie trying to hide something? Is she plotting to do something to the business?* The thought was foreign and was sour in his mind.

"Late again, huh?" Mia asked from their usual table in the corner of the restaurant.

Grunting, he slid into the booth. After taking a cursory glance at the menu, he decided on his usual and ordered it when the waitress arrived. She had already been to the table at least once, judging by the martini glass in front of Mia.

"I'm glad we're having dinner tonight." He smirked.

"Oh, dammit, Darrin, what the hell do you want?" Her glass landed on the table roughly. Mia was a tall, slim brunette. Her over-the-top antics never failed to improve his mood.

"I have a job for you."

Her expression changed from mock annoyance to genuine curiosity. He appreciated her friendship more than she would ever know. She'd been a constant in his life, even when he'd felt everything going out of control.

"Let's hear it," she said, picking up her glass and taking a sip.

Darrin explained his anxieties and asked for Mia's opinion and help. They spent dinner catching up and laughing about Mia's most recent dating disaster. She seemed to attract some interesting characters.

Afterward, starting his car, he felt slightly guilty for what he'd done and everything that would follow. But as he'd already learned once, a person could never be too careful. *Then again, if Mia does her job right, no one will ever know.*

Now he had to decide if he would tell Jackie about accompanying her on the trip before they left or let her find out once they got there. The latter, he figured, would be a bit harsh. Although he was feeling suspicious of her, that didn't negate all the good she had done—and was doing—for the company. He'd heard about how kind she was to all the people coming through their doors and how everyone wanted her to like them. But the question still nagged at the back of his mind—she was clearly flustered, and he wanted to know why.

He hated how each time he thought of her, he pictured the sprinkling of freckles over her nose or the way her navy skirt hugged the curve of her ass. The latter was something he should never notice about his employees.

Putting his car in drive, he formulated his plan.

Chapter Three

JACKIE

Jackie arrived with ten minutes to spare. There had been less evening traffic on the highway than she'd expected. She pulled up to the large mansion and parked in the spot that had been designated as hers when she'd gotten her license nearly sixteen years ago. She noticed another car in the drive she didn't recognize. With a sound of dismay, she exited her car.

Shuddering, she thought of the last time she'd attended a dinner at her parents' house and found the car of someone she didn't know in the drive. As it turned out, Jackie's mother had tried to force a random man on her all night. Perhaps the word *random* was a bit unfair—it was the son of one of her mother's friends. She and the man were equally uncomfortable by the end of dinner. Jackie had struggled not to laugh when he'd had to leave before dessert because of an emergency.

On her way up the front steps, she contemplated turning around and leaving. Too late—she'd already been spotted by Florence through the tall stained-glass window beside the door. There was no way Jackie could leave after seeing the excitement on the woman's face. No sooner had she placed her foot on the top step than the large solid-mahogany door was flung open, and she was pulled into a bone-crushing hug.

Seeing the woman up close rather than through the window, Jackie felt a pain deep in her soul. In her youth, Florence had been the mother figure Jackie had needed. Now she could see the lines on her face and the deep caves that held her eyes. She couldn't help but wonder when Florence had changed so much. Perhaps Jackie had been so lost in her own changes that she hadn't noticed those in the people around her.

Withdrawing from Florence's hug was bittersweet. "It has been too long, sweetie," Florence said.

With a misty smile, Jackie followed her into the formal entry of her parents' home. The marble floor shone brilliantly under the light of the chandelier hanging high above. The way it reflected made it look like it might be wet. If she jumped, perhaps she could dive below the surface and escape the inevitable events of the evening.

Pulling her gaze from the floor, Jackie turned back to Florence. "You are all too right. I've missed you." She reached out and squeezed the older woman's hand.

She felt guilty about her avoidance of the house. It wasn't her home anymore, and she found it hard to come back here. Judgments lay in wait for her around each corner of the massive home, ready to drown her.

Jackie cleared her throat, and they took a moment to catch up with one another. Jackie was ecstatic to hear of Florence's newest grandchild. She would be taking a couple of weeks off to go visit her daughter and meet the new baby next week.

Jackie removed her shoes and followed Florence into the family room, still chatting. She seated herself on one of the floral sofas facing the whitewashed brick fireplace with its impressive slate hearth. More slate flowed out to cover the remainder of the floor. It was one of the only rooms in the house that had maintained most of its appearance throughout the years, thanks to her father. She preferred the fireplace with the natural brick but hadn't bothered to voice that opinion when her mother had strong-armed her father into making the change. As a child, she'd always wondered why they had a fireplace if they rarely used it. Her mother hated the mess that was created from the wood and soot. Her father had preserved his stance on the cozy familial feel of the room even though it didn't match the remainder of the excessive house.

Jackie stood again and took some time to enjoy each of the framed photos around the room. There were some from her childhood and high school and college graduations. Leaning closer, she examined one of her at a grade school soccer game. She sported a toothless grin while her brother had his arm over her shoulder, holding her close. Her team had just won their first game that year, and Jackie had scored the winning goal.

Making her way down the wall, she saw one that caused the floor to feel like it was falling out from beneath her. Her stomach floated somewhere below her knees, threatening to splatter on the floor. Swallowing hard, she stepped away from the image while she forced the sadness to leave. She dropped into one of the armchairs facing the fireplace. She preferred the one closest to the hall—it let her see who would be coming into the house or down the hall.

Hearing voices, she turned to peer down the hall in the direction of her father's study, shaking her head to clear it of the gloom stealing her thoughts. The movement released a few strands of her auburn hair from the bun she had tossed it into. Perhaps the visitor was one of her father's clients or employees who owned the expensive sports car outside. As the voices drew nearer, Jackie recognized the other man's voice and jumped out of the chair to meet the two men entering the room. With a squeal of excitement, she launched herself around the end table to give each of them a hug.

"Wow, Jackie, you act like you haven't seen me in forever."

"Ha, you're so funny, Tony! I think it's been two years since I've seen you." She socked him playfully in the gut.

"You'd better watch it. I can still whoop you." The siblings embraced again.

"How was France? When did you get here? I want to hear all about it! Oh, and I love the new car."

Mischief sparked in his hazel eyes. "I sold my last car before I left. Needed something new. As for France, I'll tell everyone all about it over dinner—don't worry. In the meantime, I could use some predinner wine."

Tony chuckled and made his way over to the built-in cabinet on the right side of the fireplace. It had been converted from movie storage to a bar after Jackie started high school. Tony was five years older than Jackie. They had exchanged several letters and more phone calls than Jackie could count over the last two years while Tony was away. She loved getting his postcards. His descriptions of the food and cities made Jackie want to travel there herself.

Tony poured himself a drink and held up the bottle as an offer to the other two. Jackie shook her head while her father crossed the room to pour himself some of his favorite bourbon.

She had sneaked some of that bourbon when she was in high school. She'd taken a big gulp, thinking it was going to be delicious, and had done all she could to keep from spewing the liquid all over the floor. Her throat burned as if she'd swallowed fire.

It had been a dare from Tony. He was home from college, visiting with one of his friends over Thanksgiving break, and they were the only ones still awake. Her brother and his friend had each taken a large swig from the bottle. The easy way they drank gave Jackie the impression it wouldn't be that bad. Her coughing had caused the two boys to burst out laughing. That was what they'd been at the time—immature boys, even though they'd been twenty and twenty-one.

As their father poured his bourbon, Tony turned to Jackie, smirking. "Are you sure you don't want a drink, Jackie?"

She felt a smile curving her lips as she again shook her head.

Their father talked of his business and how well it was doing. Jackie hardly listened, spending more time gazing out the windows. But she didn't miss the way he mentioned wanting to have *both* his kids back at his company, needing them to continue his legacy.

She looked over at Tony. Sipping his glass of wine and talking with their father, he was calm and relaxed. She wondered when he'd changed. The last couple of years had been different from the rest of their lives, with Tony the farthest away he'd ever been. But even in her solitude, Jackie had always known her brother was there for her. She had always trusted and confided in him.

Maybe he was the reason her mother had called her to attend dinner. There was almost always something brewing beneath an invitation to dinner. The difficult part was finding out what it was before it could burn her. Perhaps this time, she could get away without any scars.

Jackie's mother, Bernadette, entered the room in one of her red satin dresses, with her hair and makeup done to perfection. Looking at her, people would never know she was in her early sixties. She made a habit of going to the salon often enough to ensure that no one would see the white that was overtaking her natural hair color. Her figure was slim and petite and her movements soft and elegant. Jackie had always blamed her mother for her measly five-foot height.

Upon entering the room, Bernadette looked Jackie up and down. Jackie suppressed the urge to fidget under her mother's scrutiny. She'd never been able to dress as well as her mother would have liked in any given situation. Either her hair, makeup, or clothing was lacking—usually all three.

Having given up on the hope of impressing her mother years ago, she plastered a smile on her face. She'd known, when she selected her light-weight sundress, that her mother would despise it. Jackie had chosen it anyway for its sheer comfort. Despite telling herself she didn't care about her mother's judgment, she still self-consciously flattened her hair, trying to tuck the loose strands back into their noose.

"Hello, Jaqueline. I'm glad to see you made it on time."

"Traffic was slower than usual this afternoon," Jackie said stiffly. Interactions with her mother were always stuffy and forced, especially when her mother made her feel like an incompetent child.

"Well, dinner is ready. It's time we go to the dining room." With that, her mother swiftly spun on her heel and headed for the dining hall. Her dress made a light swooshing sound like a bird's wings flowing through the air.

The room was larger than a family of four could ever need. The table was at its smallest but could be extended long enough to comfortably seat twelve. There was an extravagant floral arrangement with lilies and ferns. The walls were filled with paintings her mother had procured on her many trips around the world. The frames glittered in the light of the setting sun. The detail in both the paintings and the frames impressed Jackie. She longed to have such a gift as that of being an artist.

They settled into their usual seats. Jackie sat with her back to the large windows, which faced the back lawn, with Tony sitting across from her, their father at the head of the table, and their mother at the other end. Florence brought in their dinner. The meal looked amazing, the pot roast prepared perfectly and paired with twice-baked potatoes and a side salad.

Dinner was easy to wade through while Tony talked of all the adventures he'd had while he was away. He entertained them with his animated storytelling. He could liven up any room—he had a way of holding people's attention. When he told a story, they could envision the entire scene as if they'd been there.

Once dessert was served, it seemed Tony was out of narratives to entertain them. Silence settled in.

"Jackie." Her father spoke to her for the first time since their greeting in the family room.

"Yes?" She looked up to meet his green eyes.

"I want you to come back and work for me."

She hadn't worked for her father for close to a decade. His business had been her first job in high school and throughout college. She'd helped with filing and simple tasks. She had to give her father credit where it was due—he'd started his company by flipping houses, which soon led him to owning apartment buildings, and life had escalated from there. Now, she had no idea how much property her parents owned or what they'd sold their last project for. What had once been her father's enjoyment had turned into a job, a means of gaining financial security. Both her parents had quickly gotten wrapped up in the money his company could make. Jackie didn't want to be like that.

Her forced smile faltered. "I have a job. I don't need a different one." She should have known this was the direction the night would eventually take. She wanted this dinner to go well, especially since it was the first time they'd all been together in two years.

"It would be much safer for you. You meet with those filthy homeless people all day long. You need a job with a nice office, where you can move up." Her father gave a wave of his hand as if to brush away the people she helped. He looked sternly down the table at her between his furrowed gray brows.

"Please don't call the people I meet with filthy," she said, rubbing her temples. "They're people. People who need help. They've fallen on bad times and need a boost to get back on their feet." Her parents could never understand why she wanted to work at Hands, Hearts, and Homes. Although she doubted they'd ever even tried to understand her work.

"Jackie, don't be so dramatic. I want you to be realistic. I know you like to help people, but that place is so small. How are you ever going to afford everything you want in life? If you come work for me, I will pay you what you deserve." He looked pointedly around the room.

"I'm actually up for a promotion. It would mean moving to California, but that's what I want. I want to help the Dominics expand their business." She sat up straighter in her chair.

Jackie hated when someone questioned the value of what she was doing. Some of the people she'd met while working at Hands, Hearts, and Homes had changed her life. There were people who'd lost everything due to cancer, depression, divorce, drugs, and family conflicts. But the losses hadn't completely killed their spirits—they were hopeful for the future, and she was one small step in helping them achieve their life goals.

"This promotion is based on work ethic and dedication, both of which I have shown and worked hard to prove," she continued. "Working for you does not prove either. People will assume I'm receiving a promotion solely based on my DNA, not my capabilities. I want to work somewhere people are going to respect me for me, not for my family's influence."

"You cannot be considering moving." This time, it was her mother who spoke in a belittling tone.

"Yes, I am. I would love a change of scenery. Why is that so bad? Tony has been halfway around the world for the last two years!" She motioned to her brother on the opposite side of the table. Her patience was dwindling. She looked pleadingly at Tony for support, but he kept his head bowed, concentrating on his dessert, like if he stared at it hard enough it might engulf him and help him escape the conversation.

"He did leave, with the agreement that when he returned, he would come back to the company."

Shocked, Jackie turned back to her brother. "Is that true, Tony? You're going to work for Dad again?"

"Yes. That was what we discussed before I left."

Knowing her brother was going back to working for their father, Jackie felt defeated. She thought that if they both worked elsewhere, they could stand together. Now she realized she was the last person standing in enemy territory, completely surrounded, and retreat was the only way to escape. To survive.

"I'm sorry, Dad. I believe in what I'm doing. I feel like I can help make this world a better place where I'm working. I don't want to go anywhere else."

"Jacqueline, this is ludicrous," her mother said, ever in the infuriating calm tone. Her mother always refused to call her by the nickname she preferred, feeling that it was immature and distasteful.

"I am sorry the two of you cannot accept my decision, but that is exactly what it is. *My* decision!" Jackie said, almost shouting. With that final point, she shot up from the table, almost knocking her chair into one of the windows behind her.

"You could be making so much more money in a more senior position with me." Her father puffed out his chest.

Jackie took a calming breath. "I understand. This is not about money. This is about *me* and what *I* want from *my* life. I will not live it based on what someone else wants! Why can't you two accept that?"

"Jacqueline, sit back down so we can discuss your options," her mother said, motioning to her chair.

"There's no need to discuss any options, Mother. I've made my decision whether you like it or not." She rounded the table to leave.

Looking into her brother's eyes, she felt betrayed. He was supposed to help her, but she knew what kind of position that would put him in. She could see the hurt in his eyes too.

As she hurriedly slid her feet back into her shoes, her parents called her name. The last thing she heard as she slammed the door behind her was her father shouting that if she didn't come back now, she never would.

CHAPTER FOUR

JACKIE

Jackie's night was restless and aggravating. *How could Tony just sit there while they berated me?* She was furious with them all.

Was that the point of dinner from the beginning? And was Tony only monopolizing conversation throughout dinner to bring down my defenses? That must be what they were discussing in the study.

Damn him—she'd been so excited to see him. Whatever their plan, whatever their reason, she was not going to give in. If anything, this would fuel her resolve to continue to make her own way in life. Her family's views on money were sickening. Money wasn't everything.

Squeezing her eyes shut, she willed sleep to overtake her. Finally, at half past five, she glared at the alarm clock on the nightstand as if it were to blame for her mind's replay of the evening and the absence of rest. She got out of bed, showered, dressed, and prepared for work. The morning dragged just as the night had—she was sleep-deprived and irritable. She felt it in the way she moved. Her limbs were cutting and slicing through the air with their movements. This was exactly what she needed when she knew there was going to be a mountain of work to get done before she left. Fantastic—there was nothing like talking with people when all she wanted to do was scream.

She was on her third cup of coffee when she entered the office well before anyone else. After working for two hours, she heard a knock at her office door. She hoped she'd consumed enough caffeine to act like herself. Mostly.

"Come in," she called.

Assuming it was Margie, Jackie sipped on her coffee, waiting for the woman to join her. She choked slightly when she realized a man was entering her office. After placing the cup on the coaster on the edge of her desk, she straightened the hem of her navy suit jacket, stood, and invited Darrin to sit down in one of the chairs facing her. The email from the night before forced its way back into the forefront of her mind.

"Good morning, Ms. Martinez," he said with cool indifference.

"Hello. Please, call me Jackie." She extended her right hand, and he took it.

He held her hand a little too tightly as if to emphasize his authority. Something surged through her body. Her eyes flicked down to their joined hands.

Darrin gave Jackie one of his false disarming smiles. The willpower it took to refrain from rolling her eyes was impressive. He sat in the armchair that afforded him a direct line of sight to her. She wished she could use her monitor as a shield against his piercing stare. He motioned for her to resume her seat as well. With what she hoped would look like calm disregard, she straightened her skirt while wiping the perspiration off her hands, which had appeared as quickly as he had. She sat down again and calmly looked up at him.

"Do you have all your stuff packed?" he asked, studying her face.

"Excuse me?" Jackie choked on the words, trying to hide the fear in her voice but not successfully hiding the irritation.

Darrin Dominic did not make a habit of visiting his employees in person, especially not two days in a row. It was beneath him. He had all the intelligence, class, and attractiveness of his father. However, he was also blessed with an abundance of arrogance.

His and his father's managerial practices differed in the extreme. Charles Dominic took a personal interest in all his employees. He knew each one by name and could often ask about their family members with confidence. Jackie doubted Darrin knew the names of half the people on the company's payroll or would visit their offices and check on their families on a regular basis. But Darrin was in the process of taking over from his father and was becoming more involved in the everyday aspects of the business. Perhaps he was trying to engage with employees like his father had.

A sinking feeling settled deep in her belly. At this precise moment, she figured he'd taken over the duty of termination. Her stomach clenched in anticipation. She felt as if she were going to be sick. He always seemed to take pride in reminding people he held power over them and could fire them. Distractedly wringing her hands in her lap, she awaited his response.

"Are you all packed and ready for the trip to California Monday?" he asked, his brow furrowed with concern. His strong jaw was set.

Has he noticed my nerves? "I began packing last night. I'm going to finish up tonight so I can get on the road after work tomorrow." She gave a breath of relief and dropped her gaze to her hands.

"You're still committed to driving all that way?" Without giving her time to respond, he added, "I'll be taking the flight from Albuquerque to San Diego Sunday afternoon."

Snapping her head up to meet his gaze, she thought she heard a few vertebrae crack. She gaped at him, thinking her ears must have played a trick on her. "Y-You're going? I thought your father was attending this meeting with me."

"He has decided that since he'll be retiring soon after—if not before—this location is fully operational, I should go."

She couldn't erase the disbelief from her face.

"You don't have much faith in me, Ms. Martinez." This was a statement, not a question. Again, he continued before she could compose a proper response. "Do you agree with the rumors that I don't care about the people of this company or the work each person contributes?"

Snapping her mouth closed, she shook her head. "No. I'm just surprised that you would want to go on this preliminary trip. Your father is the one who set up these meetings with the property owners, and I thought he would want to be the one to select the finalists after everything he has put into it."

"He definitely wants to be part of the decision but wanted me to go out to the sites and draw my own conclusions." On the last few words, he brought his eyes around to meet hers.

For the first time, she noticed Darrin's eyes. They were a handsome hue of bright blue but also had a cool-gray tone. His statement felt like a challenge. *What exactly does he need to draw his own conclusions about?*

"I've also been informed that you would be interested in overseeing that site," he continued, still holding her stare.

Shock took over her face, and she averted her eyes to hide her embarrassment. He was far more direct than she was used to. Most people would ask if that were what she wanted, but Darrin dove right in.

"I've been here several years, and this feels like the appropriate next step. That's why your father invited me to join him on these meetings," she said diplomatically.

"Going to these meetings does not guarantee you will get the general manager position." Again, his eyes bored into hers, making it clear that this decision would also be up to him and not just his father.

With the smug look on his face, she had to force herself not to grit her teeth. Jackie had never assumed anything was going to be handed to her despite the way her parents thought she should be treated.

"I understand," she replied coolly, holding her head high, the embarrassment at being called out having fizzled in the presence of her irritation. "I intend to demonstrate why I would be the best candidate for the position. I've proven to be dependable and forward thinking, and I put my best effort forward every day."

"So I've heard." He let those words hover in the air before continuing. "But rumors aren't always what they appear." With that, Darrin withdrew from his chair and headed for the door, his dark dress pants and white button-down showing each muscle. She hated that she noticed.

Rumors aren't always what they appear. What's that supposed to mean? Jackie wondered if he was referring to rumors about him or to ones about her work ethic. She needed this promotion, but not for the financial stability it would offer her. Instead, she needed to prove to her parents that she wasn't wasting her time or whatever they thought. And she needed to prove it to herself. If this was Darrin's idea of lighting a fire under her to make her work harder and prove her value to the company, it was ignited and burning bright.

For the remainder of the day, Jackie prepared everything that needed to be done for the rest of the week. She moved about the office with swift precision. *How's that for being a hard worker?* she thought as she cleaned up her desk at the end of the day. Every folder was in its place, which was a rarity because there were always new applications coming in.

When she finished, the office was immaculate—not a paper clip out of place. The evening was spent packing and preparing for the trip. She compiled a dinner of leftovers, not wanting them to spoil while she was away. She'd made that mistake once when going on a trip and came home to a stench from the refrigerator and potatoes on the kitchen counter. It was unbearable. The dreadful smell had been worsened by the heat in her apartment. She hadn't seen the sense in leaving the air conditioner on and running up the electric bill while she was away. It had taken two weeks to get the apartment to smell of something other than spoiled milk and rotten potatoes.

Jackie cleared her plate and was dropping it haphazardly into the sink when her phone rang. She picked it up on the third ring. "Hello?"

"Jackie! You're still going to stop in and visit this weekend, right?" her friend Verity exclaimed.

"Of course, if you'll still have me. I'm planning to leave work at four, which should put me at your place by ten," she said, doing the calculation in her mind as she'd done multiple times over the last couple of weeks. "Will that be too late? I can always leave work early if you need."

"That will be fine. The kids all go to bed by eight. They'll be delighted to wake up to find you in the house Saturday morning."

Jackie smiled. She and Verity had been close in college and had done their best to stay that way. They'd learned that life sometimes had different plans and led people in vastly different directions after they completed their third year of college. Jackie's had led her back home, while Verity had stayed in college to complete her degree on time and was now the human resources manager at a hospital only a few miles from her home.

"That's great—I can't wait to see them!" Jackie exclaimed. "You're doing me a huge favor by letting me stay with you a couple nights."

"Are you kidding me? We're all excited to see you. To tell you the truth, I didn't tell the kids you were coming. If I did, it would be a replay of Christmas Eve last year. They would stay up all night just to get a glimpse of you." Verity had a way of bringing humor into all situations. It was one of her best qualities.

"We'll need to make sure we do something fun Saturday, then. I'll have another six hours to drive on Sunday," Jackie said with a grimace.

"No need to worry about that either. I don't think any of the little munchkins have slept in past five o'clock once."

The two laughed and spent the next several minutes catching up. Jackie thought about bringing up the explosion with her parents the night before, and the email, instead deciding she was too tired to rehash it. She would tell Verity about it the next day or Saturday. She wanted to see Verity's expression when she shared the news.

As she climbed into bed, her last thought was of Darrin. She was ashamed to admit he'd been on her mind all night in multiple ways. She'd thought about him going on the trip and the intimidating yet alluring way he dressed and carried himself—the crisp white shirts he always wore tucked neatly into the dark dress pants, each snug enough to give an idea of the man beneath.

Friday blew past her. There was so much Jackie wanted to get done that she could never have had enough hours. Miraculously, everything pressing was finished by three. The prep work she'd done the day before had put her in a good position. For the last hour, she finished up the detailed notes for what needed to be done in her absence. Reading through them, she figured she had been a bit too thorough, but one could never accuse her of not covering everything.

Jackie was checking her email for what felt like the fiftieth time. When she didn't see another email from her mystery partner, she released the breath she was holding. The swoosh sound notified her of an incoming email. Nearly choking on her next breath, she recognized the sender's name. Her heart was about to beat out of her chest as she scanned the screen. The email was much like the one from Wednesday night.

Resolve set in. She was going to talk with Mr. Dominic. There was no possible way this was a real person. Glowering at the screen, she composed an email to forward the asinine accusations. As she hovered over the send button, there was a knock at her door. This time—in case it was Darrin arriving unannounced again—she pressed the wrinkles out of her blouse and minimized the window she had open. She adjusted the hem of her plaid pencil skirt and corrected the collar of her blouse.

"Yes, come in."

Without preamble, her visitor entered and dove straight to the point of his visit after securing the door closed. "I heard you think you're going to get the general manager position," Todd said. "I've been here since the beginning. Don't get your heart set on relocating. I will have that promotion." He slapped his hand on the desk in front of her.

Furrowing her brow, she said slowly, "Todd, I have just as much right to apply for the position as you do."

Jackie's calm response seemed to aggravate him. His eyes widened as he paced her office.

Sure that there was something wrong, she walked around her desk to check on him. "Todd, what's wrong?"

"I have a great relationship with Darrin. We've been friends for years. Don't think you're going to sweet-talk your way into what should be mine."

"Look, I don't know what you're talking about, but I certainly don't *sweet-talk* my way into anything. I will be applying for that position," she said with an edge to her voice, losing her grip on her patience. "The person best suited will be selected."

"Huh. I've seen what women like you do. Come in here, throwing your bodies around to make sure the men see you. Is that how you got this office in the first place?" He spun around, looking at the room.

Rage was welling up inside her. Her skin went hot. The urge to slap his oily face was ready to boil over. "I think you need to go. Now." Holding onto the last thread of composure, she pulled the door open for him to leave. In a voice only he could hear, she added, "don't you ever speak to me like that again."

Todd left her office, making it a point to nudge the door, causing the handle to crack into her hip bone. Stunned, Jackie closed the door behind him and leaned against it. Her chest was heaving with the effort to take calm, steady breaths. Her hand stayed splayed over her pained hip.

This was not turning out to be a good week. Todd was acting strange. They'd always gotten along fine—they'd never shared a cross word.

Shaking off the nerves that had barged in, much like Todd had, she tried to force her mind to settle. As she shuffled back to her desk, her mind raced. Bracing herself on the edge, she shook her head, loosening a few hairs from her tight bun. Satisfied that she was as calm as she was going to get, Jackie started packing. She collected her hotel information, laptop, purse, keys, and files on locations of interest.

Astoundingly, she made it out of her office without dropping anything. She shifted her keys in her loaded hands and locked the door. "Have a great weekend and week, Margie. I probably won't be in the office until next Friday."

"Thanks. You too. Travel safely."

As she approached her car, a shadow loomed over hers on the asphalt. It was vastly larger than hers. She carefully tried to recall what she'd always been told to do if approached in a parking lot.

Damn! What was it? Of course. Carry your keys in your fist with a key pointing out. Ironically, keys were exactly what she was struggling to find. She'd already dropped her work keys into her purse and was searching for her car keys while balancing everything precariously on one arm. She couldn't easily turn and see who was walking toward her. Heart thumping, she struggled with shaking hands. The sound of the keys rolling around intensified her haste.

Feeling a touch on her shoulder, she gasped and let her instincts take over. She dropped everything in her left hand and spun around as hard as she could with her elbow out. She caught him square in the abdomen.

He doubled over in pain. She felt triumphant for only a moment. Her blood ran cold as realization set in.

"Oh my. Oh no. I'm so sorry. I-I panicked," Jackie stammered as she placed a consoling hand on her brother's shoulder.

Anguished at seeing him in pain, she apologized again to the top of his head. Tony's dark hair was longer than most men's, but it suited him. He always moved to the beat of his own drum. She often found herself admiring him for his self-assurance. But at present, she was watching the way it bobbed with his ragged breaths.

He coughed a few times and looked up at her with a grin. "Well, I'm glad you can handle yourself. That would have worked on anyone who tried to attack you." He laughed, wincing.

"Tony, why were you sneaking up on me, anyway?"

"I wasn't exactly sneaking. Anyone could have heard me walking over to you. It's friggin' broad daylight, Jackie," he said, making a show of looking around the parking lot. "What's got you so spooked?"

"N-Nothing. I was just thinking about my trip, off in my own world, when you touched me." She wondered why she wasn't telling him about Todd and the emails. He could help her work it out—but she couldn't do it.

"That's kind of why I'm here. I wanted to apologize about dinner before you left," he said, dropping his eyes to his polished shoes. "I knew Dad was going to ask you to come back, but I didn't know things were going to go like that. I didn't even think he was going to bring it up that soon." His earnest face eased the anxieties she'd been harboring that he was a pawn in their father's plan. "If I'd known, I would have warned you."

"Thank you."

"I'm sorry, Jackie, really. I just didn't want you leaving on your trip thinking I set you up."

She pursed her lips and glared at him.

"I'm right, aren't I?" he asked with a knowing smile. "You're so predictable. But really, I would have given you fair warning if I knew it was going to be brought up last night. Before dinner, I was actually trying to figure out a way to tell you that it was coming at some point, but I didn't get the chance." He frowned.

"I appreciate that. Now, help me clean this up," she said with a sly smile.

Tony helped her pick up the files she'd dropped. Fortunately, everything was still secured within. Once she and all her belongings were safely deposited in her car, she gave her brother a hug, promising they would get together when she got back.

"Are you still going to pop into Verity's?" he asked, leaning into the window of her small sedan.

"Yeah. I'm staying with her tonight and tomorrow night then going to the hotel Sunday evening."

"Text me when you get there, please? I don't like you driving all that way alone," he said, taking a step back.

In mock exaggeration, Jackie rolled her eyes. "Yes, I will."

"I'll get you back, just so you know. I probably have a couple broken ribs. One of my organs has to be damaged." He chuckled, tapping the roof as his goodbye.

Chapter Five

JACKIE

Feeling moderately better about the events of the last couple of days, Jackie pulled out onto the highway. She anticipated the ride ahead of her to be uneventful and mundane. She could use some peace and quiet. She needed to think. *What is happening to my life? Everything was just beginning to fall back into place, and now the pieces don't seem to fit right.* It was as if someone had poured water all over the pieces, and they'd become distorted and misshapen.

She drove half the distance before allowing herself to stop for sustenance. Choosing the closest fast-food chain to the highway, Jackie went inside to order so she could also use the restroom. Back in her car, she freed her haphazardly wrapped burger, and lettuce rained down on her skirt as she merged back onto the highway. Looking down at the green confetti, she brushed it from her lap. She would need to clean that up in the morning. The meal wasn't terrible, but she would not go out of her way to get another. She munched on the fries until they were cold and stale, at which point she tossed the remnants back into the bag and onto the floor in the back.

With her stomach sickly full from the greasy meal, she couldn't prevent her mind from racing. *Am I crazy to think I can take on the responsibilities that come with the general manager position in California?* She knew all about the actual partnership side of things, but she didn't know much about the financial side of the business. She'd taken all the required accounting classes needed to obtain her degree, but she hadn't thought about them since the class had ended.

While driving, she tried to replay all the lessons she'd been taught about accounting. She thought about balance sheets, ledgers, and cash-flow analysis. *Ha. It won't be that easy for Todd to push me out of the way of this job.* The fight was going to be tiring. She knew she needed to calm down a bit. The job ad for the position hadn't even been posted yet.

Tipping her head from side to side, she stretched her aching neck. She peeked down at her phone—one of her exits was only twenty miles away. Releasing a slow breath and a sigh, she rolled her shoulders.

After switching interstates and driving for another hour and a half, she turned off at her exit. She would be at her destination in a matter of minutes—she no longer needed to think about the drive in terms of hours. The thought was enough to make her giddy. The anticipation of seeing Verity built in her gut. Butterflies swarmed.

The temperature had only changed moderately since the sun had gone down on her way out of New Mexico. The Arizona sky was dark with the cool late-night air. Prescott Valley was beautiful. Jackie understood why Verity had moved here after college. She'd only visited a few times but was never disappointed.

Rounding the last corner, she let out a breath of relief but, in the same breath, wondered why she hadn't just flown to California. She looked forward to seeing her friend, but it was also a reminder of what she didn't have—a beautiful home or a family to share it with. Not that she'd never had the chance—it just hadn't worked out. The sadness she'd been outrunning for a long time wiggled among the butterflies, trampling their wings and halting their momentum.

She pulled into the driveway and cut the engine and lights as soon as she was parked. The kids' bedrooms were on the front side of the house, and Jackie didn't want to risk waking them up. As quietly as she could, she collected her overnight bag and purse. As she made her way up to the front door, she smiled at the hints of the people within—a small swing set with toys scattered around its base. Bikes of varying sizes lined the garage.

Thinking that she should have just texted Verity that she was here, Jackie knocked as lightly as she could and heard movement on the other side of the door as soon as she lowered her hand. The door was opened so quickly it threw her off balance. Verity, with her slender arms outstretched, pulled Jackie into her embrace. Verity had always been beautiful. Looking at her, no one would know she'd had three children. She was slim and tall with long, flowing blond hair, which looked even lighter since the last time Jackie had seen her. Verity would likely blame it on the sun, but Jackie wondered if she was going white. Verity could pull it off. She had a flawless smile and complexion—other girls in college had been jealous of her and even despised her because of it. Jackie, however, was not intimidated by her best friend's appearance. She was proud of the way she took care of herself and those around her.

Upon releasing Jackie, Verity took her overnight bag and motioned her over the threshold into the house. The entryway was filled with children's shoes and jackets—the outdoor wear was piled on top of a small bench. There was no room to sit on it. Shoes flowed out from below like the small cup of slime on the kids' play table in the corner of the living room ahead.

"Sorry it's such a mess. They're like little, tiny tornadoes each time I clean..." She laughed, motioning to the mess spread across the floor.

"Are you kidding me? I don't care," Jackie said with a gentle smile. "I can't wait to spend the day with you all tomorrow."

"You'll need to get some rest tonight to gear yourself up for that chaos." Verity laughed. Then her expression changed, and she gave a small, sad smile. Jackie knew where her mind had gone but pretended not to notice. Recovering quickly, Verity said, "Let's bring your stuff up to the guest room and then have a glass of wine."

"That'd be great." Jackie was used to getting those sorts of looks from people, as if they'd let a secret slip out. They hoped she didn't notice, but she always did.

The duo made their way up the carpeted steps, careful to tiptoe as they passed the kids' rooms. The guest room, at the end of the hall, was simple and comfortable, with a large bed and a mirrored dressing table. They were mismatched but looked cute in the small room. A floor lamp was positioned to the right of the nightstand.

Verity placed Jackie's overnight bag on top of the dressing table and withdrew from the room. "Feel free to change, and I'll meet you back down in the living room."

Jackie was still in the pencil skirt and blouse she'd selected for work that morning. Happy to be rid of the work clothes, she exchanged them for a matching-shorts-and-tank-top sleep set. Removing the claw clip from her hair, she let it flow down her back. The relief was enough to make her groan. There were few hairstyles she could accomplish without making her hair look like a toddler had attacked it with too much enthusiasm. She looked in the mirror at the way the auburn curls haphazardly framed her face. She didn't mind the chaos of her fair skin and crazy hair. Ruffling it a bit more, she smiled at herself. A spark in her eyes shone back. She wished she saw that more frequently. Sneaking her way back down the stairs, she felt like a teenager. She tucked herself into the corner of the large sofa.

Verity entered the living room with two glasses of wine and a small bowl of buttery popcorn balanced on a serving tray. She deposited the tray on the ottoman and handed a glass to Jackie. They sat together, enjoying one another's company. Jackie talked about work, while Verity talked of all the accomplishments and fun things the children had learned since the last time they'd seen one another. Jackie told her about the things that had been happening at work and the potential promotion she was up for.

"So, do you think that Todd guy is behind those emails too?" Verity asked with her legs folded under her, leaning against the arm of the loveseat, across from Jackie. Her eagerness for the details reminded Jackie of their late-night chats when they'd first met during their freshman year of college. The wine had been cheaper, the taste only bearable because of the knowledge that they were breaking the rules.

"That's what I've been trying to figure out. I mean…" Jackie gazed into her glass of wine as if the answer was hidden just below the bloodred surface. "I can't imagine that he would do that. But then again, I never would have thought he would come to my office today and accuse me of trying to sleep with Darrin."

Verity was studying Jackie. Even with her eyes narrowed in thought, the dark-chocolate irises were visible. "What would make him think there was something going on between the two of you? Also, I have to ask…" She leaned in closer and whispered, "Is Darrin attractive?" Verity wiggled her eyebrows.

Jackie's cheeks heated at the thought of Darrin's appearance. She contemplated her answer. "He is, but he's my boss, Verity. I don't know why Todd would think there was anything going on. I thought I was going to these meetings with Charles until yesterday."

"Charles?"

"Darrin's father." Jackie chuckled, seeing the puzzled expression on her friend's face.

"I just really don't like the idea of these emails. What you tell me doesn't make them sound like outright threats, but they make me nervous."

Jackie froze. The fear she'd been trying to suppress came bubbling to the surface. She had tried to play the emails off as something harmless. But now that Verity had expressed the same concerns, she couldn't bury her nervousness any longer.

"I forwarded the last one I received to Charles earlier, before Todd came to visit." She rolled her eyes.

"That's good. Then he'll know you're not trying to hide anything. But there is still something unsettling about them." The concern in her eyes was touching, and Jackie appreciated it.

"I promise I'll talk with him when I get back to the office." Finishing off her glass of wine, Jackie suggested they head to bed. She was tired from driving, from talking, and finally, from thinking.

The two said their good nights and went their separate ways. Verity's bedroom was on the first floor, next door to her youngest child. Jackie climbed the stairs as softly as she could.

In bed, she tossed and turned. Thinking. Dreading. *Is there going to be another email? Is Todd going to lose his mind if I get the position instead of him? What kind of stink will he cause? Is Todd sending those emails?*

Eventually, she drifted into an uneasy sleep.

Chapter Six

DARRIN

Darrin spent more time at the office than he should on weekends. He had nothing else to take up his time. The next day, he would be flying out to California and would be able to get a better sense of Jackie.

That day, he was going to do some research into her personnel file. It wasn't exactly typical for him to do such a thing. But the fact that she might be running an entire location validated his perusal.

She'd been with the company longer than he realized, starting only two years after he had. He'd started immediately after he graduated from college. Her original résumé showed this was only the second job she'd ever held. She'd previously worked for a property management company. It was far larger than his father's company. She'd been an office assistant there and had been hired at Hands, Hearts, and Homes for the same type of position originally. He wondered if she'd switched because of the commuting distance. He didn't know where exactly she lived but knew it wasn't far.

She'd received a degree in business administration the spring before she was hired at Hands, Hearts, and Homes. That would be good for the general manager position. Sighing, he kept searching.

There was nothing negative—not a single complaint on her yearly evaluation. He tossed her file onto his desk and rubbed his eyes. Since his visit to her office the other day, she hadn't been far from his mind. This was ridiculous.

Something about her had caught his attention more than usual. He told himself it was the nervous way she behaved. It definitely wasn't the way her breasts pressed against the front of her blouse or the way those pencil skirts always fit her ass perfectly.

"*Fuck*," he hissed. Leaning back in his chair, he tried to think of something else. Anything else.

Todd wanted to apply for the same position. It was only fair to give Todd's personnel file the same search. Todd had been hired straight out of college and had a degree in accounting. There had been a few complaints about Todd's attitude in the beginning but nothing during recent years.

The idea that Todd's and Jackie's files would make the decision simple had proved wrong. The position was to be posted next week. He didn't know the exact date, but he wanted to get a head start in determining their capabilities. It was better to get a feel for someone's work ethic when they didn't know you were looking. Far fewer false attitudes and accomplishments. Anything could be made to look like a big deal when someone was being considered for a promotion.

Darrin interlaced his fingers. Resting his hands on his head, he tipped his chair back.

"Working in HR now?"

He let the front legs of his chair fall back to the floor.

"Kinda." He smirked "Isn't the CEO responsible for checking on everything?"

Charles walked over to Darrin's desk and leaned over to read the names on the files. A brow quirked.

"If you had to pick someone today for the promotion, who would you choose?" Darrin asked, anticipating his father's answer.

Charles sat in the chair across from Darrin. "I couldn't begin to tell you."

Darrin huffed.

"I know of only two people who are interested. There could be more qualified people. Why are you so concerned about this new location suddenly?"

There were times Darrin hated how close he and his father were. There was little he could hide. His suspicions about Jackie were nothing but an inkling in his gut. He'd found a few years ago that he couldn't always trust that feeling. His internal compass had almost led him to disaster once before, and it could be wrong again.

"I'm just nervous about having someone else running it so independently. How am I going to make sure they don't fuck everything up when I can't be in both locations every day?"

"Trust." Charles stood, reaching across the desk, and patted Darrin on the shoulder. He turned and headed for the door. Then he turned back to face Darrin. "Dinner tonight?"

"Yeah, that would be great."

After Charles left, Darrin found himself staring at the folders on his desk. After returning the files to their proper places, he locked up his office and the HR offices. Twirling the keys, he found himself standing outside Jackie's office. He could probably count on one hand how many times he'd visited it. The keys spun around his finger as he struggled with his internal debate.

He turned his back on the door and left the buildinig. He would not stoop to searching her office. Her nerves didn't give him the right to dig through it. Darrin was disgusted with himself for considering it. If someone did that to him, he would be pissed.

His phone pinged with an incoming text message. Charles wanted to have dinner at his favorite diner. That was an easy choice.

After arriving back home, Darrin spent the afternoon packing and making preparations for the trip. Heading to the diner, he knew he needed to steel himself for his father's perceptiveness. He reached the diner and walked in. It had a nostalgic look to it. The way the decor could transport the patrons to a different time. They'd spent one meal every weekend there when he was a child. His mother had let him sign up for whatever sports he wanted, and she was so tired by the end of the week that they would eat out most Saturdays.

Charles sat down across from him in the small booth. Once they'd ordered, Charles fixed his intense gaze on Darrin. "Now, tell me why you really want to get so involved. Why did you need to take the trip to California? No more half answers."

Darrin shook his head. *Well, this happened faster than I thought.* "When I stopped in at Jackie's office the other day, she was acting strange. Fidgety, nervous." His brows furrowed as he described it.

"When was the last time you visited her in her office? Talked with her?"

"Well, I sometimes stop by after staff meetings." Darrin thought. He couldn't actually remember a specific instance. Jackie always appeared to be paying attention at those meetings, so he didn't focus on her much.

"Wouldn't you think that would be fair for her to be nervous, then?"

Darrin didn't want to concede that point. There had to be another reason. He would find it out.

CHAPTER SEVEN

JACKIE

"Jackie! Jackie!" two children chorused.

Their yells startled her—she'd forgotten where she was. She opened her eyes to mini versions of Verity staring back at her. "Good morning, girls!" she exclaimed on a yawn as she pulled them into a hug.

"Mommy said we could wake you up. But we had to be quiet and wait until it was eight o'clock," Olive said proudly.

"Eight o'clock," the younger of the two, Annabelle, repeated.

"Well, it's a good thing you two came up to wake me up. I could have slept all day!" Smiling, she hugged the girls again and got out of bed. "Let's go downstairs and see what Mommy and Daddy are up to."

"Okay!" The girls scrambled to the stairs.

Annabelle hesitated before beginning her descent, while Olive was almost at the bottom before Jackie had a chance to take the first step. Jackie took Annabelle's hand and helped her down the steps. Her hand was small and soft. The trio entered the kitchen to find Verity and her husband, Porter, sitting at the dining table with their youngest child in his high chair next to them, eating his breakfast.

Jackie took the chair across from Verity. Jackie smiled down at Annabelle and helped her climb onto her lap.

"Well, since someone has designated you as her chair, can I get you a cup of coffee?" Verity asked, standing.

"Yes. Please!"

Over coffee and breakfast, the girls wanted to tell Jackie all about the things they'd been learning in school. Olive, the oldest, was in third grade, while Annabelle, three years old, had just started preschool the previous fall. Their youngest and only son, Hunter, was going to be one in a few weeks.

* * *

During their talk the night before, Jackie and Verity had decided to take the kids to Prescott National Forest. It was one of the family's favorite places to go—they were active and enjoyed hiking—so they spent an eventful day in the forest. The evening was filled with stories and laughter just as the morning had been. Jackie was looking forward to her time in California, but was going to miss Verity and her family.

Jackie helped tuck the girls into bed, telling them she would be gone before they woke up in the morning. They said tearful goodbyes as she promised to visit again before the end of summer.

"They're really going to miss you," Verity said with a smile.

"I know. I'm going to miss them."

"Jackie, I hate to stick my nose into your love life..." Verity tentatively began. When Jackie didn't object to the trespassing, she continued. "Have you tried dating since everything?"

"Here and there." Jackie looked away, not wanting to meet Verity's gaze.

"I can tell you want what we have," Verity said, motioning to the ceiling in the direction of the children's bedrooms. "I think it's time you gave dating another shot."

"I just don't know if I can go through something like that again. What if I end up in the same position?"

Jackie hated to think of her past. She'd spent several years suppressing those thoughts. They were safely locked away, and she was not going to open that chest now.

Clearing her throat, she removed herself from the sofa. "I have to get up at three to leave. I should really go to bed."

"Jackie, I'm sorry. I just want to help." Verity looked down at her hands in her lap. "I just want to see you happy again."

"I am happy," she said with a smile that didn't reach her eye, as she headed for the stairs. "Thank you for everything. I had a great day."

Without a backward glance, she finished climbing the stairs and hurriedly packed. When she finally climbed into bed, she felt the tears she'd buried burn the corners of her eyes. *Dammit, Verity.* She rolled over, longing to drown the memories invading her mind.

Sleep came in short spurts. She was awakened each time by the same dream. The feeling of despair increased with each awakening. The last thing she would see was the suffocating walls of the hospital, where she lay in pain and alone. A hollowness threatened to engulf her. She had to take deep, slow breaths to soothe the rising panic.

Three o'clock arrived, and she doubted she'd slept more than four hours. With as much quiet as she could manage, she turned on the shower. She allowed the heat to flow over her body as she washed. The ache from crying remained. Turning the water to a cooler temperature, she willed the puffiness to dissipate.

She dried off and leaned on the sink. The mirror revealed the sadness in her eyes. Red surrounded her irises, giving them a gray, lifeless look.

Jackie shut off the light and went back to the guest room to pack her remaining items. She tidied the room and snuck downstairs. No coffee shop nearby would be opening until at least five o'clock on a Sunday, she remembered with regret.

Sighing, she hitched her overnight bag and purse onto her shoulder. She was almost to the front door when there was a tug on her purse strap. Startled, she spun around to find Porter standing there with a travel mug filled with piping-hot coffee.

"Porter," she whispered with exasperation. She clutched her chest as if to keep her heart from beating its way out of her ribs.

"Sorry. I didn't mean to scare you." He looked chagrined. "I just didn't get to say goodbye last night and knew no coffee shops would be open this early. Besides, Hunter was up about twenty minutes ago. I could hear you in the shower when I laid him back down. So..." He extended the mug to her.

"Thank you, Porter. I really appreciate it." She accepted the mug with a sleepy smile. "Only a six-hour drive from here." She laughed.

"Don't be mad at Verity. She told me about your conversation last night," Porter said. Jackie felt anger surge through her, but she remained silent. "She just wants to help you."

"I don't need any help," she responded through a forced smile.

"Jackie, I'm not trying to add to whatever she said to you last night. I just want you to know she was doing it with the best of intentions."

With a sigh, she closed her eyes. "Thank you again for the coffee," she said in a calmer tone. "Really. I must be going. I'll return the mug as soon as I can." She turned on her heel, but not wanting to damage their relationship, she turned back. "I know she only has the best intentions. It's just easier for me to look forward if I don't look back." She choked back tears, refusing to cry. "I love you guys. Thank you so much for everything." Saluting him with the coffee cup, she went out the front door.

Jackie drove for four hours then stopped for breakfast at a small roadside restaurant. She was enjoying the time alone. She liked being able to think. Taking a moment, she texted Tony to keep him apprised of her progress.

She ate her stack of hotcakes and enjoyed a large cup of coffee—she'd finished Porter's before she'd driven an hour. She was about two-thirds of the way through her trip and estimated she would be arriving around lunchtime, a few hours before she could check into the hotel. Sitting on the beach for a while would ease some of the tension she was feeling.

Jackie wanted to allow herself time to unwind before her meeting with Darrin. They'd agreed to meet Sunday night to determine their game plan. Suppressing a groan, she savored the final slice of bacon and hoped he would be more pleasant than he'd been in her office.

Before she knew it, she arrived at her hotel. Happy to see that the beach was within walking distance, she parked. She usually tried to avoid leaving anything valuable in her car but didn't have much of a choice that day, since taking her entire suitcase to the beach would look a bit foolish. In the parking lot, she tipped her head back to allow the sun access to her face. Breathing deeply, she relished the salty air, allowing it to seep into her skin, her lungs, her soul.

After trudging out onto the sand, she lay down the picnic blanket that lived in her car. Smoothing out the soft fabric, she felt a calm take over her body. Lowering herself onto her stomach, she took another deep breath. She reached into her tote bag and removed a book. The paper along the spine was flaking, and the pages and cover were curling at the corners. She could buy herself a new copy so it didn't look like she'd pulled it from a dumpster, but she liked the character a well-loved book offered. With a story of life and love, she was never disappointed. Happy endings—not everyone got one.

Reading on a busy beach on a Sunday afternoon proved to be difficult. There were families everywhere. Children were screaming while splashing one another. Couples were holding hands, strolling along the ocean's edge. Several well-built men were tossing a football back and forth in the water, hooting and laughing at one another. Rows of young women were lined up, working on sunning themselves while they chattered.

Giving up on the book, she redeposited it in her bag then tucked the bag under the top of her blanket to use as a pillow. She closed her eyes and allowed her mind to wander... daydreaming about her honeymoon.

She and Harmon had wanted to go somewhere quiet and not heavily populated and had decided on New Hampshire. They had enjoyed the mountains and quaint local stores. Mount Washington provided amazing views at the top. They were in no shape to hike such a daunting mountain, so driving was their best option. They parked, taking in the views each overlook point provided. Jackie took photos of everything. It was all so beautiful—she wanted to remember it for years to come. The views at the top were spectacular. It was hard to believe they were there in the middle of summer. The sun was out, but it was only forty degrees at that elevation.

They ate their packed lunch at the top. Looking out over the remarkable view, Jackie watched as a couple walked out onto the rocks below their vantage point. The man pointed out something in the distance. As the woman looked away, he dropped to one knee, and when she turned back around, he produced a box. A shocked smile spread across the woman's face, and she nodded before she ever saw the ring. As the woman turned the remainder of the way around, Jackie had noticed her protruding belly. Jackie smiled as the couple hugged and looked out at the skyline.

"How many do you want?" Harmon asked while finishing up his lunch.

"How many what?" she asked him, puzzled.

"Kids."

They'd been together since the beginning of their freshman year of college. They were about to begin their third year. They'd gotten engaged during the winter holidays of their sophomore year and wasted no time getting married. However, within all their talks, they had never discussed children. This sudden interest in children made her curious.

"I don't know… how many were you thinking?" Not wanting to say more than what he was interested in having, she wanted to hear his thoughts first.

"How about three?"

"Why not an even number, like four? Why three?"

"It has always been my lucky number," he stated as if her not knowing that was foolish. She couldn't help but laugh at his reasoning.

Jackie hadn't told him she couldn't wait to have children. She'd been too afraid he wouldn't share her desires yet. Usually, the last thing a handsome man in college wanted was children.

She leaned back on the picnic blanket, supported by her arms, so she could get a better look at him. He had a handsome profile. His dark hair was always trimmed perfectly. His brown eyes had a depth to them. Maybe they only looked so appealing because of how much she loved him.

"You know, once we have kids, you might not have time to make yourself so pretty every morning," she'd teased.

Jackie was jolted out of her musings by a sudden pain in her shoulder. One of the young men was running toward her.

"Sorry!" he shouted, making his way to his football. Before picking it up, he knelt beside her to make sure she was all right. Immediately, she felt uncomfortable but couldn't define why.

"I'm all right," she said sharply. She'd been enjoying her thoughts.

"Let me see it," he said, reaching for the neckline of her blouse.

"I said I'm fine." She pulled the neckline of her shirt closer to her neck. Suddenly feeling foolish for her modesty on a beach, she got up and started packing up her blanket.

"Sorry again," he said, looking perplexed.

The young man retrieved the football and returned to the water. Silently berating herself for her conduct, Jackie made her way back to the hotel parking lot. He was an attractive man. *Why did I act like an idiot when he tried to touch me?*

She rolled her shoulder, and the pain radiated down her arm. She knew the hit would leave a mark. Checking her watch, she was happy to see she could now check into the hotel.

Chapter Eight

THE CONSPIRATOR

Soon, revenge would be implemented. They were about to learn what suffering was. They weren't going to suffer as long, but they were going to know the pain of losing a loved one. The pain of a sudden loss would be good for them. Their lives had been so blessed and easy that it made them sick to think about it. Everything had been easy for them while others struggled to get their footing and keep their lives afloat.

The plans had all been laid out. The pivotal point would be ensuring their target acted as expected. The emails had been sent to rattle her. The conspirators hadn't been able to see exactly how she reacted, but they hoped it would distract her enough that she could be manipulated. Easily distracted. Caught off guard.

Everything had been carefully put into this plan. If one thing went wrong, if one piece fell out of place, everything would fall apart. Keeping a level head was of the utmost importance.

Even Todd had fallen into his place in the plan unwittingly, the fool. He was so quick to assume Jackie had been accepting and returning sexual favors with Darrin. He apparently didn't know her at all. She hadn't been on a single real date in close to ten years.

CHAPTER NINE

DARRIN

Darrin entered the room after hearing nothing when he knocked. She was probably down at the beach; it was a perfect day for it. He took in the room with its two queen beds.

But when he heard the metallic click of the lock, his eyes shot to what must be the bathroom door. So, she had locked the door while alone in the room. Interesting.

He looked away from the door and down at his hands as he apprehensively rubbed them together. How was she going to react to his being in her room? He was more nervous than he'd originally expected.

But then again, he hadn't expected to find her in the bathroom either. The door he stood by swung out, blocking him. Darrin nudged it closed while Jackie walked to the bed with her suitcase on it.

He was not disappointed by what he saw. She was wearing one of the hotel towels wrapped around her voluminous chest. He wondered why he hadn't noticed just how shapely she was until this last week. The bottom of the towel barely covered her ass. He couldn't suppress the rush of desire that ran through his entire body, urging him to walk up to her.

To take her. Her hair was wrapped up in a second towel balanced on the top of her head. He wanted to wipe away the droplets of water that were sliding from her scalp, over her shoulders, and down her back. He could only imagine where the water was rolling down her front.

A silent battle raged in his mind, one side telling him to make himself seen while the other—the aroused half—argued that he should stay silent. No matter his choice, he knew she was going to be pissed to be found in such a vulnerable state. But that was what he liked most about it. The thought sent a strong pulse to his groin.

His moment to notify her vanished. She turned and screamed when she saw him standing there, watching her. Feeling the guilt rising, he lowered his eyes, but not before she clutched at the front of the towel, pulling it closer to her chest, making the size of her breasts more evident.

"What exactly do you think you're doing in my room?" she asked shrilly.

"Look, Jackie, they messed up the room booking. I'm not sure how. But somehow, they booked us into the same room." Darrin kept his eyes averted but could see her fuming in his peripheral vision. She was going to rip the ends of the towel if she pulled them any closer together.

Her cheeks flushed as she looked down at the small barrier protecting her body. The sadness in her eyes made him feel like a pervert. She would be revolted by the thoughts he'd been entertaining only moments before.

"Why didn't you book another room?" she asked, seething.

Her accusatory tone made him whip his head up to meet her eyes. "Don't you think I tried that?" he asked snidely. She glared back at him, waiting. "I asked. All the rooms have been booked through the next few weeks." Taking a deep breath, he tamped down his tone. "I really am sorry for scaring you. I tried to call your cell, and I knocked on the door before I came in. I figured you were down at the beach. You came out as I came in—I swear."

Looking away from her face, he noticed a horrid bruise on her right shoulder. She slid her left hand from the towel to cover the blemish. She uncomfortably shifted her weight from side to side as he swept his gaze from her face to her shoulder.

"Darrin," she croaked. "Can you turn around so I can get my clothes out of my suitcase?"

"I don't know," he said with one of his signature sly grins. "I might like what I see if that towel slips."

She narrowed her eyes. "You think that since your father is my boss, you can talk to me like that?"

"No." He held his breath, waiting for the wrath he was sure was coming his way. He had an entire arsenal of additional dirty lines to give her. Knowing they were not appropriate and would make him look more like a pervert, he pressed his lips together.

She kept her right hand clutching her towel and used the other to grab her suitcase off the bed closest to them. Watching her drag it into the bathroom with her, he had to fight the urge to smile.

He moved over to the window to look at the ocean below. Rather than enjoying the view, Darrin was thinking back to when he'd visited Jackie without an appointment. He'd done this intentionally; he hated when people knew he was coming and would tidy their desks or pretend they were getting more work done than they actually were. He liked seeing people in their true work states, not what they thought the boss would like to see. *How many people just so happen to have a full pot of coffee brewed for possible visitors? How many people keep their desk impeccably clean?*

Jackie's desk had been covered in files, but they were all separated and organized. The office had been designed to have an inviting atmosphere and made people feel at ease. He'd always been observant, a trait he'd cultivated at a young age. People were always nice to him because of who his father was—even before starting the business, his father had been president of the bank in their city. Darrin learned to watch body language and speech patterns to discern who truly was interested in him. These skills had thus far been essential to his success. They'd only failed him once. And now he could not read Jackie as easily as others. This was cause for alarm on multiple levels.

She'd definitely been surprised to find out that he would be going on the trip to California with her, and she'd certainly been nervous when he'd entered her office. He could not figure out what had caused her to be so nervous. Not once had he heard anything bad about Ms. Martinez. People raved about her.

He had learned from their most recent conversation that she was not afraid to tell him what she thought. She was surely not impressed to be sharing a room with him. He wondered if she had a boyfriend and how she'd come by that bruise. The bastard had better hope the two weren't connected... *If there is a boyfriend*, he reminded himself.

Just then, he heard the lock release on the bathroom door, again. Darrin turned to see her emerging in a pair of tight-fitting jeans that would drive any man crazy and an equally tight tank top. He realized he had never seen her in anything other than business attire. *And a small towel.* He tried to hide his amusement.

"What?" Her tone hadn't lost any of its irritation. "So, are you going to call another hotel and get a different room?" She looked at him pointedly, raising her eyebrows. "We can't share a room."

"I tried. All the other places I called are booked up. This isn't my idea of a great way to start a week, either," he said, matching her irritation. "What? Do you think I'm going to attack you in the middle of the night?"

Staying silent, she glared at him.

"Before you file sexual harassment against me, let me explain what happened when I arrived." He took several minutes to tell her about the mistake his assistant had made when she was adjusting the booking from his father's name to his.

"The poor woman at the front desk looked like she wanted to quit when I lost my shit over the mistake."

After his explanation, she softened. Slightly.

"I didn't have lunch. I'm going down to get something to eat." She grabbed her purse off the bed and swung that strap onto her right shoulder. The moment it made contact with the contusion, she flinched. He watched as she let the strap slide down to rest in the crook of her elbow.

"That's great—neither did I." He rose from the bed and walked up behind her so he was only inches away.

His closeness had that alluring shade of pink flooding her cheeks. Quickly, she grabbed the door handle and proceeded down the hall, not waiting for him to fall into step next to her. Jackie turned toward the restaurant off the hotel lobby, but Darrin grabbed her hand. The tug caused her to cry out. Realizing which arm he'd grabbed, he released her immediately.

"Jackie." He stepped around her to stand in front of her. He hoped his eyes would relay the sorrow he felt. "I'm sorry. I didn't mean to hurt you."

"I'm fine." Her breath had a catch to it. "Why did you feel the need to touch me, anyway?"

"I just thought we could go somewhere else for dinner, go for a little walk. There are lots of places along the main drive."

"*We?* I didn't realize sharing a room meant we had to dine together too."

"I told you the room mishap wasn't my fault. I'm sorry—I really am. But you know, if you get this promotion, we"—he motioned to the space between the two of them—"will need to learn to get along. Plus, I thought we were planning to meet tonight anyway to come up with our game plan."

She looked him over, and something stirred in him as her eyes roamed his body. He was wearing a pair of dark jeans and a light-blue button-down shirt. He could see the internal fight. He didn't realize going out to dinner with him would be such a terrible suggestion.

"Please, Jackie." The sincerity in his voice surprised him. He wasn't sure why he was so determined to have her go to dinner with him, but it was suddenly all he wanted.

After another lengthy pause, she nodded. "All right, lead the way," she said, pointing him toward the front entrance.

With a small, triumphant smile, he preceded her out the door.

Chapter Ten

JACKIE

They arrived at a restaurant that promised the best home-cooked meals. She was surprised by the location he'd selected. Instead of any of the fine-dining places they walked by, he chose a small family establishment.

"Why here?"

"Why not?" he countered with a smile that had her heart skipping a beat. "Would you rather go somewhere nicer?" His smile dropped slightly as his steps slowed.

"I'm just pleasantly surprised you would choose this place over something more expensive."

"Expensive doesn't always mean better." He stepped forward and opened the door then stood there, holding it open for her. This gentlemanly gesture made her realize she had never seen him outside of work.

"Thank you." She stepped over the threshold.

The atmosphere inside was friendly. His hand grazed the lower portion of her back and caused a rush of anticipation to course through her body. She sidestepped him, and he tucked his hand into his pocket.

The young woman at the hostess stand greeted them and sat them at a small table next to the bar. She extended them each a menu and wine list. From the outside, Jackie hadn't realized the restaurant had a bar. It ran down the center of the dining room, with tables on either side and seating along the long edges. The opening of the bar faced the kitchen, with another opening directly in front of the entrance.

"Thank you," Darrin said to the hostess, brandishing one of his handsome smiles.

Jackie was stunned when a pang of jealousy surged through her body and senses. *How? How can I be jealous?* This was her boss. She had no right to be attracted to him. *Oh no. I am. Aren't I?* She looked up from her menu to meet his eyes, and a flutter of excitement rolled in her stomach.

"Know what you want already?"

"Um, no." She quickly returned her eyes to her menu. Tapping her nails on the table, she read through the options. They all sounded delicious.

"I think I'm going to get a nice, juicy steak." He placed his menu down just in time to greet their server. "Hello. Can I start with a beer? I think I saw you have a stout on tap."

"Yes, we do. And for you, ma'am?"

"Oh, I'll just take water for now. Thank you."

"I'll be right back with your drinks and then take your dinner order."

"Just a water?" Darrin asked with one eyebrow raised.

"Well, I haven't had time to look at the wine list yet."

The truth of the matter was she didn't have to drink much to get drunk. She'd never made a habit of drinking, so when she did, it hit her hard. Even when drinking with Verity, she limited her intake. Two glasses was pushing it. Anything more than that and she knew she would end up with word vomit. The last thing she wanted to do on a business trip was to look like a fool.

Their server returned with their drinks and took their orders as promised. Jackie settled on a chicken–bacon sandwich, while Darrin ordered his steak with potatoes.

"So, have you had a chance to review all the places we're going to be visiting?" Jackie asked.

"Really? We're going to talk about work?"

"This is a business trip," she reminded him.

"Right, but it's Sunday. The work week doesn't start until tomorrow," he said, smiling and taking a sip of his beer.

"I thought we were coming up with a 'game plan,'" she said, using air quotes. She saw a quick quirk of his lips.

"That's true. We have access to the hotel's conference room. We'll meet with all the property owners so they can pitch their facilities so we can choose which to visit Tuesday."

"You had that planned before we left." She couldn't help the indignation in her tone. "You could have told me that in the room."

He smirked.

She wanted to throw her napkin at his smug face.

"So, now that the business portion of this dinner is taken care of, what should we talk about?" he asked.

Glaring at him, she refused to answer.

"Fine, I'll pick. How did you get that nasty bruise on your shoulder?"

Self-consciously, she covered the mark with her hand. "It's actually kind of stupid." She looked up at him, chagrined.

He motioned his hands over the table, indicating that she should lay it all out.

"All right. Well, I got here a little after noon and decided that I wanted to go down to the beach. I didn't have my swimsuit out, and it was too early to check in, so I just went down in my travel clothes. Anyway, I was lying on the sand with my eyes closed. A group of men were playing with a football, you know, just tossing it back and forth at the edge of the water. Well, I don't know which one threw it, but the other guy missed, and it slammed right into my shoulder. I couldn't believe the pain."

Darrin started laughing his deep chuckle that made her insides defy gravity. "Really, a stray ball?" He continued laughing until she gave him a dirty look. "Okay, I'm sorry. It looks painful. You should be happy it didn't hit you in the face, though. From the looks of your shoulder, it would have broken your nose."

She laughed at the image.

"I'll be honest—I thought you had some sort of abusive boyfriend or something."

Jackie's laughter ceased. "No, I do not have a boyfriend."

Her confession made her self-conscious again, and she clammed up. She busied herself with the photos around the walls of the restaurant. Many looked like local shots of the ocean and various festivals and activities. She could feel Darrin's eyes following her every move, but she studiously avoided meeting his gaze. Something about him made her feel that she would tell him anything he asked. And that scared her.

Out of the corner of her eye, she saw his mouth begin to open, but just then, the waitress arrived with their food.

"This looks terrific. Thank you." Jackie positioned the plate in front of her just so, happy to have a reason not to talk.

She looked up from her plate and made eye contact with him. Darrin was watching her with puzzled interest. His cool-blue eyes were assessing her. She wanted to squirm under his intense gaze, which might soon burrow under her skin.

"Do I have something on my face?" She picked up her napkin and began wiping her face.

He shook his head, laughing. "You surprise me."

"Mm-hmm? How so?" she asked, eyeing him suspiciously.

"Your general behavior." There was no trace of joking in his response.

"Should I take that as a compliment?"

"I make a point of reading people. You're hard to read."

His response, again, was not what she was expecting. He was far blunter than she'd imagined. The thought of him trying to read her had anxiety rushing through her veins. She preferred it when people talked about themselves. She averted her eyes, looking at the photos around the room again. A black and white of a little girl dipping her toes in the water caught her eye. She wore a polka-dot dress and straw hat; she lifted the dress to avoid dampening the fabric. Her toes made small ripples in the water.

"And you do that." He gestured to her face. "When someone makes the conversation about you, you immediately look elsewhere. You don't like to talk about yourself?"

"No," she said, defiantly meeting his cool-blue eyes.

"See? That's odd. Most of the time, when I go out to dinner with a woman, she wants to talk all night long. All you want to talk about is... work. Or nothing."

"And I'm sure that's a long list, isn't it—the number of women you've taken out?" she said, hating how accurate and pinned she felt by his assessment.

"Or you do that. You get prissy and flip my words."

"I thought that's what we were talking about—all your escapades with random women and what they like to talk about."

Darrin's jaw clenched with anger. She knew it was a cheap shot, but she didn't like him analyzing her. He scraped his chair across the floor, stood, and then went over to the bar. While he was waiting, a woman two seats down the bar leaned closer to him. She engaged him in conversation and excessively laughed at something he said. She was busty, in a tight-fitting black tank top and denim shorts.

Unbelievable. Jackie had had enough of him, his prying questions, and his looks. And the way women gravitated to him. She shoved her plate away and pulled out enough money to cover her meal. She was not going to depend on him for anything. She tucked the money under his empty beer glass and stalked out of the restaurant. She doubted he even noticed.

Outside, the sun was shining brightly between the buildings. Maybe she would go back to the hotel, change, and go down to the beach. Turning in what she hoped was the direction of their hotel, she took some calming breaths.

Walking down the street, Jackie had the strangest feeling she was being watched. She looked over her shoulder but didn't see anyone looking at her. She assumed she'd only had that feeling because of her argument with Darrin.

The next time she had that feeling, she knew she'd heard something. But the streets were packed with people. If someone was following her, she didn't know which person to look at first.

She quickened her pace, clutching her purse to her side. *How far did we walk from the hotel?* She hated this feeling.

"Jackie!"

She was about to start running when a hand settled on her left shoulder. She froze, too afraid to scream. She was surrounded by people, but it was as though none of them saw the fear on her face.

"Jackie," the man repeated, but this time, she recognized the voice. Thankful for a familiar sound, her heart skipped a beat.

"Darrin, I thought someone was following me," she said barely above a whisper, struggling to control her fear.

"That's what I was told," he whispered back, putting his arm around her waist and pulling her close.

His statement caught her off guard. She'd thought he was the reason she felt like she was being followed. Looking up at him with a question in her eyes, she waited.

"I got back to the table to find you gone," he said, bringing his piercing eyes to hers. "I was pretty pissed, as you can imagine. Anyway, just as I sat back down, a guy from the next table over asked me if we'd been expecting someone to join us. He'd been outside, smoking, when you stormed out."

"I didn't storm out," she said sheepishly.

"Well, he said that as soon as you walked out, a guy leaning up against the side of the restaurant started walking behind you. That immediately sent up warning flags, so the first guy came in and asked if me and my wife were going to be meeting another person at the restaurant. I said no and asked him why he would ask that. He explained. I paid our tab and ran out. I was afraid someone had tried to grab you. When you came into view, I called your name. There was a man in a hoodie just a few people behind you, and he stopped dead in his tracks and then quickly turned down a side street."

Darrin whispered it all in her ear as they made their way back to the hotel. She didn't know if it was his words, the breath on her ear, or the eerie feeling she still felt that had the hairs on the back of her neck standing at attention.

"Oh my gosh. Really?" This time, she didn't even try to hide her fear. When he nodded, she leaned in closer to him for protection.

"It's okay. We're almost back." He tipped his chin up to indicate that the hotel had just come into view. "I want you to go into the hotel and go straight to the room."

"I don't want to go up alone," she whispered, her eyes pleading with him.

"Okay, let me think for a moment." His nervousness was making her even more nervous. "Most likely, it was just someone hoping to take your purse," he said with his brow furrowed.

She didn't think he believed that was the case.

"But just in case, why don't you go in and take a seat in the lobby," he continued. "Somewhere that it would be difficult to see you. I'll go to the front desk and talk to the attendant. I'll make up some kind of bullshit about not having enough towels. I want to wait and see if your friend follows us into the hotel."

He looked down at her, presumably waiting for her thoughts. She was too afraid to think, so she just nodded.

They arrived at the hotel and split up. The seating area was just to the left of the entry doors. A love seat faced the windows looking out toward to beach, with small arm chairs on either side. She chose a chair with its back to the front desk, picked up a magazine, and held it up to her face, trying to look engrossed in what she was doing.

Between the fingers of her right hand, she could see Darrin talking to the attendant in the reflection of a vase on the end table. The shifts must have changed while they were out. There was a man covering the desk. He and Darrin went back and forth a few times. A few people had entered the hotel and gone straight to the elevators. Darrin completed his conversation and took a seat in a chair across the lobby, far from her. He sat and looked ahead as if waiting for someone, with his hands folded over his stomach and fingers interlaced, his left ankle lying on the opposite knee as if he were relaxing. Turning, she watched him. She could see he was not at all relaxed.

After several minutes, he crossed the lobby and took her hand. "Let's head up."

"What were you waiting for?" she asked, nervously looking over her shoulder.

"I'll tell you when we get upstairs." He led her over to the elevators and allowed her to get in first. Instead of the third floor, he selected the second. When they stopped, he pulled her from the elevator and took her to the stairs, and they climbed the last flight.

Without speaking, he led the way to their room. Fresh towels had been deposited on the bathroom counter. He pointed to the wall behind the door, indicating that was where he wanted her to stand.

She waited as he checked all through the room. The tapping of his shoes was the only indication that he was moving around. He went back to the door, decisively flipping the lock into place. She released a pent-up breath, surprised to note that her anxiety settled quickly in his presence. Although, she was still rattled she felt strangely safe. The contradiction had her shaking her head, allowing strands to fall from her ponytail and frame her face.

Placing one hand on either side of her head, he leaned his face close to hers. She held her breath, too transfixed to move. She could feel the heat of his body flowing over hers. He moved closer until his forehead was touching hers. A rush of excitement surged through her body and settled in her middle. She was shocked by the arousal that was slowly taking over her senses. She yearned for him to kiss her.

"I was afraid something was going to happen to you before I found you," he whispered.

To Jackie's surprise, his breath smelled sweet. She tipped her head back slightly to allow her to look into his eyes. Their noses almost touched. The shift brought their lips closer; she couldn't stop the hope that he would close the distance.

They were both frozen by the intimacy. She wondered if he was as aroused as she was. If either of them gave the slightest tip of the head, they would be touching lips.

He withdrew from her. Trying to catch her breath, she leaned forward, bracing herself on her knees. His sudden departure left her wishing she'd moved those last few inches. But she couldn't.

How would it look if I started romancing my boss? Todd came to mind, dropping an anvil into her gut.

"Jackie."

She drew herself back up at the softness of his voice.

"I have no right to say this. But I want you to know I only say it to look out for you... I don't think you should go anywhere alone while we are here. It's an unfamiliar city."

Outrage at his declaration warred with her sensible side. Her irritation with him at dinner came back. "You're right," she said, going over to her bed and sitting on the edge facing his. "You don't have the right to tell me that. Like you said, it was probably just a random mugger."

"That's what I was thinking at first, but why was he waiting outside the restaurant we just so happened to be in? There are so many other restaurants on that strip. How would he have known I was calling *your* name?" He appeared to be talking more to himself than to her. "Nicer restaurants. Why would a mugger wait outside a lower-scale, cheaper restaurant? The people dining there probably wouldn't have had much money." He settled on the side of his bed so he was facing her. "Why did you leave?"

She blinked a couple of times, trying to catch back up with him. He switched topics faster than she was used to. She could see in his eyes that her leaving had hurt him.

"I figured you and that blonde wouldn't want a third wheel hanging around." Jackie was angry, more with herself than with him.

She needed to learn to control her emotions around Darrin. She knew her comment would hurt him, and she didn't want to see his face. She grabbed her suitcase from where she'd left it on the bench by the television and went into the bathroom.

While changing, she wondered why he would care if something happened to her. She'd been nothing but a pain to him. She could count the number of times they'd talked before this trip on one hand.

She heard the television. Jackie emerged from the bathroom in a thin-strapped pale-pink tank top and a matching pair of flowing pants. She rushed from the bathroom to the bed and covered herself up. It was still early, but she was exhausted. The drive. The football hit. The stalker scare. The desire that wouldn't disperse.

A struggle raged within her as she thought about telling Darrin about the emails and Todd paying her that odd visit. She didn't want to make it sound like she was accusing Todd—plus she didn't know if the incidents were related. She didn't want to come across as a whiner or as if she were trying to damage Todd's reputation in an attempt to secure the promotion.

Jackie leaned over the edge of the bed, pulling her tote bag closer, and removed the book she'd tried to read earlier at the beach. She opened it and laid it on her stomach.

"Darrin," she said softly, turning toward him. She was hesitant because she knew he must be angry. He didn't speak a word but looked over at her. "I-I just wanted to say I'm sorry. I shouldn't have said that earlier." She waited for him to say something, but he stayed stonily silent. "I, um..." She licked her lips. "Also, I, ah, need to say thank you. I don't know who that guy was or why he was following me." She gave him a chance to speak. When nothing was forthcoming, she continued. "I was terrified. I don't know what I would have done if you hadn't caught up to me." On the last word, her voice caught in her throat.

"Our first meeting tomorrow is at eight. I'll be getting up at six to shower." He turned back to the laptop propped open to his right.

Chapter Eleven

LUCAS

The phone was answered on the first ring. Lucas had hoped the call would go unanswered.

"Is it done?" asked the conspirator.

Lucas listened to his own breathing. The recipient of his call wouldn't ask twice. "N-No," he stuttered.

The yell that emanated from the phone made him almost drop his cell. "What do you mean *no*?"

"It, it wasn't my fault. I was following her back to the hotel. I was going to make it look like a mugging, l-like we had talked about. But that damn pretty boy she works for showed up. He was yelling her name. People were looking all around. I panicked. I f-found a side street and ran down it. I ditched the hoodie and went back to my motel."

"Did he see you?" the voice barked.

"I-I... no. All he could see was my back."

"This was supposed to be over tonight! Let me think. Call me tomorrow at nine." The phone went quiet.

Lucas hated to disappoint. But what was he expected to do—kill them both?

Chapter Twelve

JACKIE

Stepping out of the bathroom, Jackie could hear the gentle chirp of what she assumed was Darrin's alarm. He sat up in his bed and stretched his arms over his head—he slept shirtless. She wanted to watch his muscles flex, but she forced herself to look away. Multiple times throughout the night, she'd been thankful their room had two queen beds. If she'd been forced to not only share a room but also a bed, she might have combusted.

He wordlessly went about collecting his clothes and taking his turn in the shower. She still felt rotten for the unkind things she'd said the night before. Twice, she'd accused him of sleeping around.

With a groan, she pulled her laptop from her work bag and checked her emails. It wasn't as bad as she'd expected. But there was another email from *sixy-nine_all_night*. This one had an attachment.

After hesitating for a moment, she opened the email. The idea of an attachment was especially concerning. Holding her breath, she read the message:

I hope you are enjoying California. I've heard the weather is nice. Be careful, though. Their crime rates are higher than in New Mexico. I would hate to hear of something happening to you.

Hands shaking, Jackie opened the attachment. Her scream careened out before she could stop it, and she slapped her hand over her mouth. The image in front of her was of herself lying on the beach the day before. Darrin came running out of the bathroom in only a towel. Her mind was spinning. A weight was settling into her stomach, an anchor holding her down.

"What the fuck is going on?" he shouted, rounding the corner of her bed and arriving at her side within seconds. She didn't have time to try to hide the email. "What is this?"

Water ran down his prominent muscles. His abdomen was rippled and sexy. His arms were toned and sleek. This closer look at his physique caught Jackie off guard. She'd assumed he was well built but hadn't expected this. Stunned by the combined shocks, she was unable to speak or look away from the water rolling down his pecs.

He pulled the laptop from her hands and read the email. He looked down at her, those intense eyes searching for an answer.

"I-I don't know who's been sending the emails. But that's a picture of me on the beach yesterday, before I checked into the hotel," she said in a small, shaky voice, wringing her hands in her lap under the scrutiny of his gaze.

"What do you mean 'been sending'? How many emails like this have you gotten?"

She could have cursed herself for saying that. She took the next few minutes explaining the first two emails. They'd been more about threatening her job and saying she was performing poorly.

"Why didn't you tell me or Charles about these emails?" he demanded.

"I was afraid it might hurt my chances at the promotion when I got the first one. But when the second one came through Friday afternoon, I forwarded it to your father," she said, averting her eyes from his piercing blue gaze. "I noticed they were coming from some sort of personal or fake email address, so I thought I should ignore them. I-I thought it was just someone trying to scare me away from wanting the GM position. But I figured, once I got the second one, I needed to tell your dad." Her voice was husky from the lump that had taken up residence in her throat.

Darrin let a string of curses flow. He tossed the laptop onto Jackie's bed and paced. His back was contoured with muscles, and his broad shoulders tapered down to his waist and hips. The towel stayed in place by being tucked into itself low on his hips. The trail of hair from his chest thinned over his navel then disappeared into the depths of the towel.

She noticed he'd stopped pacing and must have said something to her.

"Sorry, what?" she asked as a blush crept up her face. She needed to stop being so distracted by this man.

"I asked if you knew of anyone who would want you out of the way for this job?" His expression showed a sliver of amusement, probably over her distraction.

Todd's name surged to mind. But she shook her head. She didn't think Todd would do a thing like this. Plus, Todd had told her that he and Darrin were quite close.

"Now that all this has come to light," he said with an edge of irritation, waving in the direction of her laptop, "I really don't think you should be going anywhere on this trip alone." Although he spoke quietly, there was a definitiveness to his words. There would be no more arguments on the matter. "We need to be taking this to the police too. Either here or back home. I'll leave that part up to you."

He stood at the foot of her bed and looked up at her, waiting for her to object. She was sitting on top of the covers with her knees bent, wearing a knee-length charcoal pencil skirt. She knew the angle of her knees allowed him to see down the space between her thighs. Her legs quaked with the urge to shift their position. Darrin turned his back on her and went back into the bathroom.

"I think you're right," she said as he rejoined her moments later, in black dress pants and a white button-down. It was simple but looked great on him.

"About what?" He removed a jacket from a bag hanging in the closet.

Dammit—he was going to force her to spell it out. "That I shouldn't be alone."

"Damn right I am." He leaned in close to her and whispered, "And I am going to make sure of it."

She couldn't explain it, but she felt there was another meaning behind what he said. That thought had a rush of longing flowing through her body. She could feel his breath on her face. Her eyes wandered to his, and she wondered if he could see the desire burning in them.

Again, when she wished he would lean in closer, he withdrew. She left her bed, feeling discarded. He had her emotions reversing on themselves faster than she thought possible. Loading items into her tote bag for the meeting, she tried to clear from her mind images that—she was surprised to acknowledge—were not related to the email.

"It's almost seven. Let's go get some breakfast." He unbolted the door but checked the peephole before exiting their room. They descended one flight of stairs before entering the elevator.

"You never told me what you were looking for yesterday," she said while they waited for the elevator to begin going down.

"I wanted to wait around and see if anyone entered the hotel and went to the third floor." He allowed her to exit the elevator first then spoke in a low whisper. "So then, after I made up the story of needing more towels in our room, I wanted to see if there was any commotion or if someone came back down from the third floor, but the elevator went from the basement to the third floor without any stops and then back to the basement. I didn't see anyone that looked like they had the same body shape as the man in the hoodie."

"That was quite clever," she said, unable to disguise how impressed she was.

"You don't have to sound so surprised," he teased.

She got her first glimpse of a smile since the afternoon before. The look in his eyes made her knees weak. No wonder he had a reputation with women—though she was now beginning to doubt the validity of most of those rumors. Multiple times, he'd had the chance to make a move on her. Granted, he had made inappropriate comments the previous day. But he hadn't tried anything with her.

A sinking feeling filled her. Maybe she wasn't his type. The thought made her want to shake some sense into herself. He was her boss. Off-limits.

Chapter Thirteen
Lucas

Lucas dialed. The phone rang once, twice, three times. He held his breath, hoping the call wouldn't be answered.

"Have you kept watch for her?" the voice asked.

A groan longed to leave his lips. "Yeah. He is glued to her side. She's never alone."

"Did you send the most recent email?"

"Yeah."

"Well? When did you send it?"

"Oh. L-Last night."

The silence lasted several moments. "I have an alternative plan. This one shouldn't require either of us to be present when she dies." A cool laugh filled the phone line.

A shiver run up his spine. He waited to hear the rest of the plan, but it wasn't forthcoming. "W-what do you want me to do?" he asked hesitantly.

"Come back to New Mexico as soon as you can." Without another word, the phone disconnected.

He sighed. He didn't want to hurt Jackie, but he didn't have a choice. No one had asked him if this was something he wanted to be part of. It wasn't. *But what choice do I have?*

He called the airport and scheduled an earlier return flight.

CHAPTER FOURTEEN

DARRIN

The day went by in a flash. They met with five different property owners, one of whom struck Darrin as being the best. Between meetings, they barely had time to discuss the properties.

When their last meeting was concluded, he and Jackie sighed with relief. The day had been tiring. So many questions, plans, details. He had so much to consider and hoped Jackie was thinking of all the same details he was. He was happily surprised to see how she scrutinized each facility. She thought of some building details he had not. She had an eye for what would be seen as essential for the people they helped. She was more in tune with their needs than he was. The next day, they would go to the properties of their top two choices. Knowing he would be able to walk around then made spending the day in a chair easier to bear.

Jackie stood from the hotel's large conference-room table. He assumed she was as sick of sitting as he was. She stretched her legs, then bent over and extended her hands behind her back to stretch her arms and back simultaneously. He was reminded of the way she'd been sitting on her bed that morning. A few of her vertebra cracked as she twisted side to side. Her shapely rear was barely out of sight in the short skirt. If she turned just slightly, he would see what kind of underwear she wore.

If she wears any. His cock twitched at the thought. Although the position was enticing, he knew she wasn't doing it to tease. It was as if she didn't know what her poses did to the men around her. Standing back up, she flattened the front of her skirt.

She confused him. As usual, she was wearing a pencil skirt, blouse, and jacket. Her jackets always appeared to be a size too big, hiding the slender figure. *Why? Why does she hide under her clothes?* The jeans she'd worn the previous day had fit her as if they were an extension of her skin, and the tank top had accentuated each of her curves.

She stumbled when she caught Darrin watching her and straightened up. "Sorry. Just feeling a little stiff after sitting all day." Her face flushed.

"Me too." He smiled as he got up from his chair and stretched as well. "All right, it's about four. Let's go upstairs, change, and get something to eat. After we get back, we can talk about what locations we want to see tomorrow."

Their habit of only taking the elevator to the second floor continued. Jackie winced as she tried to balance her work bag on her shoulder.

"Can I take that for you?" he asked.

"It's all right. I just need to carry it on the other side. I keep forgetting about the bruise." She frowned.

He hated the thought of her being in pain. "I was so pissed when I thought you were in some sort of abusive relationship," he said. Her hazel eyes seemed brighter than usual in the artificial light of the hall. "Now I see you would never let anyone treat you like that."

"Not anymore." Her response was low and quiet but brought him around quickly. He watched her snap her lips closed, and his jaw tightened. She fumbled with the room key and quickly escaped into the bathroom without another word.

JACKIE

She sat down on the toilet lid with her head in her shaking hands. Her breathing became harsh as she remembered what her marriage had become. Everything had started great—they were perfect together. Then it had become all about conceiving a child.

The gentle knock on the bathroom door pulled her back to the present, with a slight gasp leaving her lips.

"Jackie?" Darrin asked hesitantly through the door. "Are you all right?"

The concern in his voice made her feel childish for hiding from him. The last two days, he'd been kind to her except when she goaded him. And all she did was get angry with him and shut him out. Her defenses were so deeply ingrained at this point that she didn't know if she could ever stop them.

"Yes, I'm fine." She rose from the toilet to lean over the sink and splash water on her face. After patting her face dry and fixing her hair and makeup, she left the bathroom.

She found Darrin directly outside the door. He reached for her hand and rubbed his thumb over the top. "I don't know what has happened in your past." His voice was low and calm. "If you need to talk about it, I'm here." He placed his index finger under her chin and gently tipped her head back to look into her eyes.

The urge to rip her chin from his hand was almost too much to stand, but this was a different touch, and she forced herself to realize it.

Jackie immediately wanted to tell him everything. But why? She hardly knew him. She gave him an appreciative smile and cleared her throat. "I want to get changed out of my work clothes before dinner." She removed her hand from his and dropped her chin to look at the floor.

She selected a tank top similar to the one she wore the night before and smiled at him as she made her way back to the bathroom to change. When she came out, she found he'd put on a pair of dark-blue jeans but kept his white shirt on. She wondered if he ever wore anything other than button-down shirts.

She couldn't figure out why, after all these years, she wanted to open up to someone else. She'd told Verity and her brother most of what had happened, but that was it. She didn't feel like talking about it with anyone else. She'd isolated herself. It was unfathomable why she felt she could tell Darrin everything. She longed to find the words to tell him—to tell him more than she'd told the others.

She was determined to give her friendship with Darrin an honest try. She needed to allow herself to branch out from her brother and Verity.

DARRIN

He kept running her words through his mind. "Not anymore." She'd spoken barely louder than a whisper, but he was certain that was what she'd said. One day, he hoped she would be able to confide in him. He hated to think of anyone mistreating her.

Is this abusive lover the one who's coming after her now?

The thoughts were pushed from his mind when she emerged from the bathroom. An olive-green tank was tucked into the pencil skirt she was still wearing. The snug tank left little to the imagination. He could tell she'd tried to conceal the contusion on her shoulder with makeup. It was still visible, but she'd done quite well hiding it. Her hair, which had been in a clip at the back of her head, was now in a French braid that trailed down her back.

He extended his arm to her. When she accepted it, her breast rubbed against it. He looked down at the swell of her breast. She shyly took a step away from him but didn't remove her hand from his arm.

"Where to this evening?" she asked huskily.

He tried to clear his throat and mind. "I noticed a place out on the beach that has an outdoor grill. Do you like burgers?"

"Yes." She cleared her throat as well. "I haven't had a good burger in a while."

With a grin, he put his other hand over hers. The gentle touch sent a pulse of yearning through him. He hoped she felt it too. He studied the tiniest flecks of brown in her hazel eyes.

He needed to tread lightly. She already thought he slept around. He needed to keep his desire buried so she didn't think she was just one among many. Truth be told, he liked to have a connection with a woman before he slept with her—which was hard to find with some women. They saw dollar signs—or his looks—and their interest would revolve around what he could do for them.

Jackie was the one to break contact. She looked at the door, and Darrin took the hint. He, as before, unbolted the door and checked the peephole before exiting. He pulled her back to his side, and they made their way down to the second floor and onto the elevator.

They shared the small confines with an elderly couple. Jackie slowly withdrew her arm from his, though he wanted to hold her in place, making the statement to all other men that she was not to be approached.

Darrin bit back his possessiveness and trapped it in a place he didn't think another woman would ever venture. Somewhere he didn't want to think of. As they made their way to the beachside cantina grill, he didn't try to touch her again. They sidled up to the counter and ordered burgers and drinks. Then they carried their drinks back to a table with an unobstructed view of the ocean.

She looked out at the water. "It's beautiful," she whispered and sipped her margarita.

"Sure is." He was looking at her over the rim of his beer. He needed to get a grip.

A flush covered her cheeks as she looked back out over the water. He kept his gaze steady on her, studying her. He wanted to know what made this confusing woman tick. Most women, he could read quickly, especially once they found out the money his family had. Being him held advantages and disadvantages. A relationship with any of the women who threw themselves at him was the last thing he wanted. They didn't seem to realize how transparent they were. Everyone assumed there was truth behind each damn tale. Even Jackie.

Jackie, though—she seemed to drag brick walls with her everywhere she went. The urge to climb those walls raged inside him. She didn't care about the money his family had, and she didn't treat him with any special reverence. She was happy to let him know how she despised his behavior. It both aggravated and relieved him. She was a woman he could see himself getting to know—and allowing to know him.

Their order number was called out, and Darrin left to pick up their food. As he walked over, he felt the glances of other women in the vicinity. He didn't show that he noticed. He knew why they looked; he worked out most mornings. A good workout made him feel accomplished.

He returned and placed her burger in front of her. She smiled and thanked him. Indicating the women looking his way, she said, "You seem to cause a stir anywhere you go." She said it in a playful manner, and he decided he wouldn't take offense.

"Have you noticed the looks in your direction, Ms. Martinez?"

She laughed, tipping her head back and revealing her supple neck. He had the urge to kiss it, taste it.

"You don't believe me?" he asked, skeptically arching one sandy brow.

"No. I think I'm one of the last women men want to ogle," she said with another burst of laughter. The margarita in front of her was almost gone.

Is she always this giggly when she drinks?

"That's where you're wrong," he said huskily. "I haven't been able to take my eyes off you."

She visibly swallowed. "I think I'm going to get another drink," she said, indicating her almost-empty glass. "Anything for you?"

"Not tonight." He would love to get drunk with her, but he wanted to keep his wits about him. After seeing the email that morning, he knew it was no coincidence that someone had been waiting outside the restaurant.

"Suit yourself," she said, giggling, and made her way back to the bar.

He noted all the men who stared in her direction as she walked. She had no idea how crazy she drove the men around her. She came back holding another margarita.

"How is it?" she asked, resuming her seat.

"The burger? It's good."

"Thank gosh! I'm starved." She took a large bite from her burger. The juice ran down her chin.

Darrin smiled as he handed her a napkin. She cleaned up her chin and licked the juice off her fingers. The simple motion rushed Darrin with arousal. He let out a groan, and she dropped her hand from her lips and flushed.

"Sorry," she whispered, abruptly turning serious.

He finished his burger and waited as she polished off her second drink and her burger. Darrin collected the dirty trays and brought them over to the bins in the corner of the cantina. He quickened his pace back to their table when he saw a man leaning against the edge, talking to Jackie. Red-hot anger rushed through his body, and it felt oddly right. She was attractive, and he felt a protectiveness for her.

He arrived at her side to hear the man asking her if she'd like to go for a midnight swim with him. Darrin's insides boiled. He wanted to rip the man away from the table. Jackie laughed and declined the invitation. Catching sight of Darrin, she left her chair. She bade the other man good night and turned to Darrin with an innocent smile.

That one look soothed the roiling rage in his stomach. They walked back over the walkways, hand in hand. He could get used to this.

Chapter Fifteen

DARRIN

They got back to their room without further incident. He realized quickly why Jackie had avoided drinking the night before. She was much more easygoing after having a drink or two.

He enjoyed this version of Jackie Martinez. She was playful and silly—two things he had never experienced from her. She ran into the room, tossed herself onto her bed, and kicked off her shoes as she lay down. Then she turned to her side with her knees tucked up level with her hips.

"All right, sleepy," he said with a chuckle. "We need to choose the properties we want to see tomorrow."

With a playful smile, Jackie said, "I'm not sleepy, just getting comfortable." The twinkle in her eye had Darrin wishing he could take her on the bed where she lay.

"Mm-hmm." Removing the files from his bag, he had to remind himself she was off-limits.

Laying the files across the edge of his bed, he took another peek at the woman who, since last week, had been one of the first things he thought about every morning. He settled himself on the edge of her bed, by her feet, and gazed down at her. The hazel eyes that looked back at him had him enraptured.

Clearing his mind, he looked away. "You pick your favorite, and I'll pick mine. Sound fair?"

"Sure." Jackie pulled her legs closer to her chest and then swung them over the edge of the bed. She sat up next to him, close enough for their legs to touch from hip to knee. The touch electrified the desire already tormenting his every waking moment.

He cleared his throat to dislodge the longing that had settled in it. "You pick first."

She leaned forward as if thinking really hard. He doubted she needed to contemplate this much, since he'd had his top two picked before they even arrived in California—before he left the office Friday, actually. She tapped her index finger on her chin then selected the building that had just been constructed for rentable office spaces. The company had had a difficult time renting out the spots for what it was asking and had decided to put the building up for sale. It was Darrin's first choice as well.

He selected an old office building that had once housed a small law office. The attorney who practiced out of the building was retiring and no longer needed the commercial space. He and his wife were planning to travel and didn't want anything to tie them down to one place.

She wrinkled her nose at the one he chose. He found the scrunch adorable. Another pang of desire flooded his body, and he wondered how an expression of disgust could do that to him.

"You don't like it?" he asked, surprised by how much he cared about her opinion.

She smirked. "Just messing with you."

Rolling his eyes, Darrin stacked up the files. "Great. I'll email the owners of each building and let them know we would like to view them tomorrow." With jerky motions, he put the files back into his travel bag. She was going to be the death of him, or of his sanity.

"I'm going to get into my pajamas," she said, leaving the bed.

He swore she intentionally rubbed her breast against his arm this time.

She went straight to the bathroom, with an extra swish to her hips as she walked. Darrin sent his emails. He had promised to let the owners know their decision no later than seven o'clock. It was quarter of seven when he sent his last email. After closing his laptop, he went to the dressing table to find his own pajamas.

Jackie returned in the same pajama top as the night before. This evening, however, she was wearing a pair of small spandex shorts. He looked her up and down. He saw why she'd virtually run to her bed the night before. She wasn't wearing a bra, and the motion of her breasts as she walked was going to break his small thread of control. His dick was begging for attention.

"More comfortable now?" he asked, letting his eyes roll over her again.

Her hair was loose around her shoulders, and her eyes sparkled in the light of the bedside lamp. She gave him a sly smile and nodded. *Damn.* He wanted to touch the shiny fabric that peaked at her shapely breasts. She crossed the room until she was standing directly in front of him, allowing him to see down the cleft of her breasts.

Darrin leaned his head over hers slowly and watched her eyes to gauge her desire, waiting for her to object before he touched her. Her hazel eyes were begging him to come closer. He obliged, lowering his face closer to hers, and took her head in his hands, sliding his fingers through her hair. When he didn't receive any objections, he pressed his ardent lips to hers. Her lips were soft and wanting. They accepted his with eagerness. She bent her knees as he deepened the kiss. Lying down on the bed, she pulled him with her and kissed him with a passion that had him nearly coming undone.

He slipped his tongue over her bottom lip, and she granted him access to her mouth. She tilted her hips up to him, pressing into his greedy erection. He needed more. Wanted more. He put his hand on her waist below the silky fabric.

She took a quick breath.

He froze. Her body went stiff below him, which made him rethink what he was about to do. He didn't remove his hand or his body from on top of hers but lifted his head. He looked down into her eyes. They were wide with fear.

Is she afraid of me? He removed his hand and braced himself on his arms above her, his eyebrows drawn together.

She had closed her eyes, taking slow, steady breaths.

"Jackie," he said. She opened her eyes back up. "Are you okay? Do you want to stop?"

She lowered her eyes, and he knew the moment she noticed his erection fighting the zipper of his jeans. Her eyes went wide and came back to his face. "We can't do this," she whispered. Her next words were even quieter. "I can't."

The anxiety in her voice broke something inside him as he pushed himself up off her bed to stand. When he stood, the prominence of his erection was more noticeable. He heard the catch in her breath. He turned away, retrieved his pajamas, and made his way to the bathroom.

Out of the corner of his eye, he watched as she moved up onto her bed and climbed under the covers. She had a faraway look in her eyes. Her gaze never left some spot on the opposite wall.

Darrin struggled with his warring thoughts in the bathroom.

He found her rolled over to face the wall rather than his bed as if she was embarrassed. She'd flirted with him all night. She wanted him, he knew. *Why is she stopping me? Stopping herself?*

He wanted to understand her. *Why is she so... damaged?* The word had him dropping onto his bed, staring at the slight movement of the covers she hid under. That had to be it. Someone had hurt her to the point that she was afraid to be with another.

It was best that they did not get too carried away after she'd been drinking, anyway. He wanted to be with her but wanted to make sure she wanted it too. Taking advantage of her willingness when her judgment was impaired wouldn't be right. He felt anger growing in his gut as he watched her. He disgusted himself.

He felt like a heel for even trying anything. The steady rise and fall of her breathing calmed his irritation. Darrin walked over, sat on the edge of her bed, and rested his hand on her arm.

He leaned down to whisper in her ear. "I would never do anything to hurt you. I'll wait until you're ready." He kissed her on the temple, reveling in the sweet scent, then pushed himself away to return to his own bed.

"I'm sorry, Darrin," the soft voice whispered before he was able to lie down.

He went back to her. "Sorry for what?" He placed a hand on her back and rubbed his thumb back and forth.

She rolled over onto her back to look up at him. He watched as she struggled to speak.

"I think it best if we act in a strictly professional manner. I'm sorry. That was my fault." Her large hazel eyes looked gray and sad in the dim light.

"Jackie, I want you." He wanted to be with her in more than just the physical sense.

The thought was a punch to the gut, and her walls were back—he could see it in the way her eyes changed as she stared into his. "I can't." She rolled back over to face the wall.

She cared for him, he knew. Something was bothering her, stopping her. Jackie had so much going on at the moment, he reminded himself—she shouldn't have to worry about protecting herself from more than one thing at a time. With a sigh, he returned to his own bed.

He couldn't sleep. Multiple times, he noticed she awoke with a start. Not once did she get up from bed, but her increased rate of breathing told him she battled demons in her sleep. He wondered if she was like this every night. She twisted and turned in her sleep and screamed Darrin's name as she awoke.

"Shhh, it's okay." He slid into bed next to her and pulled her onto his chest. Her breathing was fast and labored. "It's okay," he repeated, rubbing his hand up and down her back.

"I-I dreamed that guy was chasing me down the street. I couldn't find you. H-He dragged me down a side street. I was yelling to you for help." Jackie's voice got shriller. Her hands clutched at his chest and shook.

He pulled her closer. "You don't need to worry about him. I won't let anything happen to you."

The promise had fallen from his lips. He'd been careful to create a façade of indifference, but this woman had him turning into anything but. Her body slowly relaxed against him. Shifting closer, she laid her head in the space between his shoulder and chest.

"That's it—just relax," he whispered into her hair. "I'm going to ride back with you when you drive home. I don't want you making that trip alone again."

His arms were still around her when her alarm sounded at five thirty. He wanted to pull her back down as she withdrew from his embrace.

Chapter Sixteen

JACKIE

Jackie let the warm water wash over her. She couldn't believe the events of the last week. She'd shared a bed with her boss last night, someone was stalking her, and she and her parents were on opposite sides of a battlefield. Nothing was making any sense. An unbelievable desire for a man she should never want coursed through her.

Everything has changed so quickly.

She tried to be conscious of how long she was in the shower so she could get out and give Darrin plenty of time. She wrapped herself in a towel. Unsure of how long she had been in, she went out into the room and stopped dead in her tracks.

"What are you doing?" she shouted.

Darrin was sitting up in her bed with her laptop in his lap. She rounded the bed to see what he was doing. He was going through her emails. Red-hot anger flooded her veins, and she had the irrational desire to shove the computer from his hands.

"Here I was thinking how great you've been the last two days. I wanted to hurry up in the bathroom to give you a chance to use it, and you've been spending the time going through my computer." The invasion of her privacy hit her hard.

"Jackie, calm down."

"Don't you dare tell me to calm down!"

"I just wanted to see if there was another email."

She let out a short, quick breath, scoffing. "I see. You didn't think I would tell you if I got another one. Is that it? You don't trust me?"

Surging to his feet, he towered over her. "You're not exactly forthcoming with information." He got so close to her they were almost toe to toe. "You neglected to tell me about them in the beginning. You keep letting things slip out that I know you would rather not tell me." His steely eyes dared her to contradict him.

"I didn't want to come across as a complainer." Backing away from him, she averted her gaze. "Do you want the shower now, or should I go back in to get dressed?" she asked, ending the conversation about herself, as he probably knew she would.

"I texted my father last night. He said you never sent him those emails. I don't have patience for lies," he growled.

A chill ran through her body. "I... I did. I remember drafting the email." Her eyes darted to her laptop.

His eyes were cold, angry. "I'll take the bathroom," he snarled.

"Was there another email?" she asked, not trying to hide her annoyance.

He went straight to the bathroom. She was relieved tonight was the last they would be spending together. She needed her solitude back. Sharing close quarters with someone like him was far too much. Her emotions couldn't handle it, and her desires were bound to get the best of her if they continued being around one another like this.

She took her anger out on her clothes as she got dressed. Each article was tugged on as if it had been the one to enrage her. She stayed on the other side of the bathroom wall so she would hear the door open before he had a chance to see her.

Maybe she should go back to work for her dad. She didn't know if she could stand to look at Darrin any more than was absolutely necessary. That would stop her from making the stupid decision to sleep with her boss.

She groaned as she settled onto her bed and checked her emails. She didn't see any trace of another threatening message. Relief settled in her middle. He could have deleted it, she supposed. She figured he would have told her if there was another one, because it would have justified him looking.

Looking into her sent emails, she found nothing going to Charles for over a week. Checking more slowly, she still found nothing. There was an email in her drafts. Dread replaced the calm she'd just felt. Revealed in the draft folder was the email she had been planning to send to Charles before Todd's visit.

She hung her head. Now both Charles and Darrin were going to doubt her word. Telling Darrin might not make a difference, but she would try.

When he came out, she was ready to go, perched on the edge of her bed, with her purse and tote bag within reach. He made no attempt to talk to her—he never even looked at her. He sat down and checked his email, taking a few notes. The silence was suffocating. She wanted to scream; this was not how the week was supposed to go.

"I checked my email drafts," she said, and his eyes never lifted from his computer. "I forgot to hit send. Someone stopped into my office. I got distracted."

He didn't acknowledge her.

Fine. If he was going to ignore her, she might as well not be here. She would go down and get breakfast alone. She headed for the door.

"Where are you going?" he barked over the top of his computer.

"Getting coffee. Do you feel you need to follow me to make sure that's really what I'm doing?" she asked snidely.

His glare could have frozen boiling water.

"Don't cancel your flight. I can drive home on my own."

Jackie left their room and slammed the door behind her. She trudged down the first flight of stairs then took the elevator. She made her way to the restaurant and ordered breakfast.

She already had her food when Darrin entered the room, dressed in another of his suits that fit far too well. His trimmed hair was perfect as always. She wanted to run her fingers through the short threads.

"Get it together, Jackie," she mumbled to her eggs.

He went to the counter and ordered his food and coffee. Then he strutted over to sit with her. "The first place we're going is the office building. We need to be there by nine." Checking his watch, he said, "We need to leave here no later than eight thirty."

She nodded.

Their breakfast was quiet. No unnecessary conversation. No conversation at all, actually. She wasn't sure what irritated her more, the silence or the desire to fill it.

They took Darrin's rental car to the sites. The silence between them was strained and awkward. She would rather have driven her own car but didn't know exactly where she was going. She spent the car ride looking out her window with her arms crossed. She was wearing a pair of navy-blue slacks, a pale-yellow scoop-neck pleated shirt, and over that, one of her shapeless jackets.

At one point, she realized that with her arms crossed that way, the shape of her slender body and volume of her breasts were visible. Darrin glanced at them when he'd had to look out her window to make a turn. The drop of his eyes had her shifting in her seat and adjusting her shirt to prevent additional glimpses.

They arrived at the site ten minutes early and walked the perimeter. It provided plenty of parking and was away from the busy streets of town but still centrally located. This was the place Jackie had liked best after reading the write-up on the location.

It didn't disappoint. The building was three stories tall, sleek, and covered in windows. The reflection of the sunrise in the panes was breathtaking. She longed to see such a sight every morning. She closed her eyes, letting herself be immersed in the idea, with the early-morning sun warming her face. She worried she wasn't going to even be in the running for the general manager position. Things just kept getting worse.

As they walked back to their car, Thomas Windsor, the owner of the building, pulled into the parking lot. "What do you think?" he asked by way of greeting.

Thomas's walk exuded confidence. His appearance wasn't what Jackie was expecting. He looked to be in his early thirties, and his head was shaved close. The men shook hands, then Thomas extended his hand to her.

"It looks nice from here," Darrin replied with his signature smile.

Since he'd responded, Jackie didn't feel her words would be required or necessary, especially since Darrin's father owned the company. *Why would they care what my thoughts are?*

At this point, she doubted she would be the one to get the GM position, problem one being that she would need to get along with Darrin. Problem two was that he obviously didn't trust her. *He has to trust me to run and entire location.* Despair began to fill her. She wanted this position, this opportunity.

She followed the two men across the threshold into the building. The entry was large and sleek. She could visualize the reception desk that would sit just inside the door. The elevator was just to the right of where she could see it all playing out. As she pictured what could be, renewed determination filled her soul. She was not going to allow Darrin's pushiness and her forgotten email to prevent her pursuit of the GM position. She'd *meant* to send that email. She just needed to prove it.

Thomas led them around each floor, showing them each office, cubicle, and bathroom. He discussed the advantages of the location and the engineering of the building. He could have been quite a successful used-car salesman.

Darrin kept his expression impassive. If he was impressed, Thomas wouldn't know it, but the subtle tics of his eyebrows hinted at what he was thinking. He liked the building.

Jackie was pleasantly surprised by how large each space was. This was going to be great. They were expecting this location to be more popular than the one in New Mexico. The larger offices would be perfect. She didn't want to but could feel the excitement surging through her. Who was she kidding? She couldn't go back to working for her father. She would be miserable.

"Now that you've seen it in person, what do you think?" Thomas asked as they left the building, looking back up at the elegant windows.

"It's nice for sure," Darrin replied with a smile. "We have another contender to view this afternoon. A decision will be made after a report is given to Charles on Friday."

"Thank you for allowing us to view your property," Jackie added. "It's beautiful."

"My pleasure. I think your company does great things for people. I would be honored to provide you with your new location."

They said their goodbyes and shook hands again, with a promise to be in touch within the next few days. Then Jackie and Darrin got back into his rental car. He started the car and began backing up before acknowledging her existence.

"What are your thoughts?" he asked.

Keeping her tone professional and even, she stated the facts. "It's located in a great place, with plenty of parking, and the offices are spacious. Plus, the gym in the basement will be a good selling point for employees."

"I agree. I don't think the other place this afternoon will come close to this," he said, motioning to the building as he shifted the car into drive. "The next meeting is scheduled for one o'clock. Do you want to stop for lunch?"

He was being civil, but she could tell it was forced. "Sure," she answered.

Darrin didn't bother to ask where she would like to go. He chose a chain restaurant with a drive-through to make it quick and easy. They ate their meals in the parking lot. The only sounds filling the car were the radio and the crinkle of wrappers.

Jackie couldn't wait to get out of his car. To get away from him. She was stuck, as if the walls were closing in around her, and she felt like she couldn't breathe. She'd never considered herself claustrophobic—this was a new feeling. Trapped in a place that provided protection. Trapped in close confinement with someone who could both ruin and validate her. The air in the car was stifling.

Shaking, she rolled down her window, welcoming the fresh air. Breathing deep, she longed for it to fill her senses—to give her a glimmer of normal life and show her things would get better. *No such luck,* she realized as she closed the window when they began moving again, entrapping herself once again.

The second location was much smaller but also significantly cheaper. The elderly man who'd previously run the space as a law office gave them the tour. It was much more crowded. Jackie's mind had already been made up when they arrived.

The parking lot did not allow many cars. The space around it required some upkeep. There was landscaping that had once been beautiful but had been left to its own devices.

They shook hands with the man and thanked him for the tour. As much as she wished to purchase the property just so he could have his retirement dreams, she knew that was not the way to make a business purchase. They promised to let him know their decision by the end of the week then made their way back to the car with a friendly wave to him.

"Thoughts?" Darrin asked again as soon as they were seated in the car.

She stated the downfalls and reasons she felt the other office would be best. He didn't say anything back. This annoyed her.

Mockingly, she asked, "Thoughts?"

He addressed her with a snide look. "Same as you."

Their drive back to the hotel was just as quiet as the rest of the day had been. They each had work they wanted to get done, so they separated in their room and took care of what they needed to do.

When five o'clock arrived, Darrin closed his computer. "Jackie?"

She looked up at him to show she was listening but refused to speak.

"Ready for dinner?"

"You go out. I'll order room service." Her chilled answer was meant to cut like daggers.

Irritation and disappointment warred in his features. Jackie knew she was acting childish, but she couldn't help it. She was in a defensive mood that she couldn't switch off. She was beginning to think of what life could be like if she gave herself to a man again. Her emotions were at war with one another, and she was taking it all out on Darrin. Her life was being flipped around, and the changes had all started because of him. Well, they'd really started with the emails.

Without another word, Darrin grabbed his wallet off the table and left. She was astounded he didn't try to talk her out of it. Disappointment settled into her body. She found the room service menu and ordered herself a sandwich and a can of cola. The food arrived within fifteen minutes. Jackie ate her sandwich while she watched an old movie that was airing on one of the television's few channels. She'd seen the movie many times but enjoyed it each time. It was one of her feel-good movies.

After finishing her sandwich, she decided to take a bath. She filled the tub and sank into the scalding water. Her skin turned red, but she didn't mind. Lying in the water, she read for a while. No matter how many times she read it, the book made the tears flow. The first time, she'd tossed it away from her when the author killed one of the characters she was rooting for. But when she got to the end, she'd accepted that death as a necessary evil.

The temperature in the water started to drop. She got out and dried off. But instead of the pajamas like she'd originally intended to wear, she put on her swimsuit. It was a pale yellow that complemented her dark-auburn hair.

She needed a reprieve from spaces filled with Darrin. The thought of her bed mocked her with memories filled with desire and comfort. After wrapping herself in her coverup, she grabbed her tote bag and headed to the elevator. She pressed the button for the lobby. She wanted to go to the beach but didn't feel entirely comfortable going alone. But she wasn't going to ask Darrin to accompany her. She stepped out of the elevator and found herself face-to-face with the man who was never far from her thoughts or presence.

"Where are you going?" he demanded.

"Swimming."

"Alone?" he scoffed.

Jackie scowled at him, and her breathing sped up. *Is he making fun of my nightmares?*

She pushed past him and headed toward the hotel's indoor pool. When she turned to look back at him, her heart sank as she realized he had gone. Twice that night, he'd left when she hoped he wouldn't.

Probably for the best, she told herself.

The pool was close to the elevator and enclosed in an area with large windows. Anyone walking by inside the hotel could see in. She needed the space to breathe but feared the unknown. If she knew who she was up against, it would be easier.

She laid her bag, which contained a towel from their room, on one of the small tables. Jackie always found the towels by pools far too small, as if they were made for children. She could hardly wrap one around her leg, never mind her chest. Placing her cell phone on the top of the pile, she assured herself that she would be able to call someone if she needed to. She removed her coverup and draped it across the back of the chair. She was relieved to see the only other people in the pool area were the elderly couple she and Darrin had shared the elevator with the morning before.

She slowly descended the steps of the pool. The water was lukewarm and lapped at her legs. Chilled bumps rose and spread across her skin; she shivered as she took another step. Her back was to the door, giving her a feeling of vulnerability. As soon as she reached the bottom of the pool, she turned and dropped herself into a backstroke. She noticed the group of young men from the beach the other day entering the room. Behind them entered a group of young women about the same age.

Jackie felt self-conscious immediately. She didn't mind her body, but she knew it wasn't as slim as it once had been. The padding around her middle hadn't been there in her early twenties. She tried to ignore the presence of the young people while she swam laps around the pool. The exercise was therapeutic. The group of girls climbed into the hot tub while the men descended into the pool. She wished she'd stayed in the room.

Her eyes were drawn up to the door when she saw another person entering. Darrin deposited his T-shirt on the second chair next to Jackie's bag. His hard abs looked better in this light than they had in the hotel room the previous morning. They were more distinct than she had originally realized. Under these bright lights, she saw more definition all over his upper body. The young women in the hot tub stirred and started whispering to one another.

Jackie stayed where she was, transfixed. She was wondering what he was doing. *Did he come down to watch over me? Did he come down to protect me even though he's clearly angry with me?* A flutter took over her mind, one she didn't want to analyze.

Her throat closed as she watched him make his way around to the steps of the pool. His legs were long and muscular. She wondered if he worked out when he was at home.

The young men had started staring as well. They were all well-built but not like Darrin. He carried himself in a dignified manner and wore his swim trunks low on his hips. When he reached the bottom step, he submerged himself in the water. The other men went back to their conversations.

He came up with his dirty-blond hair clinging to his face. He shook his head, sending water flying and making his hair spike out at odd angles. The stubble on his chin made him more attractive. Jackie felt a pang of yearning low inside her. He swam right up to her, deflating the hope on the faces of the young ladies, who turned away from him. They must have assumed Jackie and he were a couple. Most people on this trip had. Jackie had caught herself on multiple occasions hoping that were the case.

"Nice swimsuit," he said as he got closer to her.

A fire of desire swirled in her womb. She longed to wrap her arms around his neck. The small pieces of fabric she was wearing hid little. The two triangles over her breasts emphasized their size, while the bottoms barely covered her buttocks.

"Thank you," she croaked.

"I think I could get used to seeing you like this," he whispered. "Only half dressed." His breath brought her accusatory gaze to his.

"You're drunk," she stated.

He merely grinned and swam away. He was a strong swimmer, she noted. His long, muscled arms carried him quickly through the water. She could not suppress a smile. Just as she let it surface, he stopped swimming and looked back at her. She tried to avert her eyes. It was too late. He'd already caught her watching him and probably recognized the want in her eyes.

The young men were trying to race one another across the pool. Avoiding being in their way, Jackie made her way over to Darrin. "Did you come down to check on me?"

"In a way." He looked her up and down as much as was possible in the water.

She swam away from him and made her way to the steps. As she began climbing them, she felt his presence close behind her. Jackie thought she felt the brush of his swim trunks on the back of her thigh. She wanted to cover herself. She felt naked.

The elderly couple left soon after the others had joined them in the hot tub. Jackie walked as confidently as she could from the pool over to the whirlpool, feeling Darrin's heat right behind her. Heart pounding with excitement, she made her way down the steps and took a seat. Darrin slid in close next to her but made sure not to touch her. Considering how wound up she had been all day, she figured he didn't want to press his luck.

"What time are you leaving tomorrow?"

She noticed immediately that he didn't say *we*. "Six," she said evenly. "You kept your flight, I hope."

"I did, but the offer still stands to ride with you."

"I'll manage," she said stiffly. Her desires fought with the cold words tumbling from her lips. Self-preservation and stubbornness kicked her in the rear each time.

"Come on, Jackie," he whispered harshly, his breath slipping across her ear, causing a chill to run over her body. She turned to face him and found his icy eyes narrowed on hers.

"I made it here fine. I can make it back fine."

"Fine." He moved abruptly. She didn't have time to prepare herself. His lips were on hers. The kiss was hard, passionate. She let herself kiss him back. He stopped the kiss as quickly as he'd started it. "That's what I thought," he whispered.

Chapter Seventeen

JACKIE

"My flight leaves at seven. This is your last chance for a travel buddy." The dim light from his laptop illuminated his features. They appeared sharper in the semidarkness.

"I told you last night I didn't need one." She grabbed some clothes from her suitcase and headed for the bathroom.

"Fine. If anything happens to you, that'll make the GM decision a hell of a lot easier." With that, he snapped his laptop closed.

Jackie couldn't see his face well enough to make out his expression and wasn't sure how she should take that comment. After she slammed the door, she began to undress for her shower. *Why does he all of the sudden think it's funny to poke fun at my fears? If he thinks thats the way to change my mind, he has another think coming.*

She had just removed her underwear when knocked on the door. She ignored him and started the shower. She was done with his hot-and-cold behavior and his conflicting comments. She climbed into the shower as she heard him knocking louder. After the fourth time, she'd had enough.

She rinsed the last of the shampoo out of her hair and shut off the shower.

After wrapping herself in a towel, she yanked the door open. "What?" She could feel the water dripping down her body.

"I wanted to let you know I'm heading out."

She felt like the floor was dropping out from under her. His blue eyes were hard and cold as they held her gaze.

"Thank you for letting me know," she said stiffly.

"I don't want you driving alone. But I'm not going to force my way into your car." His steely eyes met hers with the true sincerity of his words, and she knew this was her last chance to tell him. She needed to tell him not to take his flight. To stay with her. To protect her.

"Okay, then. I'll see you in the office tomorrow." Jackie's pride wouldn't let her concede.

Darrin didn't press it any further. He withdrew from the doorway but looked back to her, his eyes begging her to change her stance. "Call me when you get home, please. I want to know you're safe. I'll leave my home number for you on the nightstand, just in case," he said, shrugging, just before he closed the door.

The fight in her head was giving her a headache. She knew if she spoke, she would beg him to go with her. Instead, she nodded.

She took her time dressing and pinning up her hair. Only when she heard the hotel room door close did she leave the sanctuary of the bathroom. Without him there, the room felt cold, unwelcoming. She packed the remainder of her belongings and headed to the door, managing to carry everything at once by balancing her tote bag on top of her suitcase, with her purse and laptop bag slung over her shoulder. She figured she looked like an idiot but didn't want to make multiple trips.

She was at the door when she remembered the note on the nightstand. She rushed over and picked it up. Without reading it, she stuffed it into her jeans pocket. Then she checked that her phone was fully charged and sent a quick message to Tony and Verity to let them know she was on her way home.

Jackie made her way through the parking lot and loaded everything but her purse into the trunk of her car. Only when she got into the driver's seat of her car did she notice the damage. A rock had been thrown through the front passenger window.

On the rock was a message. She spun the rock around to read it. *Safe travels.*

A cold sweat took over her body. She was shaking, not knowing what to do. She hadn't been back to her car since the day she'd arrived. She had no idea when the damage might have occurred. If she called the police, she would be stuck here alone for who knew how long. She needed to make a decision, and she needed to do it quickly.

Making up her mind, she brushed the glass off the seat, tossed her purse down, got in, and started her car. Another rush of fear flooded over her when she looked in the rearview mirror.

DARRIN

Darrin arrived at the airport just when he'd wanted—ninety minutes before his flight. He would have time to grab something to eat before going through security. On the drive to the airport, he'd turned around twice to go back to the hotel. But he was a man of his word, and he had promised her he wouldn't force himself into her car. As much as her stubbornness was pissing him off, he wasn't about to make himself seem more of an ass than she already thought he was. The woman was infuriating.

He went to one of the only restaurants open this early that served coffee. He'd already returned his rental car, so he was stranded at the airport. He couldn't go after her at this point even if he wanted to. Checking the screen of his phone, he saw that he still didn't have any messages or calls from her.

As the time ticked closer to six, he kicked himself for leaving her. If anything happened, he would never be able to forgive himself.

When the clock read six o'clock, he left his seat and headed for the security check. He got in line to get his boarding pass. Time was moving inordinately slowly. Then it was already six fifteen. She was on the road. He hoped.

He loaded his bag into the overhead compartment and took his seat. There was still another thirty minutes before takeoff. Soon, he would need to shut off his phone and wouldn't know of her safety until they landed, and even then, he wouldn't be sure. He was already walking a fine line with Jackie. *How much farther can I push it without her snapping?* Darrin decided he would text her when he landed. He closed his eyes to relax.

He was thinking back to his check-in at the hotel. He felt bad about how he'd acted. Jackie seemed to keep leaving him with more questions than answers, the largest of which being whether she wanted to be with him the way he wanted to be with her. Their work situation was clearly weighing heavily on her. Running his hand over his face, he groaned, wishing there was an easy way for this to all work out.

His phone ringing had his heart in his throat. Without checking the display, he answered.

"Hey, Darrin, I know you have your flight back today, but I wanted to call you with an update."

He couldn't help the disappointment at the sound of Mia's voice. He'd assumed it would be Jackie changing her mind.

He cleared his throat. "Hey, Mia. What did you find?"

"Well, this is one chick you don't have to worry about chasing you for money." She laughed. "You know A.J.M. Property and Realty?"

His brow furrowed. "Yeah, they've done loads of work all over New Mexico and Arizona. They own several large properties." He didn't volunteer that Jackie had worked there previously. He remembered it from his perusal of her résumé.

"Well, your girl's parents own it."

Darrin felt his eyes widen at the revelation. Her parents owned one of the biggest real estate companies on the West Coast.

"Martin Martinez started the company nearly twenty-five years ago. A.J.M.—Anthony, Jaqueline, Martin."

Mia continued listing facts of the company, but Darrin was no longer listening. *If the company is partially named after her, why is she not involved in her own family's business? Why is she so hell-bent on getting the GM position?*

"Damn it, Darrin," Mia squeaked. "Are you listening to me?"

"Shit, what did you say?" He felt marginally bad for zoning out.

"From what I've heard, she's not on the best terms with her family."

Well, that answers one question. He nodded. "Do you know what the issue is with her family?"

"No. I'll keep looking." Mia disconnected abruptly.

Once again, he'd found out one detail about Jackie that left him with several more questions. *Why is she on bad terms with her family? Would they hurt her?*

Even if she got the promotion, he wondered if it would only be a matter of time until she went to her parents' company. He would never be able to pay her what her parents could afford. A familiar sensation settled in his gut. Leaning forward, he ran his fingers through his hair. He was doomed to be hurt by her too.

JACKIE

Jackie finally relaxed when she hit a stretch of highway and could not see another car. The wind coming through the window hurt her ears. The thudding sound drove her crazy, reminding her of a helicopter ride her brother had once convinced her to go on. She was going to push the limits. She needed to get back home as soon as possible.

She had to laugh at herself now. Right before leaving, seeing a shadow in her back seat, she'd panicked that her stalker was camping out there. She'd jumped out of her car, flung open the door, and checked the seat only to find that the shadow was cast by a sweatshirt she'd forgotten about. The floor was empty except for the food wrapper from the fast-food chain she'd stopped at the other day. Jackie had let out a breath of relief and got back in her car. She needed to get out of there.

Driving as quickly as laws would allow, she weaved back through town and to the highway, with her eyes virtually glued to her rearview mirror, like a hunter constantly scanning for his victim. Except that she was worried she would be the one hunted. As she waited for this foe to appear in the mirror, something in her soul was telling her if she looked away for just a moment, he'd be behind her. The rational side of her brain warred with the paranoia living in the shadows.

She wished she'd accepted Darrin's offer. Now she had no choice. She had no one to blame for the situation she was in but herself. He'd been nothing but helpful the entire time, even though his arrogance and pushiness grated on her nerves.

She couldn't believe the feelings she was having for Darrin. She hadn't had feelings for anyone like that since her ex-husband. Soon after the night he'd struck her, she'd filed for divorce. Their marriage had been damaged irreparably. Deep inside, she knew it had been damaged before that night, but she couldn't admit it to herself, much less to him. He'd felt terrible for slapping her, but she couldn't take a chance that he'd let himself get carried away again. Putting that barrier up was the only way she knew to keep him from being able to hurt her again.

The way he'd obsessed about a child was not healthy for her. While going through the divorce, she'd left school and worked for her father. She couldn't go to the same college he was attending anymore. It was far too much to bear.

After everything that had happened, she could only imagine the rumors that would be circulating about her. It was best that she leave it all behind. She had planned to reenroll in the fall of that year to complete her education online. Verity had been the only friend who made sure to stay in touch. She would go to visit Jackie any chance she got. Their friendship had been her savior—that and her brother being there for her anytime she needed him.

Jackie smiled at the memories of her dear friend and her brother, the two people she was always able to count on. She couldn't help but wonder if that list was soon to grow.

The ding of her gas gauge brought her back to reality. She'd been driving for almost four hours. She'd been so vigilant about watching for anything that looked like a car following her that she had not been paying attention to her fuel level. She hadn't noticed anyone suspicious yet, but she was still careful as she exited the highway. Checking her navigation app, she noticed there was far too much driving ahead of her.

She kept her eye on the rearview mirror. No one followed her off the ramp. She parked at a small filling station then went inside to prepay for her gas. It was a small station with only one person working. Wandering up and down the small, dusty aisles, she selected a few snacks for the road, checking the expiration dates, worried that the dust hinted at how old they were. The station was so remote that she couldn't help but imagine how few customers they got.

Looking out the window as she paid, she watched another car pull into the station and park on the opposite side of the pump she had used. Her heart skipped a beat. She was relieved when a mother and her children piled out of the car. It made her think of a clown car—the people just kept coming. Children of varying ages chatted as they made their way into the store. She would be surprised if they all fit.

Outside again, she pumped her fuel, careful to keep an eye on anyone else nearby. Once the tank was filled, she left as quickly as she could. Again, getting on the highway, she watched her rearview mirror. Jackie tried to relax, but anytime a car seemed like it came up on her too fast and then slowed down to stay behind her, she felt like her heart was going to beat out of her chest—if she didn't have a heart attack by the end of the day, it would be a miracle. She would speed up for a while to put some distance between her and any car that was tailing her. She did this to see if they would speed up to keep her in their sights. None of them did, but it made her feel better to know.

Jackie only needed to stop one more time to use the bathroom and get another bottle of water. She was two hours away, in the home stretch. In the gas station parking lot, she messaged Tony again to let him know of her progress. He was impatient for updates. Then she placed her phone on the roof of her car to stretch and pump some gas.

As she accelerated out of the parking lot, she heard the phone slide across the roof of her car. "No, no, no," she chanted to herself, bringing her car to a stop in a parking lot across the street.

A dark pickup pulled out of the gas station, and she heard the tell-tale crunch. She jogged across the street and found her cell phone shattered on the ground. Luckily, she was close enough to home that she no longer needed it for navigation, but it would be difficult to call Darrin later.

With a groan, she ran back to her car. She was drained. She felt as if she'd run a marathon.

Chapter Eighteen

DARRIN

Darrin arrived home a little after noon. The next six hours were going to be hell. He'd picked up his phone to text her several times but always set it back down. He was worried she might not respond well to his checking in on her. *But she agreed to call me, didn't she?*

He called his father to tell him about the trip. The call only distracted him and kept him busy for half an hour. He omitted telling him that he and Jackie had shared a room. For some reason, he didn't feel his father needed to know that detail. The last thing either of them needed was for the entire building to be buzzing with the drama of them sharing a hotel room while on a business trip.

He selfishly wanted that memory to belong to him and him alone—he doubted Jackie would be telling anyone about it. Those moments together were going to be filed away, along with how she'd looked in her swimsuit the previous night and how she looked that morning, wrapped in a towel, with her hair left loose. The wet, dark waves had splayed over her shoulders, some falling between her breasts. He'd wanted to kiss her that morning before he left. It had taken all the restraint he had not to.

This train of thought did nothing to ease the want that coursed down to his dick every time he thought about her. She was still mad at him; he didn't blame her. He would have been livid to find someone searching through his computer, not because he had anything to hide but because of the invasion of privacy. The decision to do it hadn't been easy, but the desire to know the truth had won out, and he assumed her stubbornness would have kept her from telling him. In hindsight, he should have given her the chance to tell him the truth about the email herself, but then again, there was nothing to tell. And he probably wouldn't have believed her anyway.

Instinctually, he believed she had intended to forward the email to his father. But it still irked him that she wouldn't have sent it directly to him. He wanted to know who was stalking her and sending her those cryptic messages and subtle threats.

Darrin paced up and down the dark hickory flooring in the entryway. Then he rushed back to the kitchen, where he'd left his phone when he'd grabbed a beer earlier, and dialed a number that had been committed to memory for years.

JACKIE

This was it. She was getting off at her exit. She would be home in five minutes. Jackie was surprised to see she had beaten the time she thought it was going to take her.

All she had to do was make it these last three miles without incident. The relief faded from her as quickly as it had come. *What if the stalker is waiting for me at home?*

The steering wheel felt slick in her hands. The only sound she heard was her own heart beating in her chest. *Three minutes left. Where else can I go?*

Her mind raced. She was too tired to think of an alternative. She couldn't go to her parents' house. She didn't have any close friends nearby.

Her apartment was in sight. Her heart sank when she saw a car sitting out front. But maybe it belonged to one of her neighbors. She pulled in next to it and recognized the car. *Oh, thank gosh.*

Apparently too impatient to wait for a call, Darrin was waiting for her. She'd beaten her driving time by at least half an hour. *How did he know I'd be getting home soon?*

He stepped from his car and stared at the terrorized window. "What the fuck is this? You know what? I don't have time. Get in my car," he said, waving his hands around to halt her explanation. Without waiting for her to respond, he pulled bags out of her trunk and tossed them into his.

"What? Are you crazy? I just got home," she said.

"Right. Whoever followed you in California probably knows where you live."

She pulled her purse over the center console from the passenger seat and the rock from where it had been pushed to the floor that morning. "I just thought of that while I was getting off the highway. I was worried he would be waiting for me when I got here."

"Me too. I'd been here for about half an hour when you pulled in," he said, looking down at his shoes like a child admitting to wrongdoing.

"Someone needs to check through your place tomorrow before you go in." His steely eyes bored into hers, offering no moment for argument.

Jackie sighed with resignation, too tired to put up a fight. She got out of her car. Turning the key fob over in her hand, she laughed at herself. She didn't bother to lock the car since one of the windows was missing.

Splaying his hand on her lower back, Darrin walked her around to the passenger side of his car. He opened the door for her, and she slid in. The seats were warm and comfortable. She felt like she could fall asleep right there. Her mind and body begged for the reprieve.

"I only live ten minutes away. Sorry you have to sit in the car even more today." He reached across the center console and rested his large hand on her leg.

"It's all right," she said sleepily, resting her head back against the seat. For the first time all day, she felt safe.

She woke up to Darrin's hand shaking her knee. She was astounded she'd fallen asleep in such a short span of time. His house was nice, judging from what she could make out in the dark—bigger than she'd expected.

"Let's get you inside," he said.

She unbuckled her seat belt and let her feet fall heavily to the ground. He met her at her car door and helped her up the front steps of the house.

"Sorry—I forgot to turn the light on when I left. I was in a bit of a rush."

With a glance up at the sky, she saw that it was about to storm.

He led her into a large entryway and flipped on the light. The sudden brightness caused her to cover her eyes. The entry was plain. White walls, dark floors, a coatrack, and a shoe rack were all that occupied the vast space.

He locked the door and set the alarm. She was surprised he had an alarm for his house. From the entry, it didn't look like he had much to steal. She removed her shoes and placed them on the rack.

"Let's go down to my room." Putting his hand around her arm, he tried to lead her down the hall.

She froze, and her feet felt heavy.

"What's wrong?" he asked, one eyebrow raised.

"Don't you have a guest room?" she asked through the lump in her throat.

She watched as a slow smile crossed his lips, and he began to laugh. "Yes, and that is where you will sleep. I was taking you to my room so you could pick out a T-shirt and a pair of sweatpants or something to wear to bed. Sorry, I was just assuming you'd want something clean to wear."

"Oh," she said, hanging her head as she felt her cheeks burn red. Something clean to wear did sound good.

"Unless you want to sleep in my bed too," he said with a ruthless smirk.

Once she relaxed, he led her down the hall. The house was larger than she'd thought it would be. They passed several doors before they reached the third door on the right.

The room was well furnished with a large bed and matching night-stands and a set of matching dressers. There was a white chaise lounge sitting along one wall, with a large bookcase beside it. Jackie went over to the shelves and searched through the titles. Some she had read, but others, she'd never even heard of. Most appeared to be mysteries, though she recognized a few as legal dramas. A handful were so well loved she could no longer read the titles running up the spine. She picked up one she hadn't read and plopped down on the chaise lounge.

On first glance, she hadn't realized the chair was velvet. She loved it. She settled in and started to read the back cover.

Darrin looked over at her and smiled. "That was my mother's chair. She would spend hours sitting on it, reading."

"I'm so sorry." Jackie jumped up from the chair as if it had burned her.

"No, don't be. Please sit—you look exhausted," he said reassuringly, gesturing for her to resume her seat. He went over to the taller of the two dressers and opened the second drawer. "Do you want to pick, or will anything work?"

"Anything will work at this point," she said through a yawn.

"Perfect." He pulled out a plain white cotton shirt like the one he'd worn down to the pool the night before. "Any preference on pants?"

"Could I actually borrow a pair of shorts?"

"I'd never say no to having a glimpse of those legs," he said playfully.

"Have you been drinking again?" she asked with a frown.

"Jackie," he said seriously. "I was so damn worried about you all day. I couldn't think of much else. I would have hated myself if something had happened to you on your drive home. I'm just relieved to know you're safe." His eyes were filled with emotion.

"Me too. I was terrified all day, staring in my rearview mirror." She shrugged and gave a sheepish smile. "When I found that rock on my passenger seat, I nearly fainted."

"That's what broke your window—a rock?" He pulled a pair of black gym shorts from another drawer.

"I grabbed it out of my car when you picked me up—I wanted to show it to you." As she pulled the rock from her purse, she found the demolished remains of her cell phone.

Darrin set the clothes down on the edge of his bed, took the rock, and turned it over in his hand to read it. His face turned pale. "Damn, Jackie. Who is doing this?" His hand at his side flexed as he handed the rock back to her.

"I don't know," she said solemnly. "And this happened." She brandished the phone for him to see the damaged screen. "It won't even turn on."

"What the hell happened to that?" he asked, furrowing his brow at the mangled device.

"I put it on the roof of my car. And it fell. And it got run over," she said on a defeated laugh.

"We'll replace it." He extended the clothes to her and led her to the bathroom. He turned on the light and told her to feel free to shower or do anything she needed to and to call him when she was done so he could take her to the guest room.

The bathroom was almost as large as his bedroom. There was a large walk-in shower in one corner and a whirlpool tub in the other. Jackie was tempted to fill up the tub but instead settled for washing her face in one of the double sinks after she changed. She tried to make sense of all that had happened over the last few days but realized there was no possible way to make it make sense when she didn't know who was stalking her and why.

When finished, she wandered down the hall and found Darrin in a room that had to be the guest room. There was a queen-size bed centered against one of the walls. This room was also equipped with matching nightstands and dressers. Darrin stood hunched over at the side of the bed, tucking the quilt under the mattress.

He turned to look at her and whistled as she entered the room. Her cheeks ran hot. She'd debated whether to keep her bra on and in the end had decided against it. Now she was wishing she'd kept it on. The urge to cover herself ached in her muscles.

"Need anything? Water? Snack?" he asked.

"Just a water if you don't mind."

"I'll be right back."

She deposited her travel clothes on top of one of the dressers, and he returned moments later with bottled water. Jackie sat down on the edge of the bed as he brought it over to her. Rather than open it right then and guzzle down half of it like she wanted to, she set the bottle on the nightstand.

"Thank you," she said it in a way that let him know she was referring to more than just the water.

"I promised you I wouldn't let anyone hurt you." He settled himself onto the bed next to her. "Are you planning on working tomorrow?"

"I wasn't." She didn't make eye contact with him. "I was already planning to take the day off to recover from the drive."

"Okay, good. I was going to suggest you take a day of rest."

She felt so conflicted each time she looked into his eyes. Before her sat a man she hadn't liked until a few days ago, someone she shouldn't be having feelings for. Someone she shouldn't be happy to share a space with. Yet each time she looked at him, she knew she could get lost in those eyes forever.

She laid her head on his shoulder; he wrapped his right arm around her, placing his hand on her hip. They sat in silence. There was no awkwardness to the quiet. Neither felt they needed unnecessary chatter.

Darrin turned and kissed the top of her head as he withdrew. "Get some sleep. Do you want me to wake you before I leave for the office?"

She'd been hoping he was not going to go in to work, but she couldn't bring herself to ask him to take another day out of the office on her account. So instead, she nodded as she climbed under the covers. Darrin left, shutting off the light on his way out. Within minutes, Jackie was asleep.

* * *

In the daylight, the room was even more inviting than the night before. The walls were a steel blue. The bright-white trim popped against the darker hue. The bed itself was soft and comfortable. Absentmindedly, she traced the seams of the quilt with her index finger.

As she got out of bed, she checked herself in the mirror. Deciding she didn't actually care too much how she looked, she went in search of the delectable smell emanating from the end of the hall. She had no clue where the kitchen was, but her stomach and nose led the way.

The long hall was still dark and most of the doors were closed, so there was no light being let in. Jackie made it back to the entry and continued straight ahead. She entered what she assumed was the living room. It had two large black leather sofas, a coffee table, and a massive television mounted on the wall. She wasn't surprised to see there were no photos around. Darrin had never struck her as the sentimental type, although he obviously had fond memories of his mother in her chaise lounge.

Connected to the living room was the formal dining area and then, finally, the kitchen. She stood off to the side for a moment, watching Darrin move about. He had a few different pans going on the stove, and she could smell bacon and eggs for sure. Maybe some potatoes. Her stomach rolled in excitement, causing her to cover it. Darrin moved efficiently from one pan to the next, stirring, seasoning, and flipping the various contents.

There was a large island in the middle of the room, with a beautiful granite countertop. The kitchen was quite impressive. Jackie wondered if Darrin cooked much. Her ex-husband hadn't cooked unless he absolutely had to, and he'd complained every minute. She felt a pang of guilt over comparing the two men.

"Good morning," she said sheepishly from the edge of the room.

He was wearing a pair of gray sweatpants and a plain white T-shirt similar to the one she was wearing. He spun around and displayed one of his infectious smiles. Her knees buckled. With one look, he had her melting on the spot. She didn't know how she was going to survive staying with him, however long that was going to be.

"Morning." He turned back around to tend to the cooking food. "There's coffee in the pot next to the fridge. Mugs are in the cabinet above." With a tip of his head, he indicated the direction she should look.

"Thank you," she said, gratefully entering the kitchen. "I love your kitchen." She felt the edge of the cabinet before opening it. The delicate details on the cabinet's face drew her attention.

"The house is almost exactly as I bought it, so I can't take much credit for it." He laughed, slinging the cooked food into separate bowls.

She found herself a blue-and-green-ombré mug in the cabinet, along with the sugar. She hesitantly went to the fridge to look for the creamer. She felt awkward opening drawers and doors around his house. Even with the refrigerator, she wasn't sure if she should ask first or assume she had free rein.

He must have sensed her hesitancy, because he said, "Feel free to take anything you need."

Holding the mug close to her chin, she took a deep breath, savoring the aroma. The kitchen had a small breakfast bar that faced inward. The stools were comfortable. She could barely touch the bottom rung while seated, so she swung her legs.

Darrin placed all the food on the bar in front of her and took the seat next to her. He handed her a plate and fork, indicating for her to take whatever she wanted. She modestly filled her plate with the scrambled eggs, bacon, and potatoes, excited to see that both the bacon and the potatoes looked crispy.

"How'd you sleep?" he asked, selecting his own crispy slice of bacon.

"Really good. Best I've slept in days."

"Good. I'm happy to hear that." His intense blue eyes met hers, sending a stream of giddiness through her stomach. Then they roamed her body, and she felt fidgety under his inspection.

They ate the remainder of their meal in silence. Jackie helped Darrin clean up the kitchen. She washed the dishes while he cleaned up the counters. There was a stainless-steel dishwasher to the left of the sink, but since they'd only dirtied a few dishes, she didn't see the sense in loading it.

Darrin came up to stand behind her. He wrapped his hands around her waist, resting his chin on the top of her head. She hadn't realized he was that much taller than her. She stopped washing the dishes. More butterflies filled her stomach where his hands rested.

"You should stay here a few days, until your apartment has been checked out and your car has been repaired." He held her steady against him. She wasn't sure how she *should* feel in this moment, but she liked the way his body felt pressed against hers.

She could feel him stiffen, waiting for her response, no doubt assuming this was going to be a fight. Jackie couldn't blame him there. She was stubborn at times.

"I think you're right," she said quietly.

She was aware of each point at which their bodies touched. Some of the places were a little shocking. Jackie had been denying herself a physical connection with a man for years. She wasn't sure if she was ready, but she knew she wanted it. She needed to stop thinking about it as the butterflies were replaced by a desire she didn't think was wise.

He kissed the top of her head and said he would retrieve her bags from his car. While he was gone, she finished up the dishes, her mind swimming among the bubbles. *Is it foolish to be feeling this way about my boss? Of course it is,* she berated herself.

She could hear him shuffling about in the entry. Before she could clear her mind, he was back in the kitchen. She resumed her seat at the breakfast bar, finishing her coffee.

His eyes roamed her body again. They paused on her chest before they made their way up to her face. She vowed that she would only go without a bra while she slept from now on. The confusion circulating in her veins was too much.

Darrin had kissed her multiple times over the last few days, although last night and this morning, he'd stuck to kissing the top of her head. She couldn't deny she liked it. She was surprised, really; dating wasn't something she'd been interested in.

"Do you want me to stay home from work with you today?" His concern shone bright in his eyes.

This was her chance; he was giving her an excuse, an out. "I think I can manage. I could use a day of relaxation." *Damn it. Why can't I admit I want company, comfort... him?*

"I figured you'd say that," he replied, disappointment in his voice.

He showed her where the important things in the house were—phone, thermostat, remote, washer and dryer, and clean towels. She was surprised to find he had a landline—thankful for it too.

"There is also a phone book in there." He pointed to the drawer under the coffeepot. She looked at him inquisitively. "To call a tow truck for your car and to find a place to fix the window?"

"Oh, right." She nodded slowly, wondering how she could have forgotten about the vandalism. She deflated in front of him, slumping in her seat.

He covered her hands in his. "Jackie, you can stay with me as long as you like or need to, to feel safe."

She squeezed his hand in response, not trusting that she would be able to speak.

He removed his hands from hers, kissed her on the top of the head, and went down the hall. Not wanting to follow him, she decided the first thing she should do was find a tow-truck company that could take her car to the automotive shop.

She found a pad of paper and pen in the drawer with the phone book then located the number of the automotive garage she generally used and one for a tow company. Jackie wrote down both so she could call them later—she doubted either would be open this early. She set the phone book down but quickly picked it back up and, with a sigh, wrote down the number for the local police station.

While Jackie waited for the businesses to open, she decided she could read a book. She'd seen several that looked interesting the previous night. She made her way down the hall to Darrin's room and tentatively knocked on the door. It was ajar, so when she didn't hear him bar her entering, she pushed it open.

Light emanated from under the door to the bathroom. She could hear the water running. Images of Darrin showering snuck into her brain, and she had to shove them away. This was getting out of hand. She needed to remain professional. Sleeping—or imagining sleeping—with her boss was only going to make the water more muddled. Shaking her head, she looked through the titles on the bookcase again. Curious, she removed a book whose title wasn't clear.

Just as she finished reading the description, she heard the metallic click of the bathroom door opening. Jackie panicked and tried to retreat before he would see her. *How long has the water been off? Long enough for him to get dressed, I hope.*

"Jackie," he said, sounding surprised. She was at the doorway with her back to him. "What are you doing?"

"I-I was just going to borrow a book," she replied, not turning to face him, afraid of what she might see.

"I'm not naked if that's what you're afraid of," he said.

She could almost hear the frown forcing his brows together—another of his expressions she'd grown to like in the last few days. She'd seen him in only a towel and in swim trunks. She was acting foolish, but she didn't want to further confuse her mind and body.

Jackie turned back around to see that he was indeed not naked, but he wasn't fully dressed either. His black slacks weren't buttoned or zipped, giving her a glimpse of black boxer briefs. His near nakedness made her ache. She wanted to run to him to beg for his touch.

He stood his ground, as if to invite her to do just what she was thinking about. Instead, she swallowed hard and nearly knocked herself out in her haste to escape. When she turned around, she hit the side of her face on the trim around the bedroom door. *Smooth.*

Darrin rushed to her side; she could tell he was suppressing laughter. The burn of embarrassment seared her face. *How did I just walk into the doorway? How?* She could have lain down and died from embarrassment. He asked her if she was all right.

"I'm fine, thank you." She removed her arm from his warm embrace and skulked off to the living room to read while he finished dressing.

He entered the living room wearing another of his brilliant-white button-down shirts. He smiled at her disarmingly and finished collecting the items he would need for work. Each step he took in his preparations made the knot in her throat grow larger. Her ache to be held matched it.

"Do you want me to reset the alarm, or would you rather I leave it off?"

She contemplated the question. "You can leave it off. I don't think anyone knows I'm here, so they probably won't come here looking for me, right?" she asked, hoping for reassurance.

"I don't think so, but just to be on the safe side, it would be best. Do you want me to write the code down for you in case you want to go outside at all?"

"No, I think I'll just stay in."

He looked her over one last time and set the alarm on his way out.

Chapter Nineteen

THE CONSPIRATOR

Calling Lucas usually started a day off like shit. He never seemed to be able to accomplish anything he was told to do. Much like as he'd been in childhood, he was small, quiet, and fearful of being reprimanded. Which made him an easy pawn.

"Well, did she get home yesterday?" The question was more impatient than the conspirator had intended, but Lucas should have called with an update the night before.

"S-She did. B-But he was waiting," Lucas said.

"Who was waiting?"

The waiting man was probably Darrin, but Jackie's brother would be another likely answer.

"I was across the street, like we planned. Waiting for her to get home," Lucas said.

Overexplaining was a waste of time. The urge to tell Lucas to hurry up was squashed by the need for him to continue his work.

"B-Before she got home, her boyfriend showed up again," Lucas continued. "When she got there, he took her stuff out of her car. He put it in his, and she got in his car. Then they left."

The conspirator fumed, needing to take a deep breath to calm all the volatile, coiling emotions. "Well, that doesn't ruin the plan yet. Go to work. Act normal."

The call was disconnected. *This bitch is proving to be slippery.*

Chapter Twenty

JACKIE

Jackie called the automotive garage and made an appointment to get her window fixed and oil changed. They warned her it might take a few days to get the window in stock and asked for a good number where they could call her back. She realized she didn't know Darrin's phone number.

After telling the receptionist to hold, she ran down to the guest bedroom and retrieved her pants from the dresser. She removed the slip of paper she'd almost forgotten about. She read the note for the first time. Her heart fluttered.

Suppressing the urge to cry, she went back to the phone. After the appointment was set, she scheduled the tow truck.

My flight leaves at 7. I will wait until the last possible minute to board. If you change your mind, please call. I need you to be safe.

Below, he'd written his cell and landline numbers, his flight number, and the number for customer relations. He would have found a way to get back to her.

She realized in that moment how much she genuinely cared for him. She might even love him. The thought caused panic to rise in her chest.

Complications were plentiful in her life, and she didn't need more. But she couldn't control the others, and she didn't figure she would be able to control this one, either.

The last phone number on her list was the police station. She dialed it and told them of the vandalism to her car and the emails she was receiving. The bored tone of the woman on the other end of the line made her feel foolish.

The rest of the morning was spent relaxing and reading in the massive tub. The jets helped her relax and forget about her problems... only for them to sneak back in as she dried off. She wrestled with the idea of calling her father. Jackie wondered if she should tell her parents of the troubles she was having—wondered if they would even want to know. She felt like a castaway stranded on an island they weren't going to save her from. Sharing her troubles with Tony would put him right in the middle of her and their parents. She couldn't do that to him. Darrin was her only lifeline.

Deciding not to call, she finished getting dressed, putting on the pair of spandex shorts and one of her favorite tank tops. She padded into Darrin's room to read on the chaise lounge, bringing with her a throw blanket from the living room sofa. She liked the feel of the velvet on her bare skin. The caress of the fabric made her feel safe and warm. That chair was her favorite place in the house.

She hadn't realized she'd fallen asleep until she was startled awake by the sound of the front door slamming. It must be Darrin, she thought when she heard the soft beeps of the alarm panel. She lazily sat up as she heard his footsteps, but his harsh tone dropped fear into her belly.

"Jackie!" he shouted. She could feel the anger in his voice reverberating off every surface of the house. She heard him run into the guest room. "Where are you?"

"I-In your room," she replied shakily.

He stormed into the room, which made her recoil against the wall. She'd never seen him so angry. His stance alone was intimidating. She didn't need to look at his face for confirmation.

She was shaking uncontrollably.

"What the fuck is this about?" he shouted, extending a piece of paper to her.

With shaky hands, she took the paper. It was an email from that same address. She hastily read through the email once, twice, a third time. It made no sense.

She looked up to him in puzzlement and terror. "D-Darrin, I-I don't know what that email is about." She could feel the tears welling in her eyes. "I-I swear to you I haven't been conspiring with anyone." She felt the first of the tears streaming down her cheeks.

He was still seething. His imposing size had never terrified her as it did now. There was no way she could escape him. She needed him to believe her. Tears were spilling over. No matter how much she tried, she couldn't suppress them.

He exhaled, dropping to his knees on the floor in front of her. She flinched and gasped at his abrupt movement toward her.

"Fuck," he said, shaking his head. "I'm sorry, Jackie."

They sat in silence. Jackie studied his eyes. The rage that had clouded them moments before had dissolved. His breathing steadied after a few minutes.

"Jackie, somehow, he knows you're with me. He's trying to drive a wedge between us. Trying to turn us against one another," he said much more softly, bowing his head.

"And he succeeded," she said through the tears. In that instant his features contorted. She knew from the look in his eyes he regretted how he'd reacted.

He placed his hands on hers. "I'm sorry, Jackie, I just needed to know if I was being manipulated. I shouldn't have come home like that."

He climbed onto the chair and pulled her into his lap. She let him move her with little resistance. As much as she hated him in that moment, she was in desperate need of comfort. He held her in his lap.

"I'm sorry. I'm so, so sorry," he said, resting his forehead on her temple, whispering apologies into her ear.

The tears continued running down her face. She knew they would soak his shirt. She didn't care. He squeezed her tighter. She didn't know why she was so willing to forgive him. *Why am I not storming out of this place?*

She took deep breaths in through her nose and out through her mouth.

"That's it, baby," he said, rubbing her back. "I'm sorry, Jackie. I will never accuse you of anything like that again. I'll talk with you. I just snapped when it sounded like you were tricking me."

"You don't trust me," she said, her voice cracking as the hurt escaped.

"That seems to be a problem of mine," he admitted solemnly. "Can I explain?"

Jackie shifted in his lap, wanting to see his eyes, needing to know who was behind them. She gave a slight nod.

"Four years ago, I was engaged. It was two weeks before the wedding. I wanted to surprise my soon-to-be bride with a dinner date. She'd been planning and getting everything ready for the wedding virtually by herself," he said with chagrin. "I felt that it wasn't really something I needed to worry myself with. The flowers, the colors—it was all out of my wheelhouse."

Jackie listened intently. She vaguely remembered Darrin being engaged, although until he'd mentioned it, she'd forgotten. She'd never heard about why the wedding hadn't happened.

"Anyway, I thought, to show how much I appreciated the work she was putting into the wedding, I would surprise her with a romantic dinner. She'd taken the day off from work to make phone calls to get the last of the details worked out for the wedding. Or so she told me." He looked at Jackie. She was afraid she knew where the story was going.

"I got to her apartment, and my best man's car was in the drive. I assumed he was helping her with something. He was helping her with something, all right," he scoffed. "I walked into the apartment and followed their voices down to her bedroom. They were talking about how long she was going to stay married to me."

Jackie's brows furrowed. "She was planning divorce before the wedding?"

Darrin grimaced. "You see, my mother's parents had been shareholders in a corporation my grandfather started. They sold their shares for loads of money before I was born. They didn't hold enough shares to influence the company as much as they wanted. So, when the company started going in a direction they didn't agree with, they sold them all. That money went to my mother, and when my mother passed, she left all that money to me." He motioned to the beautiful home in front of them.

"My fiancée and my best man were discussing how stupid I was for not insisting on a prenup. She said, 'I'll stay with him for up to a year then file for divorce.' And he said, 'half of everything will be yours.' My best man laughed. I couldn't believe it. At first, I was too stunned to do anything. Then I lost it. I burst through the door, ready to tear them both apart. The two people I trusted most in the world were scheming against me." He dropped his eyes, covering her hands with his.

Jackie couldn't control the way her eyes widened.

After clearing his throat, Darrin continued. "Since then, I have had a hard time trusting people. It's not an excuse," he added hurriedly. His eyes looked back to hers, and she felt the plea for her sympathy.

"Wh-What did you do?" she asked, afraid to hear the answer.

"Nothing, really. I opened the door and simply said the wedding was off. I left immediately, afraid of what I would do if I stayed any longer."

"I'm sorry, Darrin. That's terrible. I had no idea what ended your engagement." She turned herself over in his lap until she was straddling him. She hugged him closely. She hated the pain he'd endured. As she began to release him, she realized the provocativeness of her position.

A quick intake of breath made her breasts seem fuller, so she leaned back. He splayed his hands across her back. Afraid she was going to fall, she gripped his shoulders as he reclined, pulling her with him.

Still serious, he looked up at her. "I want you, Jackie. I think you know that."

As he said it, she was astounded to notice the bulge wedged against her sex. He reached up to pull her down to him. Then his arms dropped, and she knew her face had betrayed the fear she felt.

"Are you ready to tell me everything? What has happened to turn you off from sex and to make you afraid?"

She slipped off his lap to lie next to him. Which wasn't easy—the chair wasn't made for a man of his size. "I'm not afraid of sex," she whispered barely loudly enough for him to hear.

"Then what is it?"

She contemplated the best way to answer his question. "I'm afraid of what results from sex," she said tentatively.

DARRIN

Darrin learned quickly that pressing her for information got him nowhere. The moment he tried to push a subject, she shut down. It was aggravating and concerning. He reminded himself to have patience with her. He was clearly still healing as well.

Darrin made lunch, and they spent the rest of the day enjoying one another's company. No more was said about the email Darrin had received that morning. They spent the afternoon watching movies and talking of their childhoods and their favorite memories.

Late in the afternoon, the phone rang. When the caller asked to speak with Jackie, Darrin when on the defensive, only to find out it was the auto garage calling about when she should expect her car back. They wouldn't be able to get the replacement window until Monday. The thought of Jackie staying with him through the weekend brightened the dismal day.

They worked together to prepare dinner. Darrin grilled steaks outside while Jackie made a potato salad. As they ate, she swirled her glass of wine.

"I was just thinking how easy it is for me to be here." She paused, dropping her gaze from his. "To spend time with you." She looked up from the swirling red liquid.

"Funny, I was thinking the same thing," he said with a wink. "We have a meeting with my father tomorrow at ten to discuss how the meetings and property viewings went."

"Perfect." She finished the last of her steak.

He wondered if he should mention that he hadn't told his father about their sharing a hotel room for three days. The evening was going so well, and he didn't want to make her feel awkward. He decided it didn't merit mentioning.

Much like with breakfast, they cleaned up the kitchen together. Then they went for a short walk. Darrin didn't seem to find it nearly as relaxing as Jackie did, but he understood her wanting to get out of the house for a few minutes. The evening was beautiful.

When they returned, Darrin queued up another movie. Jackie joined him on the sofa moments later, carrying another glass of wine.

"Be careful with that, Ms. Martinez. I know how you get once you've had a drink or two."

"I promise to be on my best behavior," she said with a sassy grin.

"Well, that's a damn shame," Darrin said gruffly.

JACKIE

The next morning, they made a quick breakfast of toast and eggs before climbing into Darrin's car. She'd forgotten her laptop bag in the entry, so Darrin went back in to get it. She couldn't help but appreciate the view as he walked back to the house. Shaking her head, she looked around the interior of the car. It was sleek and sporty. Black leather was everywhere. Getting in that morning, she'd noticed it was only a two door. It was surely a man's car and was almost as sexy as the man sliding in behind the steering wheel.

Jackie kept having to fight with herself about whether she was allowed to be attracted to him. She wasn't sure it was ethical. She didn't want to fall into the cliché of sleeping her way to the top.

They arrived at the office early enough to beat most of the others. "Do you want me to come down and get you when it's time for the meeting?" he asked.

"No. That's all right. I'll come up around quarter to ten." She needed to focus without having Darrin coming to her office again. He wasn't known to visit people, and she didn't want to add to the asinine comments of Todd. She suppressed a groan at the thought of possibly having to see Todd that day.

"All right," Darrin said, squeezing her knee just before they got out of the car. Just that small gesture made her womanhood warm with desire.

She made her way to her office. Margie wasn't in yet. Jackie wanted to see how the week had been while she was away. She needed to act normal even if nothing was.

She found a stack of phone messages on her desk and sorted through them in order of urgency. She would start making return calls at eight. Calling before then would be a waste of time.

She turned on her laptop and held her breath as she opened her emails. She let out a sigh of relief—there were no new emails from her admirer. She wondered how he'd found out she was staying with Darrin. A shiver ran down Jackie's spine at the thought of how quickly her whereabouts had been discovered. She'd kept the email printout Darrin had brought home the day before.

I see you're getting close to my little pen pal. Be careful. She's quite clever, you know. And a wonderful actress too. She acts shy and unwilling, but that's her game. She's trying to get you to sympathize and feel bad for her just to get what she wants. Just wait and see. It'll be a repeat of Jessica.

She folded the email and placed it back in her purse. Whoever this was knew about Darrin and his past. This person was the clever one. They had purposely brought Jessica's name into it. They knew the reaction he would have.

Jackie tried to push the vindictive person they were dealing with out of her mind. She needed to concentrate on work. She greeted Margie when she heard her arrive and asked her how the week had been.

"Just like any other," Margie responded with a smile.

Jackie was glad someone's life was carrying on in a normal way. She returned as many correspondences as she could before quarter to ten then climbed the stairs to Charles's office, the clicking of shoes made on each step cheering her on. She reached the landing and walked to Heidi's desk. Heidi was on the phone, rattling off information as she scribbled a note. Jackie patiently waited by the desk.

"Ms. Martinez, good morning. both Mr. Dominics are already in attendance, waiting for you. Can I get you any coffee?" Heidi rattled that off faster than Jackie had expected.

"Thank you—I'm all set," she said, swiping her hands down her skirt. It was the one she'd worn to the Monday meetings. She wished she could go to her apartment and get some additional clothes.

Jackie clutched her notes from the meetings. This would be her chance to show Charles how much effort she was putting into the new facility. Taking a deep, calming breath, she opened one of the double doors and entered his office. It was neat and filled with shelves of binders and ledgers.

"Good morning, Ms. Martinez," Mr. Dominic greeted her. He was in his early seventies. Each time she saw him, Jackie was shocked by how good he looked for his age. Darrin sat opposite Charles's desk. Jackie was starting to see their subtle similarities. Much like his son, Mr. Dominic was tall and lean. His hair showed evidence that he was significantly older than his son, but Jackie could see where Darrin got his looks.

"Good morning, Mr. Dominic," she responded.

"Oh, please call me Charles," he said, shaking his head. "Take a seat. I'm excited to hear how the two of you made out." He gestured toward the leather armchair next to Darrin.

His word choice had a blush covering her face. She felt her gaze shift to Darrin. *Did he tell his father about us sharing a room?*

She took her seat and extended a greeting to Darrin that he politely returned. Together, they talked Charles through the meetings they'd had on Monday and the tours they'd done on Tuesday. He listened patiently. They explained which of the buildings they thought best.

Charles smiled at the two of them. "I figured you would choose that one." He chuckled, leaning back in his chair and resting his interlaced fingers on his abdomen. "That was my favorite from the start.

"All right, I'll call the owner of the building and get the formalities worked out—the offer and the date and time of the closing. Then you'll both go back to California to sign on the dotted line," he said excitedly.

"Both go back?" Jackie asked.

"Well, I figure the two of you should complete what you've started."

She could feel more color filling her cheeks.

"I assume you're still interested in applying for the general manager position? This will be good experience for you both."

"Thank you." Jackie was excited, but under the surface, she felt a pull of disappointment. Her stomach sank when she thought of having to move to California.

It had sounded great the previous week, but now she knew the new position would take her miles and hours away from Darrin. She looked at Darrin and could tell he had the same sinking feeling. She returned to her office, her mind swimming with all that would need to be done.

After Jackie had only been in her office for an hour, Margie knocked on the door.

"Come in!" Jackie called, trying to sound as normal as possible.

"Mr. Dominic's secretary is on the phone. She said your meeting will be set for Wednesday the tenth. She wants to know what time of day you prefer to fly."

Jackie contemplated the question. "I think I'll drive again," she said with a smile.

She hadn't told anyone about the vandalism to her car. People knew she preferred to do things on her own, and she needed everyone to think she was fine and nothing out of the ordinary was going on outside these walls. The last thing she wanted was for Todd to have any additional opinions on her life.

"Are you sure?" Margie asked, concerned. "That's an awful long drive."

"Yes, I'm sure. Thank you."

All too soon, another person filled her open door. "How was California?" Todd leered, insolently leaning on the doorframe. "Anything exciting happen?"

The way he asked the question had her anxiety growing. She schooled her features. "It went well—thank you for asking." Jackie turned back to her computer.

The dismissal either didn't register or he chose to ignore it. "I just spoke with Mr. Dominic about applying for the general manager position." Todd walked into her office and leaned across her desk, whispering, "Don't get too comfortable. I always get what I want."

Raising a brow, she met his gaze. With a wave of her hand, she said, "I have actual work to get done, Todd. You can take your foolish threats elsewhere."

She didn't know how she held on to her composure. A vial of anxiety was teetering on the peak of a mountain she was apparently going to die on, threatening to spill everywhere.

Taking the not-so-subtle hint, Todd practically stomped away from her and out the door.

She released a pent-up breath.

Jackie set up appointments with applicants for Monday, her hands shaking with anger. Worse, she felt guilty she hadn't met with anyone all week. If she still wanted this promotion, she needed to buckle down.

Just as she closed her laptop, Darrin appeared in her doorway. "Ready?"

"Yes," she replied hesitantly. She felt odd leaving with him. But no one's eyes narrowed at them as they walked past, and no one whispered.

After they climbed into the car, Darrin turned to her, perplexed. "My assistant tells me you're planning on driving to California next week." His confused tone caused an ache in her gut. "Why?" he asked.

"I'm going to stop and see my friend again on the way. She lives halfway between here and San Diego."

"I'll go with you," he said instantly.

"No. Keep your plans as they are." She could tell this plan was frustrating him, but she needed to do it.

Without another word, he jerked the car out of its parking space and headed toward home. *How am I thinking of his house as home?* The thought stunned her.

She still hadn't heard anything back from the police station. She'd sent them all the emails she'd received and told them about the rock and note as well. Their interest in the activities in California was practically nonexistent, and they seemed to doubt the severity of the emailed threats. Since the damage hadn't happened here, they didn't concern themselves with the issue. They'd told her they would call her when the check on her apartment was completed, and she was still waiting. She'd never been part of an investigation before and didn't know if this was typical.

Their dinner was quiet that night. Darrin was still clearly upset about her refusal to let him ride with her to California.

Chapter Twenty-One
Lucas

Groaning, Lucas answered the phone with an annoyed "Yeah?"

"I have the last of the hardware. It was delivered today. I need you to install it this weekend," the voice ordered. The new plan was hatched and ready for implementation.

When is this going to stop?

"I don't want to be part of this," he said with as much bravery as he could muster. He was relieved it came out without a stutter.

"Don't you ever say that again." The growl on the other end of the phone sent chills through his body. He knew how threatening the caller could be. "You will finish this job."

There was silence for a bit, a challenge to see if Lucas would continue to argue. He knew the reasons for his part in the plan. That didn't mean he agreed with them or wanted to be part of the damn plan.

"Am I picking up the hardware?" he asked in resignation. He'd never been able to stand up for himself. He wished he'd been raised to have more of a backbone.

"I'll drop it in your car. Leave the doors unlocked."

"Okay," Lucas replied, drowning in the defeat that was his life.

Without any closing words, the line went dead.

This is it, he thought.

After this job, he was done. No more being a puppet. If he had to, he would pack everything up and move away. Looking around the dismal apartment, he knew that wouldn't take long. He could take just the essentials. He'd call his sister. She lived on the East Coast, in Boston, he thought. She called to check on him from time to time. He knew she would take him in. Grasping his last shred of hope, he unlocked his car.

Chapter Twenty-Two

DARRIN

The weekend Darrin had looked forward to ended up being nothing more than a battle between the two of them. The first problem arose when they found out her apartment had finally been checked out. He didn't know why it had taken the police department so long. He was supremely irritated with them, and it unfairly transferred to her. He and Jackie had stopped by her apartment to pick up some needed items. She hadn't mentioned staying at her own place, and he definitely was not going to suggest it.

He kept trying to persuade her to take the same flight he was taking. She was being so difficult, and he couldn't figure out why. Her excuse was the same each time: she hated flying. It was infuriating. He knew his arguments were stronger than hers, but she wouldn't budge. By Sunday night, they weren't speaking to each other. She went to bed early to avoid any more arguments.

Right before he went to bed, he stopped by her room. "Do you know when your car will be ready tomorrow?" he asked, not making eye contact.

"I'm not sure yet. They're supposed to call me."

"So, you're leaving tomorrow night?"

"Yes," she said, her voice breaking, and his eyes narrowed on hers. "Darrin, please don't be angry with me."

The pleading in her eyes damn near made him let it go. But he was just as stubborn as she. "Damn it, Jackie! I am angry. I've been doing anything I could to help you, and like every other time, you shut me out."

His night was aggravatingly restless. *Damn woman.* She pushed every one of his buttons and shoved him to the brink of insanity. No one else had ever had such an effect on him. It was both confusing and frustrating.

He could hear her as she got ready for work and packed her bags. He paced his room, trying to figure out what she was thinking. Darrin's phone rang.

"Hey, Dad."

There was a slight pause that caused Darrin to check to make sure the call hadn't dropped.

"I just got the credit card statement for your time in California." His father let the statement land in the air and distance between them. "The cost was half what I expected."

Darrin felt his throat go dry. He was a grown man. He wondered why he was afraid of how his father was going to react.

"There was a mistake in the room booking." Darrin fidgeted with the books on the shelf.

"I'm listening." His father's voice held an edge that wasn't typically there.

Darrin took a deep breath and relayed the events of their trip.

JACKIE

She hated to think of not going back with Darrin that night. She'd come to love her time here with him. Most of it, anyway.

They didn't speak on their way to work that morning. She wanted to open up and tell him everything, but she couldn't force the words out. They were close to the surface, but she couldn't find the strength to let them through the door and out into the space around them. It was as if there was something small wedged into the opening at the bottom of the door, blocking it from swinging open. She could push all she wanted, but it was never going to budge.

What if his opinion of me changes?

She looked over at Darrin, who was driving. His handsome profile was rigid. His jaw tensed. She turned away, allowing her head to fall, she rolled it from side to side. They pulled into his designated space. When the car was shifted to park and the engine was cut, he pushed against the steering wheel, staring out the windshield at nothing in particular.

"Are you going to need a ride to pick up your fucking car tonight?" He wasn't yelling, but the edge to his tone broke her.

She swallowed hard. "Yes," she said quietly.

"Call my direct line when it's ready." Without looking at her, he got out of the car.

Her sadness continued throughout the day. Jackie tried to put up a good front for everyone around her. She doubted she fooled many. Her appointments went well—she found people who had an interest in several of their partners' positions. That should have brightened her day.

Finally, around two o'clock, she got the call that her car was ready. She lifted her phone to call Darrin. It felt like it had gained a hundred pounds in a matter of seconds.

He answered on the second ring. "This is Darrin."

"It's Jackie. My car is ready."

"What time do you want to leave?" he asked impatiently.

"They're open until four."

"If you're going to be on the road for six hours tonight, you should leave sooner rather than later," he snapped. "Meet me at my car in ten minutes." He hung up before she could formulate a response.

Her heart was caught in her throat—it hurt to swallow—and her eyes were stinging with the tears that wanted to escape. She slowly packed up her work bag. She was finally able to swing it onto her right shoulder without cringing.

She arrived at the car to find Darrin waiting. After she climbed in and secured her seat belt, she told him which garage her car was at. He didn't utter a word to her the entire way to the auto mechanic.

When they arrived, she turned to him. "Are you going to wait for me before you leave?" Her voice was barely above a whisper.

His piercing eyes met hers. "No. I thought I would throw your suitcase onto the sidewalk while you were inside." He narrowed his eyes at her.

She dropped her gaze and reached for her purse. Before getting out, she sent one more longing look his way. He, however, was staring straight ahead.

She went in, to pay her bill, and collect the paperwork, notating all the work they'd done. She looked down at the papers in her hand—they looked like gibberish. She couldn't focus. After being asked a second time how she wanted to pay, she extended her debit card to the man behind the counter.

She somberly walked out to where they'd told her she would find her car. They'd cleaned up all the glass debris. No one would ever know the window had been broken. One of the many secrets she shared with Darrin.

She pulled her car up next to his, and he silently helped pack her bags into the trunk. She reached out for his arm as he was going back to his car. He spun on his heel to face her.

He didn't say a word. His eyes said it all. They were angry and hurt. After everything he'd done for her, this was a direct insult. She swallowed hard before she was able to speak.

"Thank you. For everything," she said, tears welling in her eyes. She was imploring him to understand. But how could he?

"I'm not going to feel bad right now. I offered to ride with you. I begged you to fly with me. Both instances, you pushed me away. But that's probably what you do best," he finished, almost in a whisper.

Feeling that he'd probably said all he wanted to say, she dropped her hand from his arm and turned before he could see the tears fall. She was still terribly upset, but all she wanted to do was get some rest. She would see Darrin the next day.

Her walls were quickly crumbling at Darrin's feet. Later, in bed, staring up at the ceiling, she wondered what she was going to do. The thought of him brought more feelings than she thought she was capable of having.

"I need to give this a chance," she whispered to the darkness. She would let herself be free this trip and see where things went. She would stop fighting her feelings at every turn. Hopefully, she hadn't damaged their relationship irreparably.

DARRIN

Darrin arrived home feeling like a total ass. He'd wanted to pull Jackie into a hug and kiss her. He wanted to tell her she needed to be safe and that he hated the thought of her traveling alone.

As he walked through the house, he realized, for the first time since after he'd broken up with his fiancée, he was lonely. Jackie hadn't even been there a week, and he felt differently about the house. The life she'd brought into its rooms had left with her.

He felt like he would never get her back. She was probably going to take the job in California. He was going to stay in his large house, alone as ever.

Angry with his depressive thoughts, he went to bed soon after he'd made his dinner. He cursed when she was all he dreamed of. When the alarm sounded, he only had an hour to get ready before he needed to leave. He packed and placed his suitcase by the front door. All he had to do was shower and eat.

Both tasks felt like they took all the energy he had. He was frustrated with himself for not insisting Jackie replace her cell phone sooner rather than later. The chaos of the week had caused him to lose sight of that. She'd always been within reach. Now the issue felt insurmountable.

He arrived at the airport earlier than he'd originally expected. He parked his car in the secured parking area and made his way to the security check-in line. The airport was busy but not to the point that he wanted to rip his hair out at the congestion.

He hoped like hell she was safe at her friend's house. He wanted to kick himself for not getting her friend's number. *What will I do if something happens to her?* While he waited in line, he did little more than stare at the walls.

He couldn't believe the sleep he was losing over a woman he'd known personally for not even two weeks. She had been working for his father's company for almost a decade, and they had been friendly to one another, but this last week had changed him. The walls he kept up were starting to disintegrate. He wasn't sure how he felt about that.

When it was time to get in line to board, a surge of anger went through him. He would recognize that walk anywhere—that shapely ass. He could have strangled her. She could have been through the boarding gate without him even noticing her. His mind had been wandering all morning.

He was several people behind her. He waited patiently, suppressing the rage that was threatening his very sanity. *Is this some kind of joke?*

He boarded the plane to find her sitting in the seat next to his. He grabbed her wrist the minute he took his seat. Her eyes had dark circles beneath them. They brimmed with tears the minute they reached his.

"I'm so sorry, Darrin." Tears broke over their barriers.

His anger vanished. Who was he kidding? He hated being angry with her.

"I wanted to tell you so many times. I was about to last night, but…"

"Why? Why did you do this?" He motioned about the plane.

"I've been thinking. I think whoever has been messaging me either works with us or is close to someone who does," she said, sniffling, trying to suppress her tears. "I wanted to keep my plan of flying a secret. I figured if someone was planning something, I could throw them off course."

"You didn't trust me enough to tell me?" He couldn't hide the pain he felt.

"No, it's not that. It was just the chance of a slipup. I'm sorry. I hated seeing you so mad at me." New tears were streaming down her face. "I figured the fewer people that knew the real plan, the better."

"Did anyone else know you were flying?" he asked, pulling her to him. She shook her head.

"Please don't ever leave me in the dark again."

His begging whisper caused her to shake with renewed tears. "I promise I won't."

"So where did you go last night?"

Sniffling, she looked into his eyes. "I stayed in the hotel across the street from the airport."

"You wanted to make anyone driving by your house think you'd really left." He laughed, and her look turned inquisitive. "I drove by your house before I went home. I was checking to make sure you didn't stop there first—and if you did, that you were okay. I was so mad at you, but I couldn't help checking on you."

When she apologized again, he shook his head.

"I understand. I'm sad you didn't tell me your ingenious plan. But I understand. I'm just glad you're here with me." He rubbed her arm, and she laid her head on his shoulder.

They rode almost the entire flight arm in arm. She fell asleep after they boarded their connecting flight in Phoenix. She had her arm wrapped around his, her head on his shoulder, and her left breast resting against his forearm. It took all his willpower not to peek at the view of her cleavage this afforded him. He would never be accused of taking advantage of a sleeping woman.

When they were minutes from landing, he woke her up. The sleepy look in her eyes was one of the sexiest things he'd ever seen. Her heavy lids fluttered as a smile of recognition crossed her face, all for him. It pulled at something deep inside him, something more intense than just lust or fleeting desire.

"Thanks for the pillow." She laughed as he stretched out his shoulder. He had to get some feeling back into it before he tried to carry their luggage.

Once they exited the plane, they took the shuttle to pick up the rental car. "What would you have done if I didn't forgive you?" he asked, holding the car keys. "When my flight and car were booked, Mrs. Cole told me I got the last rental car."

"I don't know," she said, casually bumping him with her hip as they walked.

"I'm sad we're only going to be away two nights this time. I think if I'd had a little more time with you on the last trip, you would have eventually fallen for my charm."

"Who's to say I haven't?" she asked with a wink, climbing into the passenger seat.

He took his seat with a seductive grin. "Have you?" He leaned in close.

In place of an answer, she leaned over the remaining distance of the center console. She wavered only a moment before she pressed her lips to his. The kiss stunned him momentarily. He slid his fingers up through her hair to hold her face close to his. He wanted there to be no question that he wanted her.

She let out a whimper that had his dick stirring in his pants. He would never force himself on a woman, but he couldn't handle much more in the blue-balls department.

"Jackie, you drive me absolutely insane," he whispered against her lips. "Do we want one or two rooms this time?"

Again, forgoing an answer, she leaned farther into the kiss. She became more brazen the longer they kissed. He would have been lying if he said he didn't love it.

"Before I burst, we should get going," he growled into her ear. When he released her, desire swam in her hazel eyes.

They arrived at the hotel, and neither of them could get out of the car quickly enough. The one they'd stayed in the previous week couldn't accommodate them this time, so they'd had to book a room at a larger, more upscale location. The lobby alone was more impressive. The chandelier hanging from the ceiling was almost the size of Jackie's car.

Darrin had his left arm wrapped around her back to lead her up to the check-in counter. "Reservation under Dominic, Darrin."

"One room, two nights?" the clerk asked.

"Yes, ma'am," he responded with a sly smile in Jackie's direction.

Once they had their key and were headed to the elevator, Jackie turned to him. "One room? You had Mrs. Cole book us one room?"

"Truthfully, I booked the hotel accommodations."

CHAPTER TWENTY-THREE
JACKIE

The room was spectacular. The walls were a light cream color with beautiful photos of local scenes. The bed was large and had enough pillows for ten. There was a desk along one wall. A large sideboard served as both dressing table and television stand. A balcony with a small table and two chairs overlooked the beach.

Jackie's eyes shot back to the bed. When she rounded on Darrin, she knew there was a fire in her eyes. This was not the fire of passion that had been present in the car.

"Jackie, don't kill me now." Darrin laughed. "I am not expecting anything. We've slept in a bed together once before without incident." He took her in his arms. "I would never force you into something you don't want to do... hey, Jackie, look at me," he said. She drew her eyes back from the bed and up to him. "Do you trust me?"

"Yes, I do," she whispered and swallowed hard.

"Can you tell me what has happened to you?"

She tensed momentarily then took a deep breath and relaxed in his arms.

"It's okay. You can wait until you're ready," he said, rubbing his hands up and down her arms.

She leaned into him. They stood there, embracing one another, for several minutes. "I want to get cleaned up before dinner," she said, straightening. He released her and allowed her to make her way to the bed with her suitcase. She tossed it on top, removed something black from her suitcase, and retreated into the bathroom.

Darrin cared for her deeply and was desperate for her to understand the depth to his emotions. He'd shared something with her that he tried to hide from everyone. He acted as if nothing had happened after he broke off the engagement with Jessica. Not wanting to amplify the betrayal he felt. His father and only a few very close friends knew the truth. It affected him more than anyone else would know.

He needed to learn how to trust her and had to find a way to get her to fully trust him. That seemed to be an impossible feat. Shaking his head, he dislodged his doubts and did as Jackie had, tossing his suitcase onto the bed and selecting his dinner clothes.

He finished dressing and was pacing the room, waiting for her, about to knock on the bathroom door, when he heard the lock click. The door opened. Jackie was wearing a short black one-shoulder dress. The dress was tight and sleek. The fabric hugged each of her curves like the caresses he wished to inflict upon her. His desire pulsed for her, and he wondered how he was going to make it through an entire dinner with her looking like this. She'd taken her long hair and sculpted it into a flowing French braid.

"You asked what I was going to do if you hadn't forgiven me," she said, gesturing at herself.

He was staring at her like a fool. With a sly smile, he said, "Remind me to get angry at you at least once a week." He crossed the room and wrapped her in his arms. "You look beautiful."

Her cheeks flushed the color of pale-pink roses. Darrin leaned down and kissed her neck; he could see her smile out of the corner of his eye. He worked his way up to nibble on her ear. She let out a gasp of surprise. He paused to make sure she didn't object. He knew pushing in any way would damage any progress they'd made.

He continued his trail up her hairline to her temple then to her forehead. Stopping there took more effort than he thought it would.

"Before I ruin everything you worked on," he said, giving her another appreciative look up and down, "let's go."

He liked this new Jackie. She was more comfortable with him. He was amazed what a week had done. The frigid wall was eroding. He knew he had to be careful before it sprang back up with renewed force.

They made their way back through the vast hotel entrance to their rental car. Darrin had a nice restaurant in mind that he'd noticed on their previous trip. Not that there was any issue with the place they'd eaten at last time, but he wanted to treat her to something special. She deserved it.

He kept reminding himself he couldn't get too wrapped up in their moments while out and about. *Vigilance*, he told himself. It would have been effortless to get lost in her eyes, but he needed to look out for anything strange.

He needed to look out for himself too. The shock of Jessica's betrayal had made its mark on him. He wouldn't allow himself to get hurt like that again... he hoped. Looking over at Jackie in the passenger seat, he knew he was too far gone. His heart sank. He was going to get himself hurt again. She was going to take the new position in California. He'd gained her trust only to lose her—he could never ask her to stay with him.

Darrin reached over and placed his hand on her knee. At his touch, her glazed eyes reached out to his. *Is she thinking about the same thing?*

"What do you think of this place?" he asked, indicating the restaurant in front of them with a tick of his chin.

The building was set out over the water. It had a large wraparound porch, which allowed for seating with spectacular ocean views. The building was almost entirely made of windows.

"This is beautiful!"

Darrin couldn't take his eyes off her when she emerged from the car. Her eyes sparked in the light emanating from the vast windows.

"Better than I ever imagined." He looked at her. He could have lived in that moment forever. Her lips met his with equal fervor. "Shall we forget dinner?" he growled.

She laughed, throwing her head back, revealing her neck as she had the night they were eating out at the beach. Taking sweet nibbles out of her neck for the rest of the night would be just as delicious. He lifted her hand to his mouth and pressed a kiss to the back of it.

They walked into the restaurant and were seated at a corner table out on the deck, allowing them each an unobstructed view. He was conscious enough to only allow himself to order one drink. He laughed as Jackie let herself unwind and have a glass of wine. They enjoyed their meals and the stories they shared. By the time Jackie was finishing her second glass of wine, Darrin had already paid, but they were in no rush to leave.

She was more talkative than he'd ever seen her. This was the real Jackie. He relaxed in his chair, taking in everything about her as she freely talked about her parents and the housekeeper who had been her mentor and shoulder to cry on. He couldn't help but compare the differences in their upbringings. It was refreshing to talk with a woman who didn't seem fazed by the money his family had. She never outright mentioned how successful her father's business was, but it was evident in how she'd grown up. He appreciated that she didn't obsess over brand-name clothes. She dressed well but never seemed to worry about which designer made what.

"Florence was actually more of a mother to me than my own mother. I remember girls at school talking about painting their nails with their mothers or going to the playgrounds with their mothers."

"You never did those things?"

"Of course I did." She giggled. "Just not with my mother—she was always too busy at some kind of function and would never have known what to do at a playground. Florence was the one that taught me to cook, do my hair, those sorts of things... don't feel bad for me," she added, watching his face. "I learned young what kind of mother and woman I wanted to be. Things were tough for a while." Jackie's tone had changed from silly to serious. Darrin straightened in his chair. "Leading up to and after my divorce, I didn't know who I was anymore. That was when I started working for your dad."

She's been married? He did his best to keep the shock off his face. "I had no idea you'd been married before."

"Yeah. We were both young, nineteen. Divorced after only three years."

He reached out and covered her hand with his. "I'm sorry, Jackie."

"If it hadn't happened, it wouldn't have led me here..." She paused as if contemplating continuing. "To you."

"For that, I am thankful." He raised her hand and kissed the top. The feel of her skin was like caressing silk. "Ready to head back?" he asked after she replaced her empty wineglass on the table.

She nodded, allowing him to help her from her chair.

On their way back to the hotel, he felt her gaze upon his face. "What's on your mind?" he asked.

"Why me?"

The question surprised him. *Why not? Can't she see all the wonderful qualities I see in her?*

"I don't know where to start." He smiled at her. "For starters, you are amazing at your job." He shot her a quick grin. "You are intelligent, innovative, conniving," he said with a mock edge to the last word. "You're beautiful, sexy, and most of all..." He parked the car back in the hotel lot then turned to make sure she was listening. "You test me more than anyone else I've ever met."

The tears in her eyes glistened in the dash lights. The sudden darkness brought Darrin back to reality. He wanted to get her back inside. Like her clever plan of not actually driving, he had kept the location of their stay private.

Darrin withdrew from the car to scan the parking lot, wondering if he was being foolish. Neither of them had received any correspondence since the email he'd gotten. Maybe the stalker was giving up. But that was likely wishful thinking. He wasn't going to let her life be gambled on a maybe.

He went to her side of the car and wrapped his arm around her waist. She leaned on him heavily for support. This made him nervous. She would never be able to run if she needed to.

With his eyes shifting, he took in each movement in the parking lot. No one appeared to be paying them any attention. Jackie kept her pace even with his, although she was less graceful than usual.

When they made it through the front doors of the hotel, a calm washed over him. The hotel felt like their safe haven, their hideout. Once they were in their room, Jackie removed their suitcases from the bed and placed them against the wall by the door. Darrin watched her movements as she sauntered up to him.

"Would you mind helping me with the zipper on my dress?" she asked, moving her braid aside.

The very thought sent a tidal wave of desire through him that crashed in his chest. He ran his hands from her hips to the undersides of her arms. When he took the zipper in his hands, he kissed the back of her neck. Unzipping the dress revealed that she was wearing a black strapless bra and a pair of matching lace panties. Her curves flowed, and the fabric of the dress slid down them like the water of a river.

When it hit the floor at his feet, he gave in to animal instincts. He spun her and pinned her between himself and the wall. The sexy heels she was wearing brought her almost up to his height.

Darrin kissed her from her shoulder to neck then across her jaw to her lips. Her tongue entered his mouth and electrified him. He lifted her to his hips and carried her to the bed. He kissed his way back down her neck. Rising, he took a moment to let his eyes devour her. She was more beautiful than he'd fantasized she would be. Her breasts were full and delectable, almost spilling over the edge of her bra. He had a hard time removing his eyes from the slopes he would love to climb. He inched his gaze lower to where her waist dipped in. When his eyes found her abdomen, her arms twitched. She looked like she wanted to cover herself.

Her hips were wrapped in the black lace. He loved the glimpses of flesh he could see through the material. Without a second thought, he dropped his head and kissed her hip bone then worked his way up her stomach.

She wiggled when his stubble tickled her stomach. He wondered if she had the same throbbing desire he did. He wanted to make sure she wanted this before he started to undress.

Continuing his trek, he made his way up her ribs. He placed his hands on her hips and slid them up her waist to her ribs then to her back. He looked deep into her eyes as he reached behind her to unlatch her bra. With each clasp, he could feel the tension transferring to his breathing. When the last clasp was released, he removed his hands from her back.

He bent over her, bracing himself with hands on either side of her head, and kissed her lips. "Do you want to do this?" he whispered in her ear.

She nodded.

"I want you to say it, Jackie," he growled. "I need you to say it. I have to know you're okay with this." If she wanted to stop, he would, even though it might kill him.

"I want you, Darrin. I want this." She gestured between them. "I want you inside me," she whispered.

She reached up to undo the buttons on his shirt but paused when it came time to pull it from the waistband of his pants. The fact that her hands were so close to his erection made it throb harder as if it was going to break through his pants by sheer will.

He removed his shirt and began to unbutton and unzip his pants. He stepped out of them and removed his briefs, releasing himself from the confines. When he came back up, he found Jackie lying farther up on the bed, wearing nothing but her heels. He'd imagined this scene so many times, but seeing it play out before his eyes was more than he ever could have imagined.

Her eyes shifted down to his erection, and he saw her breath catch. A blush filled her cheeks as a small smile spread across her lips. Darrin splayed himself between her thighs, letting his penis lie on top of her sex, just between her folds. He could feel the heat and desire emanating from her. He took one of her breasts in his hand, shaping and reshaping it. He took the peak into his mouth. She sighed with pleasure, arching her back.

She lifted her hips to press into him. She was timid at first, but she ground herself against him. The motions and moans from her were almost enough to make him come.

"Darrin, I want you inside me," she whispered.

"I want you to get on me." Seeing the surprise in her eyes, he explained, "I don't want to hurt you, and I want you to be able to end it anytime you want." He couldn't stand the thought of getting too wrapped up in the moment and hurting her.

Darrin raised himself off of her and lay down, propping his head against the pillow. She looked down at him nervously. He extended a hand to her and rubbed the sweet spot between the lips of her sex. She pushed against his hand, and he slipped a finger into her soft warmth. She shook with pleasure. He added pressure, and she responded with yearning. He made love to her with his hand. He could feel her inner walls tightening around his fingers.

She stopped him right before she climaxed. Pushing his hand away, she straddled his hips. "Condom?" she whispered.

He couldn't believe he'd almost forgotten—he'd been so wrapped up in the moment that he hadn't even paused to consider protection. Leaning over the edge of the bed, he pulled a condom from his suitcase. His wishful thinking had paid off. After rolling the condom over his length, he settled back into place.

He held himself steady as she took him into her sex. She was tight, wet, and ready. Darrin let a flow of curses leave his lips as she moved. She raised herself up and down in a rhythm he could get lost in. He wouldn't last much longer. Just as he was about to climax, she did, and all was lost. He thrust his hips up just as she came down one last time. With her hips in his hands, he held her down on top of him. The tightening from within her was all the movement he needed. Each pulse, throb, and moan pushed him over the edge.

Chapter Twenty-Four

JACKIE

The sun was shining in through the balcony doors. Its warmth felt great on her face. Jackie smiled at the memory of the night before as her eyes fluttered open. She lay in bed, covered only by Darrin's arm and a sheet.

Jackie silently clambered out of bed and retrieved one of the soft robes from the closet. It smelled of peonies. She closed her eyes as she allowed the fragrance to fill her senses. On her way out to the balcony, she leaned over Darrin and kissed him on the forehead. Taking a deep breath, she reveled in his woodsy scent. He stirred and smiled in his sleep.

She continued across the room and opened the balcony door only wide enough to fit through. She silently closed the door and slid into one of the chairs. Her legs pressed into the chilly metal. The robe flitted against her breasts in the breeze, which felt forbidden and seductive against her bare skin just as Darrin's hands had. The thought made her blush. She couldn't believe she'd denied herself the pleasure of his touch before. He'd been gentle and careful, like she was a delicate flower that might lose its petals, treating her with the most care and love she'd ever known. She was thankful she'd allowed herself to live in the moment, to allow her feelings and wants to take over. It was what she needed—to let go of the overthinking.

Resting her head against the back of the chair, she stared out at the ocean. She needed to think long and hard about what she was going to do. *How could I leave him now? If it's offered, am I going to turn down the job I've been striving for?* Before she could come up with an answer, the sound of the door opening brought her around.

Darrin stood in the doorway in only his boxer briefs. The snug fit made her aware of his manhood—not that they needed to be snug for her to notice it. The carved muscles covering his body called to her. The piercing blue eyes that had once intimidated her made her feel at home.

Darrin extended a mug of coffee to her. Jackie was touched by the gesture. She took it, allowing the warmth to spread through her body.

"Good morning," he said huskily.

Does he remember everything I do about last night?

"Morning." She saluted him with her coffee cup. "Thank you."

"You're welcome. It's just what was in the room. Not sure how good it will be." He pretended to be afraid to take his first sip. "Not bad." He chuckled.

"Not bad at all," she agreed, smiling into her cup.

"Our meeting is at eleven. What would you like to do until then?"

She knew what he was asking, and she couldn't keep the flush from her cheeks.

"By the way, what are you wearing under that robe?" he asked with a sly smile.

"Nothing. Want to see?"

"You know I do," he said, leaning across the table to capture her lips in a kiss. Their kisses melted together. She walked around the table, opened the front of her robe, and straddled his lap.

She heard his arousal from deep in his chest. He set down his cup and placed one hand inside the robe around her back, using the other to manipulate her breast. She arched her back, giving him permission and easier access. He whisked the tip of his thumb across her nipple. Just as she let out a whimper of wanting, he took her nipple into his mouth.

"Please, Darrin. Please." The rush of desire that ran through her body settled into her middle. The pulsating yearning deep within her sex was driving her crazy.

He lifted her high enough off him with one arm to maneuver his boxers and release his erection. He lowered her back down, and she shifted her hips to encase him on her descent. He let out a mutter of pleasure. She spread her legs wide to accommodate him and to engage her clit. While she rocked back and forth, he cursed in pleasure. He took her breast back into his hand then licked and kissed her nipples, switching from one to the other. Each suck elicited a gasp or moan, though she tried her best to keep quiet. He took her hips in his hands, rocking her harder, faster. It was all the encouragement she needed. The pleasure erupted with sensations all through her body. Her sex clenched his, and he moaned, which made her tighten her grip around him. He climaxed moments after she did—she felt him swell inside her as release flooded his body.

"That was amazing." He smiled. She could feel the heat surge through her face. Darrin pulled her face to his. "Don't be embarrassed," he whispered, kissing her cheek.

Jackie felt better than she had in years. She felt like she could conquer anything with him by her side. She kissed him deeply and lifted herself off him. He replaced his briefs.

"Shall we go shower?" she asked. His head whipped up to look at her. She smiled at the shock on his face.

"Did you just say 'we'?"

"Hurry up before I change my mind," she called back to him as she sauntered through their room to the bathroom.

He was only a step or two behind her. She could feel him standing behind her as she turned on the shower, dropping her robe to the floor. Standing in the shower, they kissed and caressed each other, enjoying all that was the other. Darrin was kissing her neck when his cell phone rang. With a groan, he withdrew from the shower to answer the call.

Sadness was evident in his eyes when he peered back into the bathroom. "I have to take this—I'm sorry." He brought the phone to his ear.

Deflated and alone, Jackie washed herself up, wondering who would have called—who would be important enough to end their moment together. Curious to find out who the caller was, she wrapped herself in a towel and peeked around the corner of the bathroom wall.

She could see him hunched over a pad of paper on the nightstand, scribbling furiously. *What is so important that Darrin needs to take notes like that?*

"Okay, and you said he moved where last year?" There was a pause as Darrin wrote more. "Mm-hmm." Another pause. "How do you spell the last name?" He said a name then spelled it.

A knot formed in Jackie's stomach. She silently backed into the bathroom and closed the door. *What is he searching for? What has he uncovered?* She thought she would be sick.

She concentrated on listening for Darrin. The talking on the other side of the door stopped a moment later. She could hear him walking around the room again. The dread that filled her body didn't allow Jackie to move. She wondered if he'd finally figured out her secret.

She would have to face him eventually. But she couldn't yet. She didn't want to lose him. *What if the truth makes him not want to be with me?* The thought put her on the verge of losing the little coffee she'd drunk.

"You didn't wait for me to come back?" he asked, smiling.

Maybe he hadn't found out yet, but he would. If he had the name Westerly, it was only a matter of time. "I figured we needed to get ready," she said, trying to smile but knowing it didn't meet her eyes.

He searched her face. "What's wrong?"

"Why are you worried about someone with the last name Westerly?" she demanded before she lost her nerve. Fortunately, she was already seated when she saw realization then anger cross his face.

"What did you hear?"

"Just you ask where he moved and how to spell his name." She dropped her eyes to the floor, concentrating on the grout between the tiles. "I left before I heard anything more." Jackie felt like everything they had was evaporating before her, mingling with the steam of the shower. She and Darrin were damaged by the ghosts of her past before they'd had the chance to begin.

"Anything you want to tell me about him?"

"No!" she cried out, feeling the nausea in her throat turn to a lump.

"Did you know he moved to Arizona last year? Right near Prescott Valley."

She could feel the color draining from her face. No, she hadn't. She slowly shook her head. She'd thought Harmon Westerly was still in Texas. *Would Verity or Porter have told him where I was going? Is he coming after me?* Verity wouldn't tell him where she was or where she was going, she reassured herself. But Porter and Harmon had been friends since high school. Porter could have slipped up.

She felt like she'd lost all her senses. Her vision blurred, and the room became distant. Darrin was swimming in the space around her.

"Jackie, would he have come after you?"

She felt the nausea coming back around. She rounded on Darrin. "What do you think you're doing? Are you having someone look into me? You think you have the right to do that?" she asked, her voice breaking.

"Well, fuck, Jackie!" he shouted. "I can't get any information out of you. All I get is evasive bullshit! You don't give me a straight answer to a single question I ask you. I asked you if there was anyone that would want to come after you. You failed to mention that you had an argument with Todd before you left work last Friday."

She couldn't stop the gasp before it happened. "Who told you that?"

"Margie told me, when you stayed home last Thursday. At my fucking house. I didn't mention the emails, but I asked her if she had noticed anything off. She told me Todd went to your office the other day and that you were pretty rattled when he left."

Dammit, Margie.

"I'm in the process of looking into him and what he did that week, making sure he isn't behind all this."

The conflicting emotions within her frustrated her. She felt both relief and anger. Todd didn't seem the type to be aggressive, but he had been that way with her twice now.

"He stopped by my office again on Friday." She rubbed her upper arm.

Darrin ran all ten fingers through his dirty-blond hair. "Why do you think it necessary to hide everything from me?" he asked nearly shouting as he began pacing in front of the toilet she was sitting on.

She stayed quiet. Even if she'd wanted to answer his last question, she had no idea where she would start. Her difficulty opening up was going to destroy what she was beginning to want most.

DARRIN

They arrived at the attorney's office to sign the papers at exactly eleven o'clock. Darrin had dressed in one of his white button-down shirts and a pair of navy slacks. He thought he looked professional and authoritative.

Jackie had selected a formfitting black-and-white dress. She was a knockout in it. As she walked across the parking lot ahead of him, he imagined things he likely shouldn't before a work meeting. He couldn't stop himself from watching her ass sway as she walked.

He had earnestly tried to get her to talk to him, but she'd refused. She'd closed up like a safe-deposit box he would never find the key to. He didn't know what he had to do. Even that morning, when he was virtually pulling information from her, she hadn't shared anything new.

True, he had called in a few favors to have Mia look into her past. He felt that was the only option he had for figuring out the truth. She sure as hell was not going to tell him.

Darrin was pissed—he could feel it in the way his movements were so abrupt. She pushed his buttons at every move. She was infuriating. But he'd be damned if he was going to let anything happen to her.

He needed to find out what had happened between her and Todd. He'd been working closely with Todd and thought the man was smart. *Would he go after Jackie over a promotion?*

He was contemplating Todd's capabilities when they got to the door. Todd was a driven man, and Darrin thought he knew him well. Darrin didn't want to believe that Todd was willing or desperate enough to kill Jackie to get what he wanted. Mia had told him that morning that she was still looking into Todd. Darrin had added that to Mia's to-do list after talking with Margie on Thursday.

Jackie followed the attorney's assistant to the conference room where they would be completing the paperwork. The assistant showed them to their seats and asked if she could get them anything. The smoldering look she gave Darrin on her way out didn't escape him.

He doubted Jackie missed it. But she was too angry to show she noticed or that it bothered her. The angry line that settled between her brows was adorable. He wanted to reach out and rub it away.

"You know what?" Darrin said silkily. "I'd love a coffee." He flashed the assistant one of his charming smiles. If she was going to ignore him, he was going to make it damn hard to do so.

He noticed the sparks fly in Jackie's eyes. *Good, she's jealous.* When the assistant dropped the coffee off, he gave her another sexy smile. If Jackie had been a dog, she would have been growling over the invasion of her territory.

Darrin couldn't help but smile to himself. Maybe this was the way to get her to talk.

Chapter Twenty-Five

THE CONSPIRATOR

"Answer your damn phone." *It never takes Lucas this long to pick up.*

A voice squeaked on the other end of the line.

"Why haven't I seen anything on the news about her?" the conspirator asked.

"I-I don't know," Lucas stammered.

"Did you do what I asked you to?" The question, spoken at a near whisper, carried more anger than a shout could have.

"I did. I swear I did." Lucas's voice shook with fear.

The television had been tuned to the news all night. Nothing—no missing-persons alerts, no mention of Jackie at all. This was getting ridiculous. The damn bitch just wouldn't go away.

"You have fucked things up for the last time."

"I don't want to do this," Lucas said—the second time he'd made such a comment.

He'd better not be thinking of doing anything foolish. Lucas—dear, dear Lucas—apparently needed a reminder of who was in charge of this operation. A visit would be necessary if he couldn't get his shit together.

"I need to know the moment you hear anything about her." The conspirator hung up the burner phone and threw it against the wall. *How could eliminating one person be so damn difficult?*

Chapter Twenty-Six

JACKIE

Darrin was flirting with the assistant just to get Jackie going. And it was working. She wanted to yell at the other woman—scare her off. An indignant flush filled Jackie's cheeks the next time Amanda, the assistant, came in.

Taking a deep breath, she focused on the pen in her hand. She was not going to stoop to his level. Maybe she'd been wrong about him and her feelings for him. And clearly, his for her. She could kick herself for sleeping with him—twice.

Oh God—they hadn't used a condom that morning. At that thought, she ventured a glance at him. She felt her stomach clench. The thought of life growing in her womb was equal parts terrifying and exciting. She could feel a lump in her throat.

She looked away before he saw her watching him. As she did, her hands fell to her lap and caressed her stomach. The fact remained that he didn't trust her. It was her fault. She needed to tell him everything that had happened between her and Harmon.

Furrowing her brow, she wondered who Darrin had hired to look into her past. The new thoughts did little for her discontent. *What will he think of me if he finds out about everything without me telling him myself?*

Jackie didn't know why she'd needed to go with Darrin to complete the closing paperwork. Darrin's father had everything set up and ready for them. They were at the attorney's office for a matter of two hours, and then they were on their way.

From the attorney's office, they went to the building. She could have walked right out of that conference room if she hadn't needed him to drive her back to the hotel. Standing in the entryway of their new location, she closed her eyes to clear her head.

"Jackie, are you all right?" he asked with concern. "You look like you're going to pass out."

"I'm fine," she snapped. She didn't want his scrutiny at the moment. She was doing enough examination for both of them.

They had made their way through the building while Darrin was talking about all the ways the rooms could be maximized and how he liked the gym being a facility for the employees. Nothing he said was registering. If he noticed, he didn't seem to care.

They got to the top floor and entered a massive office. "This office will be mine and the general manager's," he said.

She furrowed her brow in confusion. That statement had caught her attention.

"I've decided I'm going to split my time between the two locations. Maybe two weeks at a time in each place. I want to be as involved in this location as I will be in New Mexico. We'll likely make some managerial shifts there since my father currently acts as the general manager. That way, I can relinquish some responsibilities to allow for the travel." He watched Jackie, but she kept her features calm, impassive.

"That sounds reasonable." She averted her gaze and looked out the windows, mindlessly nodding. "I'm sure the woman at the attorney's office will be happy to hear that," she mumbled. He didn't comment, so she figured he hadn't heard. A flurry of excitement churned in her conflicted belly.

The office looked like it was three of the other offices combined. It was certainly spacious enough to fit two desks, filing cabinets, and other furniture.

Can we make a relationship work on the basis of seeing one another every two weeks? It would be better than only on weekends. She chastised herself for even contemplating being with him. She shot him a look of contempt from her position by the window. He was looking across the room at her. Jackie became aware of the light filtering through the windows. She doubted he could see the look on her face.

"Are we done here?" she asked tersely.

"Ready to go back to the hotel?"

"Yes," she said, heading for the door.

His reflexes were quicker than she'd anticipated. He reached out and grabbed her bicep, halting her in her tracks. She kept her eyes turned toward the door to his right.

"You can act like an angry little victim all you want. But you know what? I have been here by your side, trying to help you figure this shit out. I've been trying to keep you safe. You push me away every chance you get. You try to hide everything from me."

She still refused to look into those piercing blue eyes. Every time she did, she felt like he was looking straight into her soul.

"Fuck, Jackie! Can't you see how much I care about you?" He took a deep breath, rolling his shoulders.

He lessened his grip on her arm so she could easily pull it from his grip. Rather than do that, she stayed as she was—still and silent.

Releasing her, he dropped his hand to his side. He preceded her out the door and over to the elevator. He was leaving her behind. She felt the sinking feeling in her gut. As he boarded the elevator, his gaze met hers. She felt the pull toward him in every fiber of her being.

He was watching her closely, holding the door, waiting for her. Waiting for her to finally tell him. Just waiting.

It was all up to her. The stone sinking in her gut told her it was time. Taking a calming breath, she forced one step after another to join him.

Chapter Twenty-Seven
The Conspirator

The apartment looked like it had been damaged by a hurricane. "Little bastard." The shadowed figure kicked over the small trash can in the kitchen. *No wonder he hasn't been answering any calls.*

The conspirator walked through the apartment. There was even more disarray in the bedroom. Dresser drawers were left open. The bed was unmade, and blankets poured onto the floor.

After everything the two of them had been through, Lucas had run out. He was gone. Well, the plan didn't exactly require any more participation from Lucas, but there was no guarantee he wouldn't warn that little bitch.

There still hadn't been anything on the news about her. No report of her missing. Either she or her car should have been found by now. Something was off—she must not have driven.

The figure tapped the top of the dismantled dresser, releasing agitation into the wood, then sat down on the corner of the dingy bed. There, another plan was born. Lucas would be given one last chance. If Lucas wasn't in, he would be out—in more ways than one.

Chapter Twenty-Eight

Jackie

Their hotel room brought back the morning's events. The stench of betrayal was heavy in the air. Jackie had done her best to be civil at the attorney's office. She wanted to scratch Darrin's eyes out of the sockets. She wanted to hurt him. She wanted to scream at him.

But most of all, she wanted him to understand her fears. She hated that she could see his point of view in this situation. Her mind had been fighting her all the way to the hotel.

"Darrin," she said around the knot in her throat. Speaking was difficult. *How am I going to tell him when just speaking his name makes me feel like I'm going to crumble?*

"Jackie." He must have sensed she was ready to tell him. He took her hands and sat down on the edge of the bed, holding them in his. "I don't know the woman you wish you were. I only know the woman sitting in front of me. She has become who she is because of her past. I only want to know about that past so I can help you build a stronger future."

She felt his fingers below her chin. He drew her face up to look at him. A tear ran down her cheek.

"Not to judge you for those experiences," he said. "Please help me understand the woman I've come to know. The woman I care for more than anything."

She felt another tear trickle down her cheek.

"Please."

"Darrin, it's hard for me to talk about," she said, her breath shaking with the tears that longed to be expelled.

"There is nothing you need to hide from me," he said, gently rubbing his thumbs back and forth on the tops of her hands.

She exhaled, allowing herself to melt into the bed, preparing herself for the dread she would soon be feeling. "Harmon and I got married young; we were both nineteen. We just couldn't wait to start our forever story." She chuckled at the irony. "We'd only been married a little over three years when the divorce was finalized. Luckily, we didn't have any assets together." She met his eyes for the first time since she'd started speaking. "It made the process much quicker."

"What happened between the two of you?" he asked, urging her on.

"Please. Please don't make me relive that."

Anguish crossed his face. "Jackie, I'm not asking this to hurt you. I need to know so I can help you heal. Let me in. Let me do that for you." His eyes softened.

Exhaling again, she continued. "I had just begun my third year of college. I think it was the end of November. I-I found out I was pregnant."

The shock on his face let her know that was not what he was expecting. She looked back down at their clasped hands. She could feel the heat of embarrassment flooding her face. He recovered quickly and resumed rubbing the backs of her hands.

"I found out I was due mid-May. I was afraid to tell Harmon. Christmas Eve, I finally worked up the courage to tell him. I was having a difficult time eating anything. He was ecstatic. I couldn't believe how happy he was.

"The next day, we announced it to our families. Both families acted excited, but I don't think they really were. They said all the right things, but the smiles on their faces... their smiles were fake. My parents thought I was too young, although they never said it to me. They hinted it to my brother, and he told me. I could tell there was something wrong with the way they talked about the baby. Throughout the pregnancy, they asked all the right questions, but I could feel a lack of interest below the surface. They threw an extravagant baby shower. I couldn't believe the generosity. We had everything we would need."

Sadness etched Darrin's face as he listened. From what Jackie knew, he had a supportive family. She longed to know how that felt.

"I had my twentieth birthday about a month before the baby was due." She could hear the change in her own voice. It was hollow, devoid of emotion.

He cleared his throat as if sensing the change in her. Fidgeting in his seat, he leaned closer.

Her mind had been transported to a place she dreaded to go. "I had some pains and called the doctor's office. They told me it was most likely Braxton-Hicks contractions—that since I was so close to my due date, I would probably feel them from now till birth. It was just my body's way of getting ready for birth." She released a humorless laugh. "I didn't want to worry Harmon, so I didn't mention it to him. I brought it up at my next appointment, and again, they reassured me that it was probably just my body preparing. The midwife irritably offered to check the baby's heart rate and everything. I felt foolish for being so worried, so I let it go. By this time, it was only another two weeks until my due date."

She exhaled a shaky breath. She could see the sorrow on Darrin's face. But it was like she was looking at him through the lens of a camera that she couldn't quite get to focus.

"The day came. I was having severe contractions. We arrived at the hospital, got checked in, and we were taken to a small delivery room. There was a private bathroom, and the bed was near the window. Next to it was a small table scale for the baby.

"The nurse left to give me a chance to change into the hospital gown. I was told not to wear anything under it. I felt highly self-conscious but did as she'd instructed me. Harmon helped me cinch up the back. It was so cold in the room." She rubbed her hands over her arms.

"One of the midwives I had seen several times at my appointments entered. She asked me to lie down on the tiny bed and place my feet in the stirrups. I hated the feeling of being so exposed." Jackie winced. "She checked me to see how dilated I was. She informed me I was five centimeters and would hopefully progress quickly so I'd be able to push soon. But she suggested that I walk around to help the baby work its way down. I paced up and down the hall for what felt like hours. Harmon was by my side the entire time, taking each step in time with mine."

Darrin ran his fingers through his hair.

"The midwife returned and asked me to lie down to get checked again. This time, she told me I was fully dilated and that with the next contraction, I needed to push. I did, for several minutes. I felt like it was taking forever. I just wanted to have my baby in my arms." She gave a sardonic smile. Exhaling slowly, she pressed her hands into her legs, running them down her thighs. "They broke my water. A few pushes later, they told me the baby's head was out. They needed to turn the baby to get the shoulders out. I could feel the tear but not any pain. I was focused on my baby.

"Once the shoulders cleared, it was only another couple of pushes until the baby was fully out. I immediately felt something was wrong. Why wasn't the baby crying? I panicked and tried to sit up, frantic to see my baby."

Jackie paused, replaying the scene in her mind. "Harmon was just standing there like an idiot. I was furious and confused. The midwife and nurse were talking back and forth in hushed voices. I wanted to know what they were whispering about. The midwife finally came to my side. She took one of my hands and said the baby was a girl. The next thing she told me I knew before the words came out of her mouth.

"She told me she was stillborn and apologized for my loss. She asked me if there was a name I wanted them to use for her." Jackie's voice broke. But she'd started this, and she wanted to finish it. Darrin continued watching her intently. "I remember just sitting there, staring at the wall behind the midwife's head. I couldn't think. I mean, how could this be true? I didn't *want* to believe her. I don't remember what happened for a few minutes. I sort of blacked out."

She felt the sting of a fresh tear gliding out of her eyes. Darrin wiped it away with the pad of his thumb. She wanted to stop but at the same time knew she needed to finish the story. She'd never shared the intimate details of the delivery room with anyone. Verity had tried to coax her into talking about it, which had resulted in Jackie storming out of the room. Eventually, Verity had given up.

"Next thing I remember was the nurse from the delivery bringing my baby over to me. She was clean and smelled of fresh soap. I don't think I will ever forget the fragrance. She smelled of lavender and baby powder." Jackie sniffled as if she was smelling it.

"The nurse asked me if I wanted to hold her. We hadn't known what the baby was going to be. If the baby had turned out to be a girl, we'd planned on naming her Cecelia. As I took her into my arms, she looked perfect. She was just sleeping, I told myself. I had the urge to wiggle her a little to get some sort of reaction from her. I wanted to feel the grip of her tiny little fingers around mine. I longed to hear the cries of a newborn baby confused about the new place she was in. I wanted to console her, to protect her, but I couldn't. She was already gone..." Jackie's throat hurt with each word she spoke. Her voice was hoarse, and the tears flowed from her unseeing eyes.

Darrin pulled her into his lap in a deep, consoling hug. "Jackie, I am so sorry. I can't imagine the pain you endured."

For a while she just let him hold her. Now that she'd started the story, she finally had the strength to get it all out. From the comfort of Darrin's embrace, she continued in a whisper. "She looked too perfect. No name would be good enough, I remember thinking. We called her Cecelia, but I knew she deserved better. A grief counselor came in. He spent time speaking to each one of us. I honestly don't remember much of what Harmon did that day. I was so inwardly focused I don't think I could tell you where he was most of the day.

"I barely even remember calling my parents to tell them. They arrived at the hospital within an hour of receiving the call. Again, they said all the right things. I'd called only to let them know, not because I wanted them there. I wanted to shout at them to shut up while they were trying to console me. I wanted to be alone. I have never felt such a range of emotions in one day. I was overwhelmingly sad, angry, and confused. I wanted everyone to just leave me alone. My parents stayed for an hour or two. I just wanted them to leave." She shakily fidgeted with the hem of her dress then turned to look into Darrin's eyes, which conveyed their sadness at her loss. "Tony visited me late that evening. He never spoke a word—he just came in hugged me, held me. He understood me better than anyone else." Her lip quivered at the memory.

Shaking her head, she continued. "I received a few stiches and was bleeding heavily. They wanted to keep me for a few days to monitor that. They needed to check on me every few hours and would swap out the icepacks. I didn't care who saw me anymore. I felt like I was watching everything from the window. Like everything that was being said was muffled and incomprehensible."

Darrin held her tighter. He got up and carried her to the top of the bed, where he sat down with her in his lap as he leaned against the headboard. She sat sideways across his legs with her head resting against his neck and shoulder.

"After a couple days, they allowed us to leave. They had requested that I sign up for grief counseling. We got into the car, and I looked into the back seat. The diaper bag. The car seat. I had never imagined we would be leaving the hospital without a baby. I had all of the pains of someone after childbirth. It was difficult to stand for more than a few minutes at a time. I was exhausted. I felt like I'd lost my life's purpose in that hospital." She felt more tears welling in her eyes, surprised to still be crying. The floodgates of Cecelia's story were open, and she was not going to give up.

"The first day I was home, I stayed in bed all day. My breasts were sore and swollen. My eyes were puffy and stung from the tears I'd cried. As I lay in bed that night, I noticed the tears had all dried up. I didn't want anyone to bother me, not even Harmon. I felt terrible afterward. I know he was in pain too. But I selfishly didn't want to hear about it. His entire body wasn't in constant mockery of what we'd lost." Jackie's voice cracked.

"Mine was. I felt trapped. The pains in my vagina were excruciating, my stomach was stretched and sagging, and my breasts were full of milk for a child who could never taste it. Everything subsided with time. I went to grief counseling. After several days, the milk in my breasts dried up but left my breasts larger than before. After a few more weeks, the pains and bleeding subsided."

Darrin started rubbing her back. She knew he wanted, in a small way, to let her know he was listening.

"The hardest part was her room. I hated going in there. The crib was all set up—a white skirt fluttered around the bottom with a little blanket with a giraffe in the middle. The dresser and closet were overflowing with clothes. The rocking chair was collecting dust. I dreamt of sitting in it, rocking her to sleep. All of it was wasted. What was I to do with it all? I wasn't sure if I should return it to the people who'd bought it for her..." Jackie's voice had grown hoarse. She cleared her throat.

"It was in those moments, examining her room, that I realized we would never be able to make this work. I refused to have an autopsy done on her. I couldn't bear the thought of them invading and ruining her little body." She shook with the new bout of emotion surging through her.

"Harmon was angry I had denied the autopsy. He wanted answers. He needed to know why. I, on the other hand, couldn't bear the thought of finding out it was my fault. That something I did made her lose her life when it was supposed to be beginning."

"Jackie, I hope you don't think that still. I hope you're not blaming yourself after all these years."

She didn't reply. Instead, she hurried to conclude her story. "One night, probably a year and a half after losing her, we got into a massive argument. When I left our apartment that night, I never went back. Weeks after our third wedding anniversary, we were divorced."

"I am so sorry you went through that. I wish I could have spared you all that pain." Darrin held her and rocked her for several more minutes, sprinkling her forehead with kisses.

Jackie withdrew herself from his lap and lay down next to him. She was still in the tight, formfitting dress she'd worn to the attorney's office. He reached around to the back of the dress and unzipped it. She withdrew her arms and allowed him to remove the dress. Then he lay down next to her.

His eyes looked all around her body and settled on her stomach. He slid down to be even with it. She could feel his breath on her flesh and felt the chills it induced. She knew what he was doing. The stretch marks had only faded so much over the years. He kissed them.

"Thank you for trusting me." He moved from one to another and back again. "You're so much stronger than I think you give yourself credit for," he said, resuming his spot next to her and tipping her head up to look at him.

She let him hold her until she fell asleep. She knew she was in love.

DARRIN

Jackie lay next to him; her eyes were puffy. He wished he could heal the pain that had been festering inside her. His left hand rested on her cheek to soothe the last of the tears that had fallen.

It had hurt him to hear her talk of the heartbreak she'd suffered. No wonder she'd been afraid to sleep with him—she was terrified of getting pregnant and experiencing another loss.

He brushed a piece of hair that lay across her face. The instant he touched her skin, she smiled in her sleep. The simple beauty made his heart ache.

How will I bear having her live hours away, only seeing her every two weeks? He cursed under his breath. Now that he knew it all, he wanted to keep her all to himself.

Chapter Twenty-Nine

JACKIE

The morning had been busy with packing and getting ready for an early flight. They arrived back in New Mexico before eight. "Just come with me. We can ride together," Darrin said, trying to dissuade her from driving her own car.

"Darrin, I need to run a few errands, and then I'll come right to the office. I promise." She leaned in to kiss him. The moment their lips touched, she felt butterflies swarm in her stomach. A blush crept over her face.

"Fine, but let me know when you get into the office," he said, pulling her closer.

She felt the tug of sexual desire deep within her. She couldn't believe how free she felt now. She'd finally been able to talk to someone about Cecelia. When he withdrew, she wished she was getting in the car with him. Instead, she settled into the driver's seat of her own car as she tossed her purse onto the passenger seat.

DARRIN

As she entered the front door, she nearly collided with Darrin. Catching her under the arms, he steadied her. "Jackie, are you all right? What's going on?"

"I-I don't know," she stammered, allowing Darrin to take on all her weight. "My head is pounding, and I'm feeling dizzy and nauseous." Her eyes were glazed over, and she looked pale and sickly.

"We're going to the hospital." Darrin crouched down, supporting her with his right hand while he swung his left around and under her knees. He lifted her, and she laid her head against his shoulder.

Todd walked by, his brows furrowed. Darrin couldn't help the irritation he felt at the sight of him.

"Tell Charles Jackie is sick and I'm taking her to the hospital."

Todd nodded soberly. Penny, from the accounting department, opened the door for Darrin.

"I'm sorry. I don't know what's wrong with me," Jackie said.

"Shhh. It's all right. Stay calm and rest," he whispered into her hair.

He made his way to his designated spot at the front of the parking lot, glad he hadn't had to park far away. "I'm going to set you down now. I need to get the keys out of my pocket. Lean against me for support. I won't let you fall." Noticing Jackie's eyes were still closed and she hadn't responded, Darrin shook her lightly. "Jackie, I need you to say something."

"Hmm." She gave him a slight flutter of her eyelids.

Hastily, he pulled her to his chest with his left arm. With as much calm as he could summon, he fished into his pocket for his car keys then unlocked the passenger door and deposited Jackie in the seat. He secured the seat belt across her lap, closed the door with a quick snap, and ran around to the other side of the car, almost tripping over his own feet in his haste.

"It's okay, Jackie. I'm going to get you to the hospital. Just relax."

Her head hung to one side. Pushing past the urge to hold her close, to feel her heart beat against his, he started the car and backed out of his parking space in one swift movement. *Please, no*, he thought. *Please, Jackie.*

Darrin arrived at the hospital in record time, bringing the car to a jarring halt outside the emergency room. He went around to remove Jackie, relieved to see she was sitting up with the door open.

"I think I can walk in."

He eyed her warily. "Why don't you let me help you to make sure."

"All right." Smiling faintly, she wrapped her right arm around his back while he placed his left hand around her shoulder, holding her tight to his side.

"Let's get you inside." He pressed a kiss to her head.

Together, they walked through the automatic doors into the quiet emergency room. There was one other person in the waiting room, a haggard-looking man with his head buried between his knees, supported by his shaking hands. Passing by the man, they reached the reception window.

A woman with a kindly face moved the glass partition to one side. "Good morning. What brings you in this morning?" she asked serenely.

"Jackie arrived at work today barely able to walk, complaining of a headache and dizziness." Darrin was shocked to hear the emotion in his own voice. It sounded foreign. The realization heightened his anxiety.

"Okay. I'll need you to fill out these forms. I'll notify you when we're ready for you to come into an examination room." After handing him a clipboard with the indicated forms clipped to it, she closed the glass partition.

Flexing his hands, Darrin fought the urge to open the glass and demand Jackie be seen immediately. His heart pounded, and he thought about what might be happening to her.

"Come on—I see a double chair." Darrin weaved through the other chairs in the waiting room to get to one wide enough for them to sit in side by side. Though still supporting Jackie, he was able to move with surprising agility. Jackie looked up to him with a wan smile. "Okay, Jackie, you're going to have to help me fill out these forms."

As they worked their way through the forms, Jackie seemed to be getting a better hold on herself. With the forms completed, Darrin left her in the chair, not wanting to ask her to get up until it was necessary, and brought the forms back over to the receptionist.

Darrin had only just resumed his seat and his hold around Jackie when a nurse stepped out of the hall. "Jacqueline Martinez?"

It only took the nurse a moment to zero in on Jackie and Darrin. He studied them as Darrin again assisted Jackie to her feet. The two followed the nurse through the double doors into the examination room.

"Are you her husband?" the nurse asked.

Darrin's neck cracked with the sudden turn of his head. "No," he said, more harshly than he meant to.

"I am then going to need to ask you to return to the waiting room while I examine Ms. Martinez."

This time, it was Jackie's head that spun around quickly. "No, I nee—I mean I want him to stay with me."

The nurse carefully searched Jackie's face before consenting to let Darrin stay.

While getting settled, Darrin watched the nurse set up his computer and look over the form they had filled out. He was a handsome man, with dark curly hair slightly longer on top than on the sides and emerald-green eyes.

"All right, Jaqueline, my name is Dalton. I'm going to need to get your vitals and blood pressure. Then we'll begin with a few questions about this morning."

Nodding, she said, "Please call me Jackie."

The smile she sent the nurse sent a pulse of jealousy through Darrin. His arm possessively tightened around Jackie's waist. If she noticed his sudden tension, she didn't acknowledge it. He hated how ill at ease he was with her around other men. He'd never had trust issues until Jessica.

"There are a few preliminary questions I need to ask you. What was the first date of your last period?"

Jackie's whole body stiffened. "May 19."

Darrin noticed her reluctance to discuss such private matters. He rubbed his thumb on her back to help relax her.

"Are you taking any medications we need to be aware of? Vitamins, supplements, prescriptions?"

"No."

"Birth control?" With that question, Dalton's eyes shifted to Darrin.

Jackie's face flushed with color and then went back to the pallor of that morning. Now Darrin was curious about the answer to that question as well.

"No," she answered reluctantly, settling farther into the chair next to Darrin as if taking cover from the arsenal of questions.

Her answer sank like a rock in his stomach.

"Is there any possibility you're pregnant?"

Is this his idea of a joke? Is he deliberately trying to embarrass her?

"No," she replied stiffly.

To check her vital signs, the nurse motioned for Jackie to move over to the examination table. Once they were all settled in, Dalton leaned forward, scrutinizing her. His closeness did little to appease Darrin, who was now seated in the chair alone. She was getting some of her color back, but under the bright lights, she looked pale and weak. This was the first time Darrin had looked at her eyes in a while. They were sad and bloodshot. He wondered if that was from whatever was wrong or from all the crying of the night before.

Leaning in farther still, the nurse began his inquisition. "I am going to need to ask you several more questions. Have you had a history of headaches?"

"No."

"What other symptoms were you experiencing?"

"Dizziness, nausea."

"What were you doing this morning when the headache began?"

"Running errands before work."

"Okay. Were you doing anything out of the ordinary? Doing anything overly strenuous?"

"No. I had a few bills I wanted to pay and ran to the bank." She sounded exhausted, her voice barely audible over the steady hum of the air conditioner.

The questions continued for another several minutes. Darrin looked around the room. Photos on the walls showed organ damage caused by bad habits. The hazardous-waste disposal bin for needles was hung on the wall along with several boxes of blue medical gloves. He hated hospitals—the smell, the bright lights, all of it. He knew the necessity for them to be sterile, but it felt inhuman.

"Our next step will be to have you go down to the lab. You'll have a few vials of blood drawn. After that's completed, I would advise you to go home and rest."

"Good. I could use some sleep." Jackie's voice had grown steadier.

Darrin got up and drew Jackie back to his side. The lurch in his stomach was a direct result of the fear in her eyes. She leaned against him. He kissed the top of her head, breathing in her floral fragrance.

He couldn't stop himself from wondering what she would do if she did end up getting pregnant and was surprised to find that the thought didn't terrify him. He'd been so caught up in their moments together that he hadn't thought about birth control. He was always so careful. He was astounded by his own carelessness.

She let Darrin guide her down the hall toward the laboratory services department. He steadily became more and more aware of the tug in his heart. The feel of her slim waist against his hand felt right—the way she was tucked under his arm and the feel of her pressed against him and how she kept resting her head on him. It was intoxicating. He was afraid to admit how terrified it made him to think she might not want to be with him for the long haul.

When the blood draws were completed, Darrin drove her back to his house. He wanted to watch over her the rest of the day in case something happened. He took her down to his room and laid her in bed. She was exhausted, yet as time passed, she appeared to be feeling steadily better.

When Darrin brought her some toast and water, she was just about ready to fall asleep. He lay down next to her. She looked deep into his eyes.

"Thank you." A smile fluttered across her lips.

"Jackie, I would do anything for you," he said, pulling her close. "If you start feeling worse, let me know."

"What did you say to the hospital staff before we left?"

He stiffened next to her. "I told them they'd better get those results to us as soon as possible and that if anything happened to you because they didn't do those tests quickly enough, I was going to make their lives a living hell."

Her brows pinched together in question as they always did when she didn't understand something.

"I guess it's my turn to have an admission of sorts. I have a hard time with hospitals," he admitted slowly. "It was my junior year in college. My mother was in the hospital. I was planning on going to see her on Monday. They'd told me Friday she was doing well. I had coursework I needed to do that weekend anyway, so going Monday would be easiest. However, Sunday morning at eight thirty, I received the news of her passing."

He cleared his throat. "I knew I would have the time, but what I didn't know was that she wouldn't. I learned a hard lesson—don't wait. Don't tell yourself it can happen when it's convenient for you. That might not be the case. Someone who's sick isn't going to wait for you to say goodbye."

"Is that why you wanted to make sure they did the testing?"

"Yes. I could tell you were beginning to feel better, but I didn't want to risk it. I don't blame the hospital staff for my mother's passing. I know they did all they could. I just felt like I was shorted. I never got my chance to tell her how much she meant to me."

Pulling her head out from under his chin, Jackie looked up at him. "Darrin, if you treated her with nearly as much care as you have shown me... she knew."

A single tear trekked down his cheek. Jackie hugged him close.

Chapter Thirty
THE CONSPIRATOR

Excitement surged. Jackie had been taken to the hospital. Maybe the plan had worked after all. While driving around, looking for the little bastard who'd run out, the conspirator had noticed Jackie's car in the parking lot by the airport.

Everything circulating about Jackie had said she would be driving to California again. But she hadn't. That was why her body hadn't been found yet.

That sneaky little bitch.

This was going to end, and it was going to end soon. Once Lucas was located and taken care of, the remainder of the plan would be finished. No one ran out and got away with it.

Maybe that little tramp would perish on the way to the hospital. The thought inspired another rush of pleasure. Retribution was enthralling.

CHAPTER THIRTY-ONE

DARRIN

"Darrin, thank you for coming up." Charles replaced a binder on the shelf behind his desk.

Darrin's brows furrowed as he sat in the chair across from his father. They hadn't spoken much since the conversation about him and Jackie sharing a hotel room. His father had not been pleased.

"Todd told me you took Jackie to the hospital yesterday."

Darrin nodded.

"Is she all right?"

"She seems much better this morning. She's staying at my house for the next few days, watching things."

Charles placed his elbows on the arms of his chair and steepled his fingers. "Are you going to be able to remain unbiased when selecting someone for the general manager position?"

After a brief pause, Darrin nodded, but he knew his father had seen him falter.

"I like Jackie, Darrin, but I will not allow you to be part of the decision if you allow your personal feelings to intervene."

The threat didn't sit well with Darrin, but he knew he was walking a fine line. His father knew Darrin didn't typically allow women into his life, never mind his home.

"Think about what I've said. I am not saying she can't get the position because of whatever you two have going on, but I've heard some grumblings."

"Todd?" Darrin snapped.

Charles lifted one brow. "Yes."

Darrin needed to get ahold of Mia. She was taking too long to get back to him.

"I know there's more going on with Jackie than I've been told," Charles said, and Darrin shifted uncomfortably in his seat. "I'm not asking you to betray her trust. But I want you to know I'm here to help you both." Charles stood, making his way over to the window and looking down at the traffic. "People will love who they love. I'm not going to threaten her job or tell you not to be with her. I can see a change in you already."

Darrin nodded. "Me too. I feel different with her. She's been through a lot and is going through even more." Darrin told his father about the stalker.

"What have the police said?" Charles's brow furrowed as he walked back to his desk.

"Nothing. She called them about the man following her and vandalizing her car while we were in California, but since it didn't happen here, they haven't done anything."

"Keep me informed."

Darrin left his father's office with mixed feelings. Taking a seat at his desk, he let his fingers run through his hair. Holding his head in his hands, he considered everything his father had said. He desperately wanted to be part of the hiring decision, but he would certainly side with Jackie over Todd at the moment. Todd was acting in ways he didn't agree with.

As he pulled his cell from his pocket, it rang in his hand.

"Finally. What have you got?"

"Wow, Darrin. It's good to hear from you too. I've missed you," Mia snarked.

"Sorry. I've been stressed." Running a hand over his face, he took a deep breath. "I've missed you, too, Mia. How have you been?"

"Good! You're about to be good too. I have some news for you. Todd Manaker…" she paused for effect. She loved to push his buttons. "Well, he's married, has two kids."

"Damn it, Mia. I know that shit. Get to the point."

"Okay, okay." She giggled.

Darrin rolled his eyes, wondering how he'd remained friends with her all these years.

"Sorry. I don't usually get the pleasure of hearing you so wound up," she said.

Darrin was relieved to hear there was no way she could connect Todd to the emails or anyone in California. He couldn't wait to tell Jackie. Although this was good news, he was still disappointed they were no closer to finding the culprit.

The next best thing was to get the IT staff to see if they could do some digging into the emails. Darrin didn't know why he hadn't thought of enlisting their help sooner. Jackie wouldn't want any more people at work to know about the emails, but this could lead them in the right direction.

He would talk with Jackie that night.

* * *

"Ms. Martinez?"

"Just a moment, please," Darrin said into the receiver as he made his way down the hall.

He'd just walked through the door. Jackie had stayed home the last two days. She was lying on Darrin's mother's chair when he handed her the phone.

She looked at him quizzically. "This is Jackie," she said, still looking at Darrin, confused.

He wished he could hear what was going on. The silence filling the room in turn filled him with dread. It had to be the hospital calling her.

"Th-Thank you. I'll make sure to have it checked out." She listened. "Okay, I'll be there tomorrow at ten a.m." Her eyes glazed over the moment she disconnected the phone.

He felt his heart sink and dropped to his knees, bringing his face level with hers. "Was that the hospital?" he asked, taking her hands into his.

"Yes. It was carbon monoxide poisoning. I have to go in for some additional testing. Neurological testing. I'm not sure what that means." She rubbed her forehead.

"What? How?"

"They said there might be something wrong with the exhaust on my car. They suggested I have someone check it out."

"It's going to the garage I choose this time." He surged to his feet and retrieved the phone from where she'd dropped it and retreated from the room.

He paced the kitchen while he made the call to his friend's tow-truck company and garage to get Jackie's car an appointment as soon as possible. They guaranteed him that they would look at her car the next morning.

When he reentered the bedroom, he held her close to his chest, kissed the top of her head, and let her know that he was having her car looked at to see what was wrong.

"You think it was my car?"

"That's the only thing you did that I didn't. If it was something on the plane, don't you think I would have gotten sick too?" His stomach clenched. He needed to know what was happening. Whoever was after her was determined.

"I guess," she said slowly. She studied his face as if trying to pull something from him.

"I'm going to go down to the garage while they're going through your car."

She looked up at him with sadness in her eyes. "I'm scared, Darrin."

* * *

"You should ask one of your parents to attend your doctor's appointment with you."

"We're not exactly on speaking terms." She pushed her eggs around her plate.

"This might be a good opportunity for you to reconnect with them. I won't pretend to understand that relationship. But if they knew what was going on, I bet they would want to be here for you."

Jackie tapped her fork on the edge of her plate. "I don't think I'm ready to talk with them."

"When did you guys stop speaking?" Darrin leaned on the opposite side of the breakfast bar.

"The night before I left for California the first time."

Darrin nodded. "Can I ask what happened?"

A disgusted laugh left Jackie's lips—this was a strange laugh for her. "Well, to sum it up, they think I need to be working for them. Money is the only factor they consider, so because they could pay me more, they think I'm wasting my time."

"Well, shit. That's a bit harsh."

"Clearly, I refused to work for my father. That was not received well." Her eyes clouded with unshed tears. "On my way out the door, my father told me not to bother coming back again."

Darrin placed his hand on hers and gave a gentle squeeze. "I'm sorry. I can't imagine."

Jackie gave him a sad smile. "Oh, I almost forgot. Guess what showed up?" Before he could make a guess, she bounded off the stool and out of sight. Darrin wasn't sure if he was supposed to follow her.

Stepping around the breakfast bar, he saw her coming back into the kitchen, the sadness from moments ago no longer visible. She wiggled a small white box in the air.

"New phone?"

"Yes." She ripped into the packaging. She'd been able to retrieve the sim card and memory card from her shattered phone. Darrin could barely believe both were undamaged. "I'll get it set up before my doctor's appointment."

Kissing the top of her head, he reminded her to reset the alarm on her way out and to text him when she got to the doctor's office. She was going to be using one of his father's spare cars while they waited to find out what was happening with hers.

Darrin arrived at the garage an hour early. He could see Jackie's car still loaded on the back of the tow truck. The garage had been owned by Clem, one of his father's friends. Clem's son had recently taken over.

"Morning, Kane," Darrin said as he walked through the bay door of the garage.

He could see the mechanic's steel-toed boots under the only car in the garage. Generally, customers were not allowed within the bays. However, Darrin and Kane had grown up together. They'd known each other since they were in diapers. They might as well have been brothers.

"Darrin!" Kane shouted, coming out from behind the late-model sedan he had on the lift. He was a stocky man with chocolate-colored hair. His clothes and hands were covered in grease. Darrin didn't mind the grunge as he pulled Kane into an embrace. "So, I hear there is a problem with your lady's car?"

Darrin looked at him through slitted eyes. "She's not exactly my lady."

"The way your dad talked about it, he was ready to start planning a wedding," Kane said around a laugh as he clapped Darrin on the shoulder.

Darrin rolled his eyes but otherwise ignored the comment. "There have been some weird things happening to one of my coworkers," he said, chancing a glance at his friend. He saw a smirk materialize on Kane's face, one that would have been in place when they were kids trying to find a way to sneak out for a night of underage drinking.

"She and I came back from a business trip. She got into her car after it had been in the airport secured parking lot and left to run some errands. She showed up at work two hours later, feeling extremely dizzy and nauseous. We just found out yesterday it was carbon monoxide poisoning."

Kane's smirk had disappeared. "You think there's a problem with the exhaust." He chewed his cheek. "I'll bring her car in next."

"Thanks, man."

The two talked as Kane finished working on the car on the lift. When that one was finished, he parked it outside in one of the customer parking spaces and had another mechanic help him get Jackie's car off the tow truck. Darrin watched from the doorway of the garage. He'd left Jackie sitting in the kitchen, eating breakfast. He'd explained that he was good friends with the mechanic and was going to head to the garage early, letting her know he should be back in a couple of hours.

The car was brought in and put up on the lift. The mechanics found the problem within a minute. Darrin excused himself to make a few phone calls.

Darrin left the garage earlier than he thought he would. He stopped and picked up some groceries on his way back home. He didn't park his car in the garage as he usually did. There was a strange car parked in the drive. Darrin couldn't put his car in park and get his seat belt off fast enough. Not bothering to take the groceries out of the car, he raced through the front door in time to hear Jackie scream from the kitchen.

Oh no—I should have had her come with me. He raced through the living room, where the kitchen was visible.

He came up short when he saw a man hugging Jackie at the kitchen island. The hot rush of jealousy couldn't be contained. He took the last few steps into the kitchen, barely touching the floor, not making a sound. Neither of them had noticed his entrance. *Is this what she's doing whenever I leave—entertaining other men in my house?*

He grabbed the man's collar and pulled him around and out of Jackie's embrace. Her eyes widened to the size of grapefruits.

"Darrin," she said breathlessly. She must have been shocked by his sudden appearance.

His angry eyes shot to hers. Hers had gone from shocked to angry in moments. *How in the hell can she be angry with me?*

"What are you doing?" the man demanded. He was slightly taller than Darrin but equally handsome. Darrin quickly assessed that the man was well toned. They would be fair opponents.

"I think the proper question is what the fuck are you doing in *my* house?" Darrin said.

"Darrin, let him go!" Jackie tried to push her way between the two men. They were both much larger than she. Neither budged while she tried to separate them. "Dammit, Darrin! He's my brother!" she shouted.

At the shout, he looked down at her. He looked from her stunning hazel eyes—which were begging him to let go—to the man whose shirt was still tight in his grip. The eyes were the same. Realization replacing rage, Darrin released the man's shirt and relaxed his other fist.

Taking a calming breath, Jackie introduced the men. "Darrin, this is my brother, Tony. Tony, this is Darrin." She waved her hand between the men. "What the hell were you going to do?" she asked, looking at Darrin.

"I was going to beat the shit out of him," he said, frowning at her.

Tony scoffed.

"I heard you scream when I came through the front door. I thought something was wrong."

Jackie started laughing. "No, Tony had just told me he was hopefully going to be taking on an administrative position at our father's company—one he's always wanted to have—so I was excited for him." She blushed.

Tony patted his sister on the shoulder and took a seat at the breakfast bar. *Make yourself at home*, Darrin thought irritably. He felt embarrassed for having acted as he did and angry that Jackie's brother clearly thought he was entitled to lounge around his house.

"Why didn't you tell me he was coming before I left?"

"She didn't know I'd be coming," Tony spat.

Jackie strategically placed her hand on Darrin's chest to stop him from responding. Her touch had a sense of calm washing over him.

"All right, you two. Cut it out," she said, dividing a look between them. "Darrin, I didn't have any plans to see my brother today. The day I left for California the first time, Tony came to see me at the office. He didn't want me to be angry with him."

She gave her brother a caring glance. Darrin had never had any siblings, so he didn't know about what kind of bond they might have.

"He's been trying to call my cell, as well as the office, the last couple days. When I checked my email this morning, I saw that he had resorted to emailing me to check on me," she said, chagrined. "We've been so busy lately I hadn't had a chance to reach out."

"I was getting pretty damn worried, Jackie." Tony's eyes narrowed just like Jackie's did when she was trying to make a point. "You seemed pretty sketched out that day I met you in the parking lot."

"You startled me," she said, lowering her eyes.

"Don't give me that crap. I didn't push it that day, but I could tell you were upset," Tony said.

"I had a confrontation with a coworker just before I left that day." She looked over at Darrin. "That was the day Todd stopped by my office."

"What did he say?" Tony asked.

She nervously shifted her weight from one foot to the other. "He wanted to make sure I knew he was fighting for the position in California. He was telling me all the ways he was more qualified, and he also made it clear that he thought I would do anything to get the position..." she said hesitantly, glancing at Darrin again. "He was insinuating that everyone in the office thinks Darrin and I are sleeping together and that if I get the job, that would be the only reason."

"Asshole," Tony spat under his breath.

Darrin appreciated the way Jackie's brother immediately took her side. He needed to feel him out a bit more but was disliking him less as the minutes progressed. He pulled Jackie into a hug. Over her shoulder, he locked eyes with Tony. He could tell from the look in his eyes that Tony didn't think Darrin was good enough for his little sister. They scrutinized one another. Darrin reminded himself that they were on the same team—they both cared about Jackie.

Breaking their staring contest, Darrin kissed the top of her head. "I picked up some groceries while I was out. I need to go get those out of the car."

"Do you need help?" she asked.

"No. Sit, visit with your brother," he said, turning on his heel and heading back through the living room and out the door.

He made the trip quick and was back in the kitchen within two minutes. Jackie helped him unload the bags, and he could feel her brother's eyes watching the two of them move about the kitchen. By this point, Jackie knew where just about everything in the house was. He wondered if her brother thought it odd. He shouldn't have cared what Tony thought but knew that deep down, he did. Darrin was in love with Jackie, and the first time he met one of her family members, he'd almost assaulted him. *Great.*

"Jackie, have you told your brother about everything that's been going on?" Darrin watched as every muscle in her body stiffened and Tony's intense eyes bored into hers. That was all the answer he needed.

"I was going to after he told me about his new job," she practically hissed.

"I think we should all go in the living room and talk," Darrin said, leaving the kitchen and taking a seat on one end of one of the sofas.

If they moved at Jackie's pace, her brother wouldn't find out what was going on until Christmas. And that would likely be too late. He was hoping Tony might be able to shed some light on who might be trying to hurt her, and with how protective her brother seemed to be, he needed to know what had been happening. Jackie took a seat next to Darrin, and Tony sat on the opposite end, scrutinizing everything the two of them did. The scrutiny drove Darrin crazy.

Looking at Tony, he explained about the events of their first trip to California and the emails Jackie had been receiving. During the explanation, Jackie occupied herself by picking at her fingernails. Tony periodically looked over at her with his jaw clenched. When Darrin started telling him about the trip to the hospital earlier in the week, he shot to his feet.

"Jackie! Are you shitting me? You didn't feel telling us you were taken to the hospital was important?"

"Well, you heard them when I left—they said not to bother ever coming back. If I died, what would they care?" she said, matching the anger in his voice.

"I would care, damn it!" he shouted. "I was the one..." Tony's chest was heaving with indignation.

Darrin didn't ask what he was going to say. He figured that was a family issue and assumed his inquiry would make the situation worse.

"We found out yesterday that it was carbon monoxide poisoning," Darrin continued as if the outburst hadn't happened. "I called a friend of mine that owns a tow company and automotive garage and asked him to take a look at Jackie's car."

He turned to face Jackie. "Someone rerouted your exhaust into the trunk of your car. The whole time you were driving the other day, the fumes were seeping into the cab of the car."

Darrin felt the emotion well up in his throat. He'd known the tampering had to be intentional, but he couldn't bear thinking about it.

"What?" Jackie ran her fingers through her loose auburn hair. "I could have died on the side of the road."

Tony shifted in his seat. "What did they do to the car?"

"They bought some sort of flex piping that was attached to the end of your exhaust pipe. Whoever did it was pretty clever about it. They bored a hole into the compartment in your trunk where the spare tire is so that no one would notice it while looking in the trunk."

She sank back into the sofa, pulling her knees to her chest as if to protect herself from what she was hearing. Tony was watching her every move.

"Who would do this?" Tony finally asked.

"I don't know," Jackie said shakily.

They all sat in silence for a while. Darrin had put his arm around her waist and pulled her close. She rested her head on his shoulder.

"So... what is going on between the two of you?"

"Tony!" Jackie shouted.

"Well, you tell me some coworker is insinuating that the two of you are together, and from what I've seen"—he motioned at the way they were entangled—"it sure as hell looks like there is something going on."

Darrin didn't feel it was his place to answer the question. He waited for Jackie to say something.

"I'm not entirely sure," she said, gazing up at Darrin from her position on his shoulder.

This was apparently not the answer Tony had thought he was going to receive. The tension in his jaw intensified, and his angry gaze shifted between the two of them. Jackie wiggled under Darrin's arm. Darrin was hurt by what she'd said, but they hadn't talked about labels. He'd assumed they were dating and their relationship was exclusive. That would be clarified soon.

"Nothing was *going on* between us until after our first trip to California," Darrin said stiffly.

Tony's slitted eyes settled on Darrin. He nodded. "Mm-hmm. And how would anything work if you two are living twelve hours away from each other? I swear to you, if you are using her..."

"Stop!" Jackie shouted, jumping to her feet. "Tony, can I talk to you outside, please?"

Not waiting for him to answer, she marched to the front door and held it open for her brother. He stood from the couch and followed her motion to step outside.

Staying inside felt like a prison sentence. But Darrin refused to allow himself to follow them out. It would certainly be intruding on a family matter. Running all ten fingers through his hair, he forced himself to relax. He pushed himself up off the sofa. Reluctantly, he went to the kitchen to work on lunch.

Knowing Jackie liked a good salad with a nice cut of steak, Darrin aggressively chopped vegetables. There weren't any that were the same size. He didn't realize how anxious he was until he almost cut through one of his fingers. Putting the knife down, he took a few deep breaths. *Is her brother telling her not to be with me? Is he trying to get her to go back to their parents' house with him?*

He didn't figure she would go. She'd told him small bits about growing up and the poor relationship she shared with her mother. Her father was a smart man who wanted his kids to follow in his footsteps and wanted to guarantee their success. Darrin's father wanted the same for him but had approached that wish in a vastly different manner.

Mia had informed him of Tony's move back to the US and that he was residing with their parents. Darrin had initially wondered if her brother would hurt her, but after this meeting, he cleared Tony from the list. He was obviously the protective sort of brother. There were five years between the siblings, and after Jackie's divorce, she'd spent a large amount of time with Tony, and he'd helped her heal from the scars of another man who'd been supposed to protect her.

It had to be hard for Tony to see yet another man taking over. Darrin wondered how he had liked Jackie's ex-husband. From what Darrin had been told, Harmon was actually a nice guy—which only annoyed Darrin. He didn't want her ex-husband to be nice and kind. Mia hadn't found out much more on Harmon. He seemed like an upstanding citizen.

When Darrin heard the front door open, his head snapped up in attention. He was listening for their footsteps. He heard none. He wondered if she was collecting her things from the house.

He rounded the corner leading to the living room to find Jackie leaning against the end table. She looked dazed.

"Did Tony leave?" Darrin asked, peering around the corner to look out the front window. If his car was still out front, it was positioned so as not to be visible from the entryway.

She nodded. Her tear-filled eyes met his. "Who is Mia?" she asked in an angry whisper.

He couldn't stop the guilt from showing on his face. His stomach suddenly felt like he'd swallowed a ton of rocks.

"Please don't jump to conclusions. Jackie," he said, reaching for her hand as she began to withdraw. She turned to go back out the door. Darrin pulled her back and pinned her between himself and the entry wall.

"I trusted you!" she shouted. "I told you things I have never told anyone before. I trusted you." She crumpled to the floor. Each tear was a stab to his heart. "You got what you wanted, didn't you? I finally slept with you."

The rocks exploded in his gut. It felt like the shards were trying to cut their way out. As if she had hit him, he stumbled back.

"You think all I wanted was sex? You think that was what all this has been about?" he shouted, motioning to the house and between them. "Fuck, Jackie! I love you. I've made that clear, haven't I? But here we are once again—something comes up, and you're pushing me away. All I've done is try to protect you." He took a deep breath. "Mia is an old friend from high school. She and I were close. I won't lie—we gave dating a shot early on in college but decided that we were only meant to be friends. We have *never* slept together, Jackie."

Darrin searched her eyes. He hoped what he saw was a glimmer of hope. Squatting in front of Jackie, he implored her to believe him.

"Mia and I remained friends all through college and beyond. She became a detective for a while and has recently become a private investigator." He let the information sink in.

"I thought you just casually asked around about me, it would have been easy to come across my ex-husband. But you hired a professional. So is that who you were talking to on the phone that day?"

He didn't need to ask what day she was talking about. "Yes," he said from his squatting position on the floor. They needed to be honest with one another. Even if she couldn't, he would have to.

"Apparently, she's been asking around about me. Turns out she ran into one of my brother's friends. Before she realized it was my brother's friend, she mentioned you and the work your father's company does. When she realized there was a connection, she asked him all kinds of questions about my family. But she was most interested in me. Set off all sorts of warning bells. She must not be particularly good... he called my brother right afterward, and my brother, in turn, tried to get ahold of me."

She remained leaning against the wall with her bottom resting on her heels. Darrin hated the hurt he was putting her through. He also now knew why her brother had been wary and suspicious of him.

"I had to find out about you," he said.

"Why didn't you call it off after I explained everything to you?"

Running his fingers through his hair, he let out an exasperated huff. "I was going to, really. But she's the one that checked into Todd, and she's looking into anyone we think of as suspects. The police haven't done shit for us. I guess I figured it was best to have as many eyes out there as possible, just in case she found something that might help us figure out what is going on." He dropped to his knees to bring himself closer to her level.

"I hate you." She shifted her eyes to meet his. "I fucking hate you right now," she said even more forcefully. This was the first time he'd heard her swear. "You couldn't wait for me to be ready to talk to you? What else have you heard about, Darrin? Any other findings you would like to share?"

The words stung, and he knew he deserved them. He returned to his feet, extending a hand down to her to help her up. "Once it was found that the exhaust was rerouted, I called the police station. You have an appointment with a detective Mia recommended first thing on Monday morning. I wrote his name down. It's in the car."

She ignored the hand he had extended to her and stood on her own.

Feeling the defeat roiling in his soul, he asked, "Do you want me to take you somewhere else?"

Chapter Thirty-Two

JACKIE

Jackie arrived at the police station to give her official statement. Darrin had offered to go along with her for moral support, but she declined his offer, though he did convince her to let him drop her off, saying he had errands to run in town anyway, and he would be back in an hour.

Her soul felt like it was being torn in two. She wanted desperately to be with this man who both drove her senseless and would eventually break down all her walls. Each option was terrifying, posing its own threats. If the past stayed where it was and she didn't bring it up, she wouldn't have to relive it. Or at least, that was what she'd been telling herself.

After telling Darrin about Cecelia, she'd felt freer. She wondered why she'd never been able to tell anyone else those same details. *I've been doing my beautiful daughter a disservice by not talking about her.*

Her options had been limited, but she ultimately knew where she wanted to be, regardless of how angry she was with Darrin. Besides, she was afraid to go back to her apartment and knew her parents hadn't changed their minds about her going back to their house. Tony was in the process of moving into a studio, and she didn't want to impose on such small living quarters, although he would have taken her in in an instant.

Another of the bombshells Tony had shared with her: her mother had instructed Florence not to allow Jackie into the house under any circumstance. Jackie would never make Florence choose between her livelihood and Jackie. Which was likely part of why Jackie had reacted so violently toward Darrin—he was the easiest target.

She made her way across the parking lot, feeling strangely nervous. She pushed open the heavy metal door and was greeted by the front desk clerk.

"Ms. Martinez?" he asked in a gruff voice.

"Yes. I need to talk with Detective..." Nervously, she looked at the wrinkled sticky note in her hand. Darrin's barely legible scroll pressed another dagger into her soul.

"Gilbert. Yes, he's in the second interrogation room down the hall on the right, waiting for you. I'll show you the way." He was brisk with his responses.

Made more uneasy by the unfriendly clerk, she shuffled down the hall, straightening her clothing and hair as she went. She didn't want to appear as if she was hiding something. She took a deep breath before entering the room.

"Ms. Martinez," an authoritative voice called through the door.

Jackie sat down at the small table across from the detective. He had a friendlier face and demeanor than the man at the front desk. There was no mistaking that this was his domain.

"Good morning, Detective Gilbert." Jackie tried to keep the fear out of her voice.

His steely eyes met hers. She didn't know why she was so intimidated by being at the police station. She'd done nothing wrong. Someone had tried to kill her. *I have no reason to be nervous.*

"Would you like anything to drink? Coffee, tea, cola?" he asked.

She gave her head a quick shake.

"I need you to start at the beginning and tell me everything that happened." He consulted his notepad. "Wednesday, June 10."

"I had just gotten off my flight coming back from a trip to California. I'd been out of town for a few days and needed to run some errands."

"Where did these errands lead you?"

"The bank on Eastern Avenue, the electric department, and the general store to replenish some toiletries." She tried to be specific in her descriptions of where she needed to go that morning and why.

"Do you remember what time your headache began?"

"It was right after I left the bank drive-through." She paused, trying to pinpoint the exact time. "I think it was right around eight thirty, maybe closer to eight forty-five." She hated second-guessing herself. Her hands fidgeted in her lap. They were cool and clammy—probably a bad sign for a witness.

"How long had you been in your car at that point?"

"Probably close to forty-five minutes."

He took notes longer than she thought would be necessary for such a small question. "Can you think of anyone who would have tried to kill you?"

Startled by the sudden change in questions, she looked up from her hands to assess the detective. "No."

"Is there any reason they would have rerouted your exhaust?"

"I don't entirely understand your question."

"Why would someone reroute your car's exhaust when your usual commute is only five minutes? You would have needed to breathe in those fumes for... my guess would be three or more hours to cause severe damage."

Sudden realization took over Jackie's mind. "Someone must have done this before I left for my trip last week. You see, I was originally supposed to drive out to California for a business meeting. Darrin—my boss," she said, clarifying after seeing the silent question on his face. "He was flying out, and I decided to take the same flight instead."

The detective's pen scratched the pad. "That would have made sense. You would have been away from home and most likely in the middle of nowhere when symptoms became troublesome." He seemed to be talking to himself and not expecting her to respond. "You consented to have your medical records released on Saturday, after they found out it was an intentional carbon monoxide poisoning, correct?"

She hesitantly confirmed his question. The way it was stated didn't sit right with her. She met his challenging gaze. He was unrelenting, so she looked away.

"When was the last time you had suicidal tendencies or thoughts?"

This question hit her like a slap to the face. When she'd given her consent to release the forms, she'd thought it was only the results from the blood tests. Rage welled up inside her, extinguishing the anxiety she'd entered the building with.

"How dare you ask me that?" she shouted and sprang from her chair. She felt like she needed to escape. She was quickly losing her faith in this detective.

"What I am asking is, was this another of your suicide attempts?"

"No! I stopped taking antidepressants almost four years ago. I have not had any suicidal thoughts or tendencies. My psychiatrist signed off on it."

"I have those records too," he replied calmly, letting his steely eyes bore into hers once more.

"Then you know I have not been suicidal for years."

"What I know, Ms. Martinez, is that you lost your baby, and approximately a year and a half afterward, you tried to commit suicide. You were subsequently saved and required to attend counseling." This time, he stood, and Jackie realized how large he was—his height and muscle mass took her by surprise. He took a step closer to her, allowing his shadow to swallow her. "So I'll ask again, Ms. Martinez." He enunciated each word through clenched teeth. "Who would have wanted to kill you? Who knew you were planning to drive to California and would know you would be in your car for hours on end? Or was this just an elaborate plan to commit suici—"

The interrogation room door was slammed against the opposite wall. The intruder froze in the doorway. She wondered if he'd heard the accusation. He stormed into the room. Those blue eyes, ablaze, landed on her.

She felt her heart rate accelerate. She was terrified Darrin had heard the discussion. He crossed the interrogation room in fewer steps than Jackie thought possible for anyone.

"Are you insinuating that she rerouted the exhaust on her car and then pretended to be terrified and not know what was happening?" he demanded at a near shout. Before allowing the detective time to regain his composure, he continued. "Is she being charged with anything? Are you arresting her for a false police report?"

"No, I am trying to get to the bottom of the matter," the detective stated, pulling himself up to his full height, which was several inches shorter than Darrin. Jackie could feel the anger emanating from him.

"In that case, instead of browbeating Ms. Martinez, why don't you go try to find the person that actually did this?" Not intimidated by the detective's stern look, Darrin grabbed Jackie's arm and pulled her out of the room. "Since you're not charging her, I am taking her home so she can get some rest."

She wanted to run from the station. *This isn't right. How could he accuse me of such a heinous act?* Darrin's hard profile told her he was beyond angry. She was thankful for his interruption, but she couldn't stop the dread and guilt building walls back up, brick by brick.

He pulled her back past the impudent front-desk clerk and out the door. He didn't release her arm until they got to his car. Then he climbed into the driver's seat and turned to her when she got into the car. His eyes held a mixture of anger and something else she couldn't put her finger on. But rather than say anything to her, he averted his eyes and started the car.

He didn't take her back home as he'd said he would but, instead, drove to the office. With his long, fast strides, he preceded Jackie into the building—keeping up with him was virtually impossible. Darrin gave each person a curt greeting, trying to behave in his typical manner. But Jackie knew he was far too angry to convincingly act like today was just another day. He strode into her office then stayed by the door, waiting for her to enter.

Once she was past the threshold, he spoke with Margie at her desk just outside and slammed the door shut. Jackie had gone to the far side of her office to look out the window, afraid to meet his eyes. She was too far away to hear what he'd told Margie.

He stood there by the door, seething, waiting for her to acknowledge him. When she finally looked around at him, she figured out the other emotion his bright-blue eyes were emanating—shock. Apparently, his dear friend Mia hadn't come across the fact that Jackie had tried to commit suicide.

His gaze enveloped her, and she couldn't look away. "Would you like to explain to me what I interrupted in there?" he asked through clenched teeth barely above a whisper.

"No," she whispered, tears brimming, her eyelids dropped. She didn't want him to look her in the eyes. Tears spilled over the edges.

"This is the bullshit I have been getting irritated about with you almost every day since I met you. You have until I leave this room to tell me before I tell you I cannot do this anymore. You need to tell me right now, or this will be it for us. I can't keep chasing you, begging you to trust me every day for the rest of our lives." He spoke slowly and barely above a whisper. "Was anything he said true? Did I just make a mistake, yelling at a federal officer on your behalf? Did you have anything to do with that hose?" His last question came out as a harsh hiss.

She couldn't help flinching. Fresh tears were racing down her smooth cheeks. "No, I didn't have anything to do with that hose."

Jackie had hoped she could hide those memories too. She'd worked so hard for years to suppress them. She'd overcome them and didn't see the need to prove her emotional distress further.

He let out a calming breath. "What about the other things he said?" he asked, making his voice as calm as possible.

"Darrin, I can't." Her voice cracked with the emotions she could feel welling up in her throat.

"Dammit, Jackie!" he shouted. "You've tried to commit suicide?"

She widened her eyes at him, then looked at her office door. Somehow, she found the strength to talk. "I can't. I've worked so hard to get over my past."

"So it's true." The words came out of him on a release of breath as if he'd been struck. He staggered back to lean against the door.

They both stood in silence. Jackie resumed her spot at the window, her tears flowing heavily, suffering in the silence. *Did I live and work through everything just to be killed by an unknown enemy?* Wasn't that ironic—the thing she'd wanted all those years ago was now her ultimate fear.

Why had she changed her mind? Watching the traffic across the street as the sandwich shop opened and began greeting its first patrons of the day, she got lost in thought. *Was it my job? Was it the feeling of purpose it filled me with? Was it the strength I gained?* Maybe it was the man standing on the other side of the room.

As if reading her mind, Darrin crossed the room in quick strides, covering the distance between them. He wrapped his arms around her and pulled her tight to his chest. She could feel the strong muscles under his pressed shirt. She allowed herself to melt into his embrace. She wondered if he could feel how small, fragile, and broken she was. She began to shake, with the tears flowing freely.

He bowed his head to allow his lips to rest on the top of her head and spoke into her hair in a gentle, loving whisper. "It's okay—I've got you. I won't let anything happen to you."

He kissed the top of her head once, twice, three times. She looked up at him. The tears had dried; they had left small riverbeds down her face. She tipped her head back farther, pressing the lower half of her body into his.

He moved his hands slowly up her back and neck and into her hair. Holding her head in place, he met her lips. The connection sparked a fire within her. She let him kiss her. His caresses were soft at first. Her lips parted, inviting him in. She wanted him just as he wanted her. He searched her mouth as if looking for the secrets she kept buried. Jackie responded with passion, pressing herself against the front of his pants—the passion was clearly welling up inside him too.

She kissed him hungrily. Rising to the tips of her toes, she allowed his sex to press against her own. A growl of want was expelled from his throat.

The sounds of his ardent passion startled her. She immediately stopped kissing him and tried to take a step back. He was still cradling her head in his strong, eager hands. Her heart was pounding in her ears. They should not be doing this, especially not at work.

"We can't do this," she whispered, tears once again filling her eyes.

She slipped her hands up between them and placed them on his chest. Her hands on him confused what she needed to do and say. He took a step back from her but didn't release her head. Instead, he used the pad of his finger to wipe away the fresh tear that slid down her cheek.

"We're in the office." She cleared her throat, looking around nervously.

"I will never hurt you." The care in his eyes made her believe him. "I don't think you're in the right state of mind to be working today. Why don't I take you home so you can relax?"

* * *

Darrin dropped her off at his house and went back to work. She'd become used to him referring to his house as home. *How will I explain this next part to him?* Jackie couldn't bear the thought of losing him but didn't think she had much of a choice. He was the first person to care enough to push her into the uncomfortable truth. Verity had tried but would give up when Jackie got defensive or began to shut down. Darrin seemed to be the only one who knew how to get her to talk. He wouldn't fail this time, either. The sooner she accepted that, the sooner she could come to terms with needing to speak about what had happened to her.

CHAPTER THIRTY-THREE

DARRIN

Darrin couldn't stand himself as he paced his office. Even the sound of his own footfalls on the hardwood floor set his teeth on edge. He was a hypocrite.

How can I keep telling her I'll never hurt her if I'm so quick to lose my patience? What is wrong with me?

He'd always been so good at keeping his emotions in check. He'd gotten angry with Jessica and Leo, but he hadn't lost control. He'd been able to think things through, call the people necessary to get everything canceled for the wedding. He'd lost a lot of money—the deposit on the venue, the caterer. They had been sympathetic but couldn't give him a refund. Truly, he hadn't cared. He'd been thankful to have seen her true colors before going through with the wedding.

He'd helped pack and remove all of Jessica's belongings from the apartment he'd been renting. Packing might not have been the right way to describe it—most items had ended up stuffed into a trash bag and thrown at her feet when she turned up to get her things. Leo had driven her to pick them up. In one afternoon, Darrin had lost his best friend and the woman he thought would become his wife. It had ruined his ability to trust most people.

New people were held at arm's length. He entered all situations as a cynic, held himself proud, and often intentionally made himself seem superior to others. Most people didn't dare approach him, which suited him just fine. Or so he told himself. Arrogance had been his standing defense mechanism.

The only time he'd really lost control of his emotions was when his mother passed. He just could not wrap his mind around her passing—she was meant to be there for all his failures and victories. She was the one who'd dropped him off at his first day of school. He still remembered clinging to her leg and her encouraging words: "This is only the first step of many in a long journey, one that I know you can conquer if you only allow yourself to try. You can do this." And then she had led him up the front steps.

He remembered the graveside service, the way he had stood in a haze. It had been days since he'd slept well—probably since before his mother died. He'd been allowing himself to marinate in his sadness. The problem was, he did not care what day of the week or what time of day it was. He drank.

The morning of the funeral was no exception. He stumbled to the side and cried heavily in the middle of the service. Refusing any help from his father, he had let his life spiral into a pit of despair where his wounds were king.

He began crying and swearing lavishly during the service, cursing everyone and everything for the loss of his mother. His father calmly put his arm around him, silencing him for the remainder of the service. The party afterward had been filled with people staring in his direction as if he was going to explode again.

The sound of his office door opening pulled him out of his musings—none too early, he assured himself.

"I could hear you wearing out the carpet from the other side of the building," Charles chided, spinning the chair on the opposite side of Darrin's desk to sit facing his son. "Care to clue me in on whatever has you so restless?"

"I'm torn." Darrin ran his fingers through his sandy hair.

"I see. Am I right to assume this indecision has something to do with Jackie?"

Darrin shrugged, not knowing where to start or how to explain everything that had happened between the two of them. His father remained seated, waiting him out.

When it became apparent Darrin was not going to elaborate, Charles rose from the chair and placed his hand on Darrin's shoulder. "You two will find a way if you want it bad enough."

"I love her—I do. I just feel like I have to fight to learn anything about her." He shook his head. "How can I be with someone if she can't talk to me?"

Charles rubbed his chin. "That's fair, but have you considered how many other people she may have opened up to? Is it a rarity for her?" His expression changed to the one he'd used when reprimanding Darrin as a child. "You two are only beginning. It takes a lifetime to find out everything about a person. And vast patience."

Darrin pushed himself back in his chair. "I know that, but I just... I've fallen so fast and feel like it's been years,"

"Patience."

Darrin stared up at his ceiling while his father watched him. "When do you think you'll be ready to make a decision on the general manager position?"

"Soon." Charles sighed. "Too bad there aren't two of you. That would make things easier after I retire." He laughed, leaving Darrin to examine the ceiling in peace.

As if struck by lightning, Darrin surged around his desk to catch up with his father. Inspiration had struck, and he was not going to wait to discuss it.

* * *

Darrin arrived home happier than he'd been in days. He had it all figured out. He rounded the corner to the kitchen to find Jackie sitting at the bar with a highball glass filled with an amber liquid he recognized.

"Jackie? Are you all right?" he asked hesitantly.

Her eyes were bloodshot and glossy from tears she'd shed in his absence. "All good," she replied, saluting him with the glass in front of her and taking a large sip. "Hope you don' mind." Her speech was a little slurred.

Looking around nervously, he wedged himself between the two barstools. "How much have you had?"

She began laughing uncontrollably. "Not enough," she managed to reply, almost falling off the barstool in her fit of laughter. "I still remember everything."

"Let's put that away. I don't think you need anymore." Darrin gently pulled the glass from her hand.

For someone who'd had too much to drink, she retained an amazing amount of strength. She furrowed her brows, watching him pour the remainder of her drink down the drain.

"I was drinking that," she said, pouting.

She reminded him of a small child confused by why their parent told them they could not have any more sweets. Running his thumb over the spot, he tried to remove the wrinkles from her forehead, which only made her scowl deepen. He couldn't stop himself from laughing.

"All right," he said, raising his hands above his head to stretch.

The sudden movement caused her to cower and cover her face.

"Hey, Jackie. What's wrong?"

"Nothing! I'm sorry." She began to cry, not removing her hands from her face, and curled into a small ball.

Stunned by her sudden outcry and reaction, he froze. There was only one reason he could think of that she might act like that. "Jackie, you know I would never hit you, right?"

He gingerly removed her hands from her face to look into her eyes. Glossy and red, they looked larger than ever. Slowly, she nodded.

"I was only stretching because I was going to carry you down to the bathroom and draw you a bath. Does that sound okay?"

Worried about what had caused her to drink so heavily, he lifted her into his arms and brought her down to their now shared bedroom. She felt so small and fragile in his arms.

After laying her down on the bed, he went into the bathroom to start filling the tub. Looking over his shoulder, he watched her as she sat up and swayed slightly, clumsily pulling her shirt off and discarding it on the floor. Her pink lace bra followed lazily. She slouched over, resting her elbows on her knees and her face in her hands. Her whole body shook.

He rushed to her side and pulled her to him. Laying one hand on her bare back and the other on the side of her head, he brought her head to rest on his shoulder. "Shhh. Shhh. It's okay, baby. I've got you."

Slowly, her racking sobs subsided, and Darrin lifted her again and brought her into the bathroom. He set her down on the floor, and she removed the sweatpants and underwear she still had on while he tested the water and shut it off, satisfied with the temperature. Offering her his hand, he helped her climb into the tub.

He sat down on the steps to the tub and kept a close eye on her. Jackie slid down into the water to submerge as much of herself as possible, keeping only her face above the surface. Her hair swirled around in the water like smoke in the sky, the movement smooth, graceful. Free. The way it swirled was mesmerizing. If he reached into the water, he wondered if he would actually feel it or if, like smoke, it would drift away.

He brought his eyes back to her face, his heart breaking to see her like this. He knew in that moment he loved this woman more than anyone before her and would do anything to help her heal. She needed someone to help her through whatever this was.

Jackie stayed beneath the water for several minutes, keeping her eyes closed. He wiped the last remaining tear from her cheek. Her eyes lazily opened, and she blinked a few times, focusing on him.

"Thank you," she whispered.

Knowing she would probably not hear his reply with her ears submerged in the water, he simply smiled, but his love for her was swimming in his eyes. He told himself he was going to be more patient and trusting.

JACKIE

The next morning, she awoke to find that she was dealing with one of the worst hangovers she'd ever had. *Why did I drink that whiskey?* She rolled over to discover Darrin was not in bed. She didn't remember him being in bed with her at all the night before. Checking her phone, she saw that she had an hour to get ready for work.

Wearily, she lifted herself from the bed and ventured out to the kitchen to get herself a glass of water and hopefully find some painkillers. She carried the glass to the bathroom then checked the medicine cabinet. Antacids, mouthwash, floss... knocking over a bottle of cold medicine, she spotted the tablets she was looking for.

Jackie shook two into her hand and hastily washed them down with a large gulp of water. Hearing motion behind her, she spun around to see Darrin standing in the hall, watching her through the doorway. She smiled at him sheepishly.

"Not feeling very good?" he whispered.

"No," she said, cringing.

"Come on back to bed." He held his arm out for her to go back with him.

Tucked under his arm, she loved the way it felt to be pressed against his ribs. "Darrin," she began, her voice catching as they climbed back into bed. "Th-There is something I need to talk to you about. If we're going to do this..." She gestured at the room, the house, and finally the space between them. "There are things you need to know before you agree to being with me."

"We don't have to do this now." The calmness of his statement shocked her, after he'd been pressing her to be honest with him.

"I want to," she choked out. Sighing, she admitted what she'd known last night. "I need to." She took a deep, steadying breath. Wanting it over with, she dove in headfirst. "Harmon wanted a baby after we lost Cecelia. Sex became nothing more than a mating ritual. There was no fun to it anymore. The only thing that mattered to him was his climax. I dreaded him coming home. Each night was the same. He didn't even notice my lack of interest. Couldn't he see the pain it was inflicting on me?"

Darrin pulled her closer to his chest.

"I felt guilty for my inability to conceive. After a few months of nothing, I sat down with him, trying to talk some sense into him. We both needed to concentrate on completing college and getting jobs. I told him we needed to cool it on trying to have a baby. I didn't think my body was ready."

Tracing his abs with one of her fingers, she allowed the distraction to obstruct the images of the past.

"He argued that the doctors had all said everything was fine. Anger always bubbled to the surface when I tried to dissuade him. But finally, I had to tell him I wasn't ready. He accused me of suddenly changing my mind, like I was the one obsessed with replacing her. His face turned a sickening shade of red. He shot from his chair—it rocked before slamming back down. He crossed the kitchen and grabbed my chin to force me to look at him. His dark eyes looked empty." She moved her hand from Darrin's chest to her chin.

Darrin gently removed her hand, lacing his fingers with hers.

"I told him he was hurting me. To let go of me. I was trapped between him and the wall. I could do nothing to get out of his grip. His thumb and index finger dug deeper into my chin, making me want to cry. I tried to push him away. He wasn't much bigger than me, but I was emotionally and physically drained. I think he realized the disdain I had for him. I think that's what caused something to snap inside him. He let go, but only to pull his hand back enough to slap me across the face."

Darrin's fingers flexed against hers.

"We were both stunned. The cracking sound of his palm on my face somehow pulled him back to his senses. I bolted out of the chair and shoved past him. My strength was momentarily restored."

She felt the subtle shift in Darrin's posture as his back straightened, as if he could sense this was the point she needed to get to. "He lost it, and then so did I... I saw my chance, and I ran into the bathroom and locked myself in. He was at the door, apologizing, telling me he didn't mean to. And I actually believed him. I don't think he really meant to hit me, but I couldn't trust that he wasn't going to do it again. I wanted to escape him, my sadness, all the people who looked at me with pity in their eyes."

Taking a shaky breath, she continued. "So I went through the cabinets in the bathroom. I found regular pain medication, the antidepressants they prescribed after I lost the baby, and some sort of painkiller from having my wisdom teeth removed, among other things. At first, I just stared at all the bottles in my hands." Jackie looked down at her hands, which were now intertwined with Darrin's.

"I set them all down on the edge of the bathtub and then grabbed the glass I usually used to rinse after brushing my teeth, and I filled it right to the brim with water. I leaned against the wall and let myself slide down to the floor." Her eyes stared fixedly on their hands, unseeing. "The tile floor felt cold on my legs. All I could think was that I wasn't going to have to worry about these feelings—or any kind of feelings—much longer."

Darrin's hands tensed in hers, pulling her back to the present—to the man in front of her and the future she hoped would be waiting beyond this admission.

"I took each bottle in turn and poured a few of each kind of pill into my hand. Then, taking two at a time, I washed them down until they were gone. I remember closing my eyes, thinking the next time I opened them, I would be seeing my sweet baby's face. But the next thing I remember was waking up in the hospital. I was hooked up to all kinds of machines, and they were doing regular tests, checking my blood. Checking my liver function."

He was looking at her with tears in his eyes. "I'm so sorry you went through all of this, Jackie. I should have had more patience. Talking to me about everything—I know this can't be easy."

"No, it's not. You're the first person I've ever actually explained every-thing to," she said, averting her eyes.

Verity had tried to get her to talk, but she just couldn't. She didn't want to feel like she was blaming Harmon for everything that had gone wrong. He and Porter were friends and had been for years, and she didn't want to risk tarnishing that relationship.

"I tried to tell both Verity and Tony but couldn't get the words out. If I'd told Tony that Harmon put his hands on me, I think he would have killed him."

"Thank you for trusting me enough," Darrin said with a sad smile, tucking a stray hair behind her ear while kissing her forehead.

"The rest of the time I was in the hospital, they kept a very close eye on me. I told everyone it was an accident—that I hadn't meant to mix the drugs. If they didn't believe me, they never said so—the hospital staff knew differently, but my family took my explanation at face value, except for Tony. He is the only one that knows it was not an accident, but he never pressed me to explain it all.

"I made it clear to Harmon he was not welcome in the hospital. When I was released, the first thing I did was file for divorce, and I had my brother help me collect my belongings from the apartment I shared with Harmon. In the beginning, Harmon begged for a second chance, but then he realized my resolve and backed off. The only contact we have anymore is on Cecelia's birthday. He sends me a floral arrangement every year." She swiped a tear from her cheek. "Since the hospital knew the real reason I was hospitalized, I was required to see a psychiatrist—again, Tony knew about these appointments. I was working for my parents at the time, and Tony helped me with excuses."

"I can't believe you suffered through all that alone," he said, shaking his head. He pulled her to him and held her tight to his chest. "I am so thankful you survived everything, Jackie. I love you."

Chapter Thirty-Four

Lucas

Did you really think you would be able to just pack up and leave and I wouldn't be able to find you? How stupid do you think I am?" The conspirator's sneer was unforgiving. "I hope you know they've found out about the exhaust being rerouted. It's only a matter of time before they trace it back to you."

"I-I'm done with th-this. This is-sn't my fight. I've met h-her a few times, and she's nice." Stuttering had been a problem for Lucas from a young age. He hated how ignorant it made him sound.

"Fine. You want to be out? Here's your ticket." Looking down, Lucas saw the barrel of a pistol rising toward him. "This is a one-way ticket. Last chance—make a decision."

Lucas turned and ran back down the narrow alley but stumbled against the brick exterior of the building next to him. The vacant old farmhouse he'd been hiding in was just beyond the hill ahead of him. The last thing he heard was "Coward!" shouted at his back and the ringing of a gunshot at far too close a range.

CHAPTER THIRTY-FIVE

DARRIN

"The communications equipment is being set up and is almost done at the California location," Charles announced in the large staff meeting. "This means we'll be sending our new general manager out there soon to get things in order and get this ball rolling." He smiled at everyone around him. "We'll be announcing who will be appointed to the GM position on Friday."

Charles looked over to Darrin for acknowledgment. Darrin nodded once in confirmation and watched Jackie take a deep breath in the back corner of the meeting room. He wanted to know what she was thinking. Todd stood in the center, smiling up at him and Charles.

Charles concluded the meeting, letting everyone know that if there was any position they might be interested in taking at the California address, they should submit a letter of interest to Darrin by Friday afternoon to allow time to get transfers set up and to know what positions would need to be posted and hired for in both locations.

On their walk back upstairs, Charles asked Darrin if he was ready to make a final decision on who would be the general manager and if he'd talked with Jackie about what they'd discussed the other day.

"I have to talk with Jackie tonight before I make anything official or start drafting any contracts," he admitted, feeling foreign nerves take over.

He had ideas for that night that would hopefully put her in a good state to discuss his plans. Taking a few minutes to map out his plan, he smiled, knowing it would all work out in the end.

Darrin took the stairs two at a time. He was saddened to think Jackie was afraid he would decide he didn't want to be with her because of her past. She still feared she might not be able to conceive and that it would be a breaking point for them. He'd assured her that there were other ways to have children if that was something they wanted in the future.

"Hi, Margie. Is Jackie in a meeting?"

"Good afternoon, Mr. Dominic. I don't believe she has another meeting until two o'clock," Margie said, smiling up at him.

"Thank you," he said, gently knocking on Jackie's office door. He went in and closed it behind him. "Hey, you, would you happen to be available for dinner tonight?"

With a small giggle, Jackie pretended to consult her calendar. "Tsk. You know what? It just so happens I had a cancelation and have an opening."

"What luck," he replied with a wink, placing a quick kiss on the top of Jackie's head and then heading back to the door. "Pick you up from here? Say, four?"

The last week had been a breeze. They hadn't had one disagreement since Jackie had laid out everything for Darrin. They'd stayed home together all that Saturday, choosing one another's company over anything else.

Jackie wanted to take things slow but agreed that they would see where the relationship took them. They were going to keep their interactions to a minimum at work, but he couldn't help coming to see her. Asking her on a date over text would have been too impersonal.

This was harder than he'd thought it would be. They shared a house, a bed, and most mornings, a shower. He was relieved and proud that she now felt comfortable with him, but his body was ready to burst. Watching her lather herself up in the shower every morning had him wishing he was spreading the soap over her breasts. The thoughts crossing his mind needed to stop, or he wouldn't be able to walk back to his office in a dignified manner.

Just as he was reaching for the door, he heard Jackie's phone ring. Not many calls went straight to her phone—usually, they would get routed through Margie. This strange occurrence prompted him to stay a moment longer.

"This is Jackie. How can I help you?"

There was a long silence during which Jackie's face turned an ill shade of white. Her doe eyes looked up at Darrin with silent pleading. She needed him.

He moved to her side, bracing himself on her desk and the back of her chair as he leaned down to hear what was being said on the other end of the call.

"… Garage to check their cameras for the entire time your car was in their possession. The owner states he does not know entirely how to work the camera system, but he will ask his son to come help him work out the kinks. He is supposed to be burning all the video for us, so we will have a copy, and we can also scan it for anything suspicious."

"Thank you for letting me know. Please, ah, let me know as soon as you find anything else out." She mechanically hung up the receiver. Turning to Darrin, she said, "They said they were able to find part of the flex tubing in the dumpster at the auto garage I sent my car to when I got the window fixed. Apparently, they don't have their dumpster emptied very often. What is stranger is one of their employees disappeared and hasn't been to work in almost two weeks."

The revelation made his skin crawl. This was a place she'd been taking her car to for years.

"It'll be okay, Jackie," he said, rubbing up and down on both of her arms. "Maybe he got scared and ran away." Darrin had hoped that this would all be wrapped up by now. He hated to have the looming thought that someone was watching her and she would be afraid to turn each corner and find her stalker lying in wait.

Smiling up at him weakly, she nodded. She was still not one to complain or be overly forthcoming with information, but their time together had given Darrin the keen ability to read her. She was nervous.

"Do you want to skip going out to dinner and do something at home?" he asked tentatively.

"No. It might be good to go out to eat somewhere. Take my mind off things for a moment," she said, returning to the work on her screen.

This was quite the internal quagmire. He couldn't decide if he should propose his idea that night or wait until another time. The clock was ticking, mocking him. He didn't have much time to talk to her about it before the announcement on Friday.

JACKIE

"Jackie, I have some messages for you from during the staff meeting," Margie said, peering into Jackie's office. She must have sensed there was something off when Darrin left, because she'd waited several minutes before approaching.

"Margie, you should have gone to the meeting. I didn't realize you stayed behind to keep working," Jackie said apologetically. She'd been so distracted by her own life drama lately that she hadn't even noticed Margie wasn't in the meeting. *Does that make me a poor supervisor?*

"It's no matter. I know I'm not going to get that new GM position," Margie said with a wink. She seemed a bit off. Although she said all the right things, she didn't seem to be herself.

Chuckling, Jackie took the stack of phone messages from Margie and resumed her seat at her desk. Before Margie had knocked, Jackie had been looking out the window. She'd been thinking about Officer Thompson's call. The thought that someone at the garage had been the one who'd rerouted her exhaust disturbed her. She'd been taking her car there for years. She'd even referred one of the men working there to the company through the partnership program. She was trying to remember all their names and what they each looked like.

"I'm going to have to leave half an hour early tonight, Jackie, if that's all right."

"Absolutely. How has everything been for you lately? I feel terrible. I've been so busy that we haven't had a chance to have one of our lunch dates." She turned to give Margie her full attention.

"Everything is good. I just need to check on one of my kids tonight—that's all," Margie said with a sweet, motherly smile. "I know you've been busy, and there've been things you needed to take care of outside work too."

"Yes, there have," Jackie said, nodding. "Margie, strictly, as a personal opinion, can I ask you something?"

"Yes. What is it?" Margie asked with a slight edge to her voice. Maybe it was because Jackie was delaying her.

"Do you think I could be a good general manager?"

"I think you would do great. You're great with people and are a natural leader." Smiling, Margie exited and closed the door behind her.

Jackie pushed up from her desk and searched her filing cabinets for the file on the automotive garage. It wasn't there. She flipped through each file. It could have gotten stuck to another folder. But again, her search turned up nothing.

Sitting at her desk, she searched the depths of her mind. She couldn't remember the last time she'd seen the file. No one had been hired there for almost two years, from what she could remember.

Checking the time, she knew Margie would be gone by now. Being alone again, Jackie started to sift through the pile of notes and respond to interested potential partners, complaints, and a message from her gynecologist to give her a call. It must have been about the appointment for her to begin a birth control regimen. It had been a while since it had been necessary, and she didn't know what her options were anymore. Things changed so quickly.

Deciding to call the interested businesses first, she got the official applications sent out to them. She called the unhappy employer back about the woman who had begun working for them the week before. The woman had been getting in late and was causing a bit of a problem with the other employees. Jackie promised she would call and talk with the young lady and hopefully get these things figured out and let the chiropractor's office know how much she appreciated them being a partner.

This felt good. She felt like she was doing something right in her life. She hadn't felt that way in a long time. *But what is the next step? Do I still want the general manager position?* It felt like this was to be a turning point in her life. She would have to choose the man she was falling in love with or fight to take the position she'd been pining for over the last year. Each was a once-in-a-lifetime chance.

"Are you ready?" Darrin asked, lazily leaning against the doorjamb, letting one hand hang while resting the other on his hip.

Startled by the flutter of excitement in her stomach, Jackie knocked over the penholder on her desk, sending highlighters, pens, and pencils rolling all around the room. Feeling her face burn, she jumped up to pick them up. "Almost."

How is it that tonight, I'm acting foolish when I've been living with him for weeks? Is it the nerves thinking about making it permanent and not wanting him to reject me? Maybe it was the fact that she knew she would be on her birth control soon, and she was, for the first time in a long time, looking forward to sex.

"Let me help you," he said, crouching down and picking up the pens that had rolled close to him. "I think that's good enough for tonight." He replaced the cup on the desktop.

Jackie felt a shift in his demeanor as he became rigid in his movements. He almost seemed angry.

"Shall we?" he asked, extending his right arm.

Taking his arm, she followed him out the door, wondering what could have inspired such a change in him.

Chapter Thirty-Six

DARRIN

Darrin?" She was looking at him inquisitively. "Is everything okay?"

He had not been himself on the drive home or while getting ready for dinner. Although at home, they had been able to fall into an easy banter, he'd been strangely silent in the car.

"Sorry, it's just been a long day. But I do need to tell you something before we leave." He sat on the sofa, motioning for her to follow suit.

"What is it?"

"I think your office is bugged. I saw something on the underside of your desk when your pens spilled," Darrin blurted.

The color drained from her face. "Then this could be anyone. I have meetings with different people all the time. I only lock my door when I leave at the end of the day." She groaned, dropping her head into her hands.

"That's what I was thinking."

She rubbed her hands over her face. "A couple years ago, we placed someone with the garage I used to take my car to. I couldn't find the file today, and I don't remember the young man's name."

"I'm going to call Mia," he said hesitantly. "If that is okay with you." Jackie nodded. "I would like to meet her sometime."

Darrin let a small smile show at the way she was willing to get to know his friend—to work through their issues. He rose from the sofa to make his calls. He hoped Mia would be able to find the bastard.

* * *

"I still want to take you to dinner," Darrin said later, pulling her from the sofa. "I refuse to let this ruin a perfectly good night."

They got into the car and headed to one of Darrin's favorite Italian restaurants.

Jackie placed her hand on his thigh and rubbed the inside with her fingertips. This was going to be a problem. Her hand inched up and brushed the bulge in his lap. Feeling her touch, he cleared his throat and straightened in his seat.

"Something wrong?" she asked a little too innocently as she brushed against him again. The sly grin spreading across her lips had him aching to touch her.

"There's going to be if you keep that up." Gripping the steering wheel tighter, he narrowed his eyes at the road. Looking at her would break his concentration.

"Keep this up?" she asked, running her hand over the fly of his pants. He knew she could feel the bulge of his sex growing as she slid her hand back over to his thigh.

"Yes. That." The next turn was taken faster than intended. "You do realize I won't be able to get out of the car for dinner if you keep doing that?"

"Hmm. That does pose a problem, doesn't it?" she whispered in his ear as she kissed his neck.

Only another few miles till we're there. He looked down, checking his speed. He didn't want her to stop, but he definitely didn't want to wreck his car. "Can you wait until we get home?"

"I could. But what fun would that be?"

"That would be more fun for me," he grunted, shifting in his seat to relieve some of the pressure on his growing erection.

Jackie laughed and threw her head back against the seat. He loved it when she laughed like that, exposing the sensitive and seductive skin of her neck. It made him want to pull over right there and take her in the car.

No. He told himself he was an adult and was not going to behave like a teenager.

"Jackie, if you don't stop, I'm not going to be able to keep my hands off you when we get home." His warning was gruff, and he could see the bumps it elicited on her skin.

"That's the plan," she whispered in his ear then kissed his earlobe. Her words had an immediate effect on his already strained jeans.

He let out a sigh of pleasure when she placed her hand on his manhood again. "Ahhh, Jackie?"

"Yes?"

"You touch me like that again, and I'm turning this car around."

Laughing, she gave him a gentle squeeze.

"That's it," he said, taking a sharp turn to get off the interstate and go in the opposite direction.

The gate at the drive was a welcome sight and the porch even more so. The car had barely come to a stop when Darrin slammed it into park. Careful to make sure the gate had closed behind them, he unlocked the front door, disengaged the alarm, and reset it for the evening. He wanted no interruptions and was tempted to take the phone off the hook as he passed it.

Turning to grab Jackie, he realized she'd already disappeared down the hall. "Jackie?"

"Down here," she called. It sounded like she was in the bedroom.

Glancing in, he couldn't see her. He checked the guest room, but there was still no sign of her. He was turning to go back to the living room when he saw a shadow behind him in the hall.

Spinning around and almost knocking them both down, Darrin extended his arm to clothesline the person hiding in the shadows... only to notice, in the nick of time, who it was.

"Fuck, Jackie, you scared me." He pulled her close and bent to allow his lips to meet hers.

They had shared chaste kisses the last few days. This was different. She kissed him back eagerly with a fiery passion. She slipped her tongue into his mouth, eliciting a deep growl of need.

The fire within her was awakened, and he didn't want to miss out on a moment of it. Taking one thigh in each hand, Darrin lifted her and carried her to the bed. His hands held onto nothing but smooth skin. Only then did he notice she was only wearing a small black bra-and-panty set. Setting her down on the bed, he looked her up and down. The set was silky to the touch. His hand slid over the material, gliding over the surface like water off a duck's back. The desire that surged through him was doubled by the slow, seductive way she was unbuttoning and unzipping his pants.

"Are you sure you want to do this?" he asked.

"Yes."

Not needing any more encouragement, he stepped out of his pants. His erection was pressing hard against his boxer briefs. Jackie was pulling at the buttons on his shirt. Darrin tugged at the top on each side, releasing most of the buttons from their holes and sending some rolling across the floor. He shrugged out of the sleeves and let it drop to the floor.

"Jackie, you are so beautiful," he said, leaning over to thread his fingers through her hair and laying her down on the bed below him. He kissed her cheek and worked one of his hands under the shoulder strap of the silky lingerie. The strap slipped down one shoulder easily and then the other.

Her breath hitched as he lowered the cups of her bra and kissed his way down to their center. She arched her back, giving Darrin easier access to her breasts. She gasped as he took her nipple into his mouth. "Darrin."

Smiling, he looked up at her. "Yes?"

When she didn't reply, he lowered his mouth back to her raised nipple and took her back into his mouth. With his hand, he reshaped her other breast. He enjoyed watching her squirm below him.

"Darrin, please."

"What, darling?"

"I need you. I need you inside me."

Her pleading sent another surge of desire through him, propelling him to remove his boxers and nestle himself between her legs. His tip was at her opening. "Are you sure?" he asked, gently brushing the most sensitive part of her opening with his thumb. Teasing.

Her hips lifted to meet his touch. Darrin brushed gentle circles around her clit with his thumb and teased her entrance with his index finger, pressing the slightest bit. She whimpered as he pulled away.

"Do you want this, Jackie?" he asked, pressing into her again as her hips bucked against his hand. He could feel her muscles tightening around his fingers.

"Yes, yes." Her eyes conveyed her need as much as her words.

Keeping his fingers inside her, he leaned down and flicked his tongue over her sensitive clit. The gasp she released had him on the verge of losing his mind. Teasing her a little more, he licked the bundle of nerves again.

"Darrin!" she cried out.

He lined his erection up with her opening. He was rocked by the pleasure that surged through him as he inched his way into her. She lifted her hips to allow him to push deeper. He let out a low growl of pleasure. She threaded her fingers through his hair, pulled his face to hers, and kissed him with all the love she had. Her breath grew more labored; her pleasure was building. The knowledge of that brought Darrin closer to his climax.

He tried to pull out, but she lifted her hips higher still to keep him buried deep within her. She finally crested the hill to reach her orgasm. The sensation took over his mind before he had a chance to catch up. All he could think about was that she was warm, wet, and tight. The pulse from her sex to his held him captive as he followed her to his climax.

Afterward, tired and satisfied, they lay together.

"Jackie, I need to ask you something," he said.

She tensed next to him.

"It's nothing bad," he said rubbing her back. "If you say yes, it's actually a good thing." He hoped.

JACKIE

Jackie had finally allowed herself to enjoy the company of a man fully. She didn't have the fear in the back of her mind. She knew if she got pregnant this time and lost the baby, she would have the support she needed.

Perhaps I can't have children, she thought. She rolled over and brushed the hair off Darrin's forehead then ran her thumb across his eyebrows. The hairs were coarse and didn't stay down.

She'd been staying with Darrin for close to a month and hadn't taken the time to really look at him and appreciate everything about him, although of course, she knew he was handsome and sexy. Under his right eyebrow was a faded scar. She ran her index finger over the small indent. Time had faded it, so it was not noticeable to most. She hadn't even noticed it until her second week staying with him.

"I love you," she whispered, tracing the length of his jaw.

He lazily rolled over, put his arm around her, and pulled her close. "I love you too," he whispered into her hair. He kissed the top of her head. Leaning back, he looked down at her. "Last night was amazing."

A smile spread across her lips. Butterflies took flight in her stomach. The feeling of being with the person she was meant to be with was sensational.

"How did you get that scar on your eyebrow?"

Chuckling, he rubbed the scar in question. "Well, I was probably seven. I was playing on a dirt road with my childhood best friend, the one that owns the automotive garage, Kane. We were racing our bikes up and down this road. There were some bigger rocks, and that's what made us think this road was so great—the rocks would make us bounce all over the place. A few times, we would hit a rock wrong and tumble off our bikes, but nothing happened that would prevent us from getting right back on... until one afternoon." He gave a nostalgic smile. "We decided to race down a large hill on this dirt road. We couldn't pedal our bikes up this hill, so we had to walk and push them. We got to the top and started going down as fast as we could. I was in the lead, and I lifted my feet from the pedals. I was going too fast to be able to keep up with their speed."

He shook his head. "Kane was starting to gain on me. I could hear him coming up behind me. I leaned over the handlebars, trying to make myself more aerodynamic. I chanced a look over my shoulder, and when I did, I must have turned my handlebars a bit, too, because my tire caught on one of those big rocks, and I went flying over the front. I remember irrationally thinking that I was going to die."

Jackie smiled at the image.

"I landed face-first on yet another of those damn rocks. Looking back on it now, I know it could have been much worse. But I landed right on my face. It was bleeding profusely. Kane was panicking and trying to help me up. I had to do everything I could not to cry. Crying in front of my friend would have been second place to death in that instance."

"This is quite dramatic," Jackie quipped.

Laughing, Darrin added, "The real drama started when I got home. The walk home was probably close to a mile. By the time I got there, the bleeding had slowed, but my shirt was drenched. I walked up the drive and noticed my mother in one of her flower beds. Hearing us coming up behind her, she turned around, and she screamed when she saw me. I was fine until she did that. I lost all composure, started blubbering and trying to explain to her what happened. Kane was afraid of getting in trouble, so he said his goodbyes and went home. Naturally, my mother took me to the hospital, and they gave me a couple stitches. They said if I had landed just to the right, I could have lost vision in that eye with the force I came down on it."

"That's terrible. It isn't all that noticeable," she said, lightly tracing the faint pink mark with her index finger.

"It used to be much worse. When I'd get tired, it would get all puffy and make me look like I had a lazy eye." He laughed. "Now, that was embarrassing."

Jackie leaned over and pressed a kiss to the mark. Then they lay together in silence.

Jackie fiddled with the hangnail on her thumb. "This is going to sound odd, but I finally feel like me. I've been so worried for years about getting too close to someone else that I haven't allowed myself to enjoy life. I feel like I'm finally waking up after walking around in a haze."

Tipping her head back, Darrin laid a seductive kiss on her lips. Their kiss slowly increased in passion. Knowing now wasn't the time to get too caught up, she pulled away slowly.

"Should we get ready for work?" Jackie asked.

With a groan, Darrin rolled out of bed.

CHAPTER THIRTY-SEVEN

THE CONSPIRATOR

Chances were dwindling. The police would likely add up the clues eventually. *But how to do it?*

Making it look like an accident would be best. She was never far from Darrin, which complicated things. The meddling prick. Once the promotion was announced, perhaps that would make things easier. Only another day to wait.

The bug installed had provided little information. Aggravating as the situation was, each night was spent listening for any kind of detail. Listening to the bitch talk of all her plans for her future.

This evening's recordings did not provide any new information. Darrin was heard entering the room and telling her he wanted to talk with her about the general manager position. He'd told her he wanted to take her out to dinner to discuss the upcoming announcement. The answer was just beyond reach.

This was frustrating. Patience was a must. But at the same time, time was getting short. It was only a matter of time before the clock ran out.

Maybe there would be a night soon when Darrin would leave her home alone. *The little hussy. She went on a business trip with him and came back to his bed?* Some people were just handed all the advantages in the world, while others struggled for everything they had.

Those same advantaged people would often be the cause of others' misfortune. Entire families would suffer at their hands. It was time for the tables to turn. The Martinez family would soon recognize the pain of such disasters.

The taste of revenge would be sweet.

CHAPTER THIRTY-EIGHT

JACKIE

"Will this all work out?" she asked her reflection on her dimming computer screen.

Jackie had noticed subtle changes in her appearance since opening up to Darrin. She was able to smile more genuinely. Granted, the pain was not erased, but it brought about a new clarity. She'd been afraid no one would accept the past she'd so studiously kept hidden for years. She'd feared she was too damaged for another to love. She undoubtedly had Darrin to thank for these changes.

Soon, Darrin's plan would be announced to the entire office. A tizzy of excitement swirled all through her body. She was abuzz with the prospect of her future. Taking a deep breath, she stood from her desk to join everyone else at the staff meeting.

"Good morning, everyone, and thank you for joining us." Darrin spoke from the head of the conference room table.

The long wooden table could seat up to thirty people. Each chair was filled, as well as the space along the walls. The turnout in the conference room was the best they'd gotten at any of their meetings.

The company had the support of several of its partners, who were dispersed throughout the crowd, some of whom had branches of their own businesses in California. They had already expressed their interest in extending their partnership to the new location. Jackie had done some investigating as to who might be good partners for them. She'd done so much to get the new location ready.

"As you know, we'll need a general manager at the new location. We gave careful consideration to who would be best for the position. We need someone with leadership skills. Someone who would not only do what is best for the applicants we assist and the business owners but would also care about Hands, Hearts, and Homes. Without further ado, I would like to announce who will be taking on the general manager position." Darrin paused and looked around the room. "Todd has been chosen to take the position. We will give him a couple months to get things settled here and move out to California."

Todd stood to wave at all the others around the room. Brief murmurs sprang up around the room. Jackie was relieved to see that people quieted the moment Darrin cleared his throat. Several had their gazes fixed on Jackie. She smiled politely at the looks she was getting.

"There will also be a few other changes in people's positions. Jackie," Darrin said, holding her stare, "will be taking on a newly created position. She will now be the vice president of operations." Many faces grew confused. "She will be with me most of the time. We will travel between the two locations, assisting and checking on the overall operations of the business."

Darrin had proposed the idea to her the other morning before work, and she couldn't have been more excited. She was relieved to learn that Darrin and Charles had spoken with Todd about his behavior.

DARRIN

They smiled at one another. Darrin only realized he was staring when his father cleared his throat. Returning his gaze to the room as a whole, he announced that he, Todd, and Jackie would be sorting through all the people who had indicated they were interested in transferring.

"We'll do another meeting such as this one when those people have been selected. In the meantime, Jackie will be going out to the location in California to get things underway. When the situation allows, Todd will go out to join her."

Again, murmurs sprang up around the room. Jackie and Todd joined Darrin and Charles at the head of the table.

"Thank you, everyone, for taking the time to come to this meeting. Does anyone have any questions about the coming weeks?"

Darrin, Jackie, Todd, and Charles spent the next several minutes answering people's questions. The crowd dispersed, and Todd excused himself when he saw one of his staff members wave him over.

"I knew the two of you would figure out a way to make this work," Charles said with a smile. "The two of you heading this company will lead to great things." He patted Darrin on the shoulder on his way out, leaving him and Jackie alone in the conference room.

Darrin turned and took her into his arms. "I'm so glad you accepted my offer of this position. I was nervous to ask you."

"It was a much better outcome than I'd thought could happen." She laced her fingers together at the base of his neck. "I was so distraught to think that no matter what happened, our relationship would suffer. This was a brilliant idea. Judging from what your father just said, this was all your idea, wasn't it?"

He nodded. "I couldn't bear the thought of only spending every two weeks with you—that would never be enough time," he said, brushing her hair away from her face.

He never thought he would consider marrying a woman again after what had happened with Jessica. But here he was, perfectly content, picturing himself with her the rest of his life.

The only problem was the stalker. Darrin had a plan, but they needed to do it just so. Since they were alone, this would be an opportune time to bring it up.

"Jackie, I think I know how we can use that damn bug under your desk," Darrin said, watching Jackie's expression change to anxiety. "We're going to talk about how you're going to go out to California alone, but the real plan will be that I'll go with you."

Jackie nodded slowly. They discussed how they would make it work. Jackie's agreement was hesitant. She didn't want to make herself an easy target. Darrin wanted to give her time to contemplate how the plan would work.

Charles approached them. "Darrin, there are a few items I need you to take care of to get yourself changed over to CEO."

JACKIE

The new plan made butterflies swarm her belly and fear settle into its depths. She hoped their plan to draw out her assailant—whoever it was—would work. The stalker wasn't Todd—Mia had cleared him and was still keeping tabs on him. Jackie was coming around to the idea of Mia keeping watch over people, especially since the police weren't helping much and were still waiting for camera footage. Jackie's inability to locate the garage's file nagged at her. Margie had said she'd never seen it since she began working there.

Harmon was living in Arizona, and Jackie figured if he truly wanted to try something, he would have done it when she was visiting Verity and Porter. Plus, how could he have gained access to her office? Mia couldn't find anything showing Harmon had traveled anywhere in the past several months. And Jackie still believed his physical abuse had been an isolated incident.

She couldn't think of anyone else who would gain anything by her demise. She doubted someone was jealous of Darrin's attention since they hadn't been involved until after the first emails were sent. Looking at him now, she knew she was lucky. She'd escaped so many demons and was blessed to be with this man. He might have gone about a few things in ways she would have preferred he didn't, but she knew the reasoning behind his actions—love. Pure and simple.

What possibilities were left? Someone she'd crossed without realizing it, no doubt. She'd stayed in contact with Tony but still wasn't speaking to her parents. They had no idea she'd even been hospitalized; Tony had promised to keep it to himself. The last thing she wanted was for this to be all over the news.

Back in her office, Jackie took a seat. The itch to check on the listening device under her desk was almost too strong to ignore. She wanted to rip it out of its hiding place, to throw it in the trash, to smash it. She wanted to send a message to show she was not going to give up. This was her life. She was finally happy, and she wanted to keep things that way.

A knock at the door brought her attention back to her current tasks. "Come in."

"Jackie, I want to talk to you about next week." Darrin dropped himself into the chair across from hers. He angled himself to check that the device was still in place then nodded.

"What about next week?"

"Things have changed, and I won't be able to go with you to help with some of the preparations. I'll need you to go ahead of me, and then I'll be along in a day or two."

Jackie could feel anxiety welling up inside her, but this was their first step toward achieving an end. "That'll be fine, Darrin. I don't need you to go everywhere with me," she said with a laugh she hoped would convey more certainty than she felt.

"I'm glad you feel that way. You'll fly out on Saturday, and I'll join you on Tuesday evening."

"Sounds good. Should I book the hotel room, or will you be taking care of that?" She took a sip of water.

He shook his head.

Jackie needed to do something with her shaking hands—they were beginning to sweat. She didn't want to bring attention to it by wiping them on her pant legs as she normally would. She wanted Darrin to know she could handle this. Things were going to be fine. They were going to get through it all—she just knew it.

Smiling, she asked, "Was there anything else you wanted to discuss?"

"Not while we're in the office." Winking, he stood and kissed her on the cheek. "I'll see you at four." Leaving the office, he closed the door securely behind him.

She tried to calm her nerves by taking several slow, steady breaths. Once moderately relaxed, she called Margie into her office.

Chapter Thirty-Nine
The Conspirator

They'd made one fatal mistake—hopefully, it would truly be fatal. The laugh that escaped the conspirator was as cold as the menacing plan coming to life. The plan they'd made in the office was the same as the one they shared with other people, with one small change.

This could prove to be troubling. It might be another of her clever tricks. By flying instead of driving on her last trip, Jackie had ruined what was to be her perfectly planned demise.

The sound of tin being crushed brought the present back into focus.

"That conniving little bitch got the best of me once. I will not let it happen again."

The empty beer can landed in the bin at the far side of the room, and the plan began to develop further. This would be easier to pull off with help. There had to be a way to let some unsuspecting fool alleviate some of the stress of this plan. It would just take some thinking.

"Of course." The conspirator retrieved the burner phone from the end table and dialed. It rang only three times. It was time to put a bit of charm to use.

CHAPTER FORTY

JACKIE

Just as Jackie had feared, the weekend was going by much too fast for comfort. Saturday was all but over, and there was an urgency inside her that made her want to be as close to Darrin as possible. Sensing her nerves, Darrin had been extraordinarily patient with her the last two days. He'd helped her pack what she would need for her trip. They intentionally discussed the solo trip in her office but with misleading details. She would actually be leaving on Monday. It was true that Jackie would be arriving without Darrin, but she wouldn't be alone. Mia and one of her old detective friends would be at the airport to watch for anything suspicious at the time Jackie's flight would have been leaving on Saturday. Thus far, they'd heard nothing.

They'd changed their original plan after Charles told them he needed Darrin to go work on getting names changed for the CEO position. The company's fiscal year was nearly at an end, and Charles wanted everything changed before then.

After her conversation in the office with Darrin, Jackie had called Margie in to ask her if she would like to go out and get lunch together. It was a much-needed rendezvous. The two women hadn't had a chance to do this in several weeks. Over lunch, Jackie asked Margie if she would be willing to go out to the California location with her since Darrin would be detained. The other option would be to have her brother go with her, but with him starting the position he'd been dreaming about, she didn't feel right pulling him away from his opportunity. The last thing she wanted was another reason for her parents to despise her.

Margie had seemed shocked by the idea. She stammered, creating a few excuses, but eventually agreed to go. Jackie was relieved to have the comfort of Margie joining her but did not feel entirely secure. Her fears were manifesting themselves in the form of different desires. She wanted to be with Darrin in the most emotionally intimate of ways.

They had spent all day Saturday outside, going for a walk and having a picnic. The entire time, her mind had been distracted by various fears. The lapses in their conversations were like a birthing ground for her anxieties. The what-ifs played out in her mind at an alarming rate. Each time Darrin's phone went off, she wanted to know if it was Mia with an update.

Pushing her doubts aside, she tried to focus on Darrin. He was lounging on the couch. They'd just finished watching a movie, and she was borderline asleep. She removed the pillow from below his head, holding his head up, then placed his head down on her lap.

"You all right?" he asked.

"I'm fine." Smiling a nervous smile, she couldn't help the way her voice betrayed her.

Darrin sat up and looked into her teary eyes. "If you're not comfortable with this, we can change the plan. You don't have to go at all until I can come with you." He pulled her over to him and draped her smooth legs over his lap.

Laying her head on his shoulder, she let the tears fall. "I want this plan to work. I want the person behind this to get caught. I'm just scared. I'm going to do what needs to be done to get this resolved. I haven't heard anything back from the police yet about the video from the auto garage, and I'm starting to doubt their capabilities." By the time she finished, she was sobbing so hard she was hiccupping.

Darrin's hands tightened around her waist. "I want this finished, Jackie. I hate seeing the fear in your eyes when you look around. I know you think I don't notice it." One hand released her waist and moved to her chin. His gentle touch pulled her gaze up to his. "I haven't said anything, but I know you check the back seat every time we get into the car, and each night, you get up to make sure the doors are locked and the alarm is set. I will continue to do anything I can to ensure your safety." His eyes glistened with the emotions he felt for her.

Jackie felt herself leaning into his lips before she consciously decided to kiss him. She kissed him with urgency. She needed to be with him again before she left. She pressed in closer, deepening the kiss.

He let out a low sound of arousal, which created a warming sensation throughout her body. She removed her legs from his lap and spun around to face him, straddling him. She braced herself against the back of the couch, gripping it on either side of his head. The desire in his eyes matched her own. Jackie could see herself swimming in their depths for the rest of her life. She felt his desire beneath her.

His hands slid up her thighs under her sundress, turning inward. When his thumbs met the border of her lacy underwear, he ran his hands along her thighs to hold her hips. Their kissing intensified. She could feel his hands making their way higher, stopping short when he ran into her belt. Jackie hastily unbuckled it and tossed it across the room. She couldn't help but notice the sly smile spreading across Darrin's face.

"You're not wearing a bra today, are you?" His hands moved farther up her waist.

Jackie's halter top was not conducive to wearing a bra. "I guess you're about to find out." Holding his gaze, she leaned into his hands, allowing her breasts to fill his cupped palms. His gentle touches encouraged her nipples to tighten. A small moan escaped her lips.

"Jackie, you are so damn beautiful." He removed his hands from the inside of her dress and reached around the back then eased the zipper down while Jackie unlatched the strap at the base of her neck. With both released, the front fell away from her breasts.

Darrin muttered some appreciative curses and lifted her breast enough to guide it to his mouth. Jackie arched her back to push herself closer to his lips.

"Can I do something for you?" Darrin asked, smirking.

Feeling slightly embarrassed by her brazenness, she pulled back slightly.

"Don't withdraw. I just like hearing you say what you want." He moved his free hand to her back to bring her back to where she had been.

"I want you to…" Jackie looked down at her breasts, at a loss for words.

"Luckily, it's the same thing I want." He took her distended nipple into his mouth.

Jackie sighed at the feel of the gentle tugging, and a rush of excitement streamed through her body. He let his tongue tickle the delicate tip.

When he released her, she moved to her feet, pulling the dress off. She stood in nothing more than lacy underwear.

Following her lead, Darrin stood and began removing his khaki shorts, revealing his depth of arousal. It matched her own. Jackie watched him as he took off his shirt and discarded it in much the same way she had her belt. She reached out and touched him through his briefs. Holding him tight, she stroked him, encouraging a growl of desire from his lips.

"I think this would feel better if I removed these." His thumbs were in the waistband of his briefs. Stepping back, he lowered them to give way to his erection.

It almost took her breath away. She didn't know why she was being so shy. They'd slept together already. But that night felt different.

Wanting to take charge, she nudged him back down onto the couch. His brows jumped in surprise as she knelt between his feet. His breathing slowed, almost stopping as she took the smooth head of his erection into her mouth.

Darrin released a long breath as she pumped him with one hand and her mouth slid up and down his length. She almost released him from her mouth each time she lifted. Swirling her tongue around the tip, she heard his breathing hitch, and a string of curses dropped from his lips. She continued the slow torture.

"Jackie, fuck, that feels so good. I want to feel your pussy around me now." His demand had her desire building.

She stood to pull her underwear down, but Darrin grabbed her hands to stop her. He stepped out of his briefs, looped his fingers into the elastic around her hips, and lowered her panties to the floor. She stepped out of them just as Darrin lifted her and laid her down on the couch. He knelt down between her legs. The gentle caresses of his tongue caused her breath to catch in her throat. He licked up along her opening. Her orgasm was on the brink of release as he continued his slow course. The moment she thought it couldn't feel any better, he slipped a finger into her. She felt her walls grip his finger.

She gasped. "Darrin."

"It's okay."

"No, I... I want you... I need you inside me." She pulled his face up to look into her eyes. "Please," she begged.

With a smile, he pulled himself up and pressed into her in one fluid motion. The passion she was feeling spread to all edges of her body. Instinctively, she lifted her hips to receive him with each movement. She met each of his thrusts with a greedy thrust of her own.

"You feel so good, Jackie." His earnest words sent her mind into a tornado of joy from both physical and emotional pleasure. She felt herself reaching the brink of her desire.

"I love you," she choked out huskily. They climaxed simultaneously. Then they lay together, enjoying the feel of one another.

DARRIN

"Should one of us get that?"

For a moment, Darrin wasn't sure what she was referring to. But then he heard it—the doorbell. It was one of the things within the house that needed to be upgraded. The quiet chime was hard to hear in the back of the house. With a slow release of breath, he kissed her forehead and tossed the blankets aside.

Hurriedly, he checked the time. Then he retrieved a pair of sweatpants from his dresser and pulled them on. They did little to hide his erection.

"Can we pretend we didn't hear it?" Jackie asked.

"No," he said with a smirk.

She slid out of the bed and pulled on a pair of jeans that had been folded on the chaise lounge, followed by one of Darrin's T-shirts.

"I love seeing you in my shirts," he said with a wink as he went to check the door.

By then, Jackie was in the bathroom, brushing her hair, which was more unruly than usual—their sexual explorations had continued once they got to the bedroom the night before. She wet her brush and tried to smooth it out as much as possible. Turning the water off, she could hear muffled voices in the other room. Curiosity getting the best of her, she ventured out to the living room.

The voices were growing louder as she neared their origin. The only thing she couldn't determine was whether these were happy or angry voices. She all but screamed when she saw who was there.

CHAPTER FORTY-ONE

THE CONSPIRATOR

Everything is packed. I'll meet you at the hotel. That's when you can transfer everything over to me."

Clearly nervous, Stanley was silent.

Finesse. Patience.

"Are you sure about this?" Stanley asked.

"Of course I'm sure. I need you to bring it when you drive over since I can't take it on the plane."

Stanley hated to disappoint anyone, which was why this was a brilliant plan. He would never back out. The conspirator let out an impatient breath to show Stanley he was causing an inconvenience.

"Yes, I'll meet you at the hotel. What time do you think you'll be getting there?"

"Two o'clock. I'll meet you in the parking lot."

With the time and place taken care of, the phone went dead. Stanley wouldn't be allowed much time. He would need to drive almost all night to get there in time. He couldn't be trusted to contemplate the plan any longer. Time to think would lead to doubts.

The fool would be breaking more laws than he likely knew. He was the registered owner of the handgun and would take the fall if everything worked as it should.

Chapter Forty-Two

Jackie

Thank you so much for coming to spend the day with me!" Jackie said, teary-eyed, to Verity and her family.

She'd been completely shocked by Darrin's secret plan. She had not seen it coming. When she got out to the entryway, she discovered that the yelling was the kids asking where Jackie was.

Verity pulled her into one more hug. "He's a good one," she whispered.

"I know," Jackie said with a sad smile.

"He's good for you." Verity smiled as Jackie watched Darrin.

Jackie could feel the blush filling her cheeks. "He really is." She smiled sheepishly. It felt good to admit it out loud. It would still take some time, but she knew she was getting better by the day.

His thoughtfulness touched her. The tears in her eyes were due as much to the love she felt in her soul for the man standing next to her as for her dear friend leaving. She could actually see herself marrying again. She'd never dreamed this day would come.

Turning, she took in Darrin's profile while he wished Porter well on their travels. His strong jawline was relaxed in an easy smile. The girls each gave Darrin a hug, and Annabelle gave him a kiss on his cheek. Her grin overtook her entire face—both girls were completely taken with him.

He'd never really been around kids much but did great with them. He was completely at ease talking or running through the yard with them. They all blended so well.

Jackie felt the relief melting throughout her body, extending to her limbs. She'd been nervous about introducing Darrin to people as her boyfriend and worried about how well he would fit in. She'd thought people would compare him to Harmon, especially Verity and Porter. They'd been a group of four for years. Jackie had been worried they would not welcome a stranger into their pack.

But she realized there was no comparison. She and Harmon hadn't been right for each other. Or maybe they had been for a while, but people changed. She and Harmon had become strangers and no longer had the patience for one another. Her relationship with Darrin was completely different.

Verity, Porter, and the kids left to continue on to Verity's parents' house, a little over an hour away. The empty house felt oddly quiet compared to the sound level of only a few hours earlier.

Sighing, Jackie lay down on the couch. "I always forget how tiring those kids can be." She laughed.

"Is it hard for you?" He slid onto the couch to lie next to her and held her face in one hand.

"Sometimes," she said, nodding slowly. To most people, she would never admit that. She would never want Verity to feel guilty when visiting. She let her eyes roam around the room. "I find myself thinking of who she could have been. Where would she be? Especially when I see people with kids of a similar age."

With his thumb, Darrin wiped away the single tear rolling down her cheek. Then he leaned in and kissed the spot where it had just been. "Jackie, I hope you know you can always talk to me about her. I might not fully understand, but I will always try. I'll always be here for you."

"I can't tell you how much that means to me. Some people pretend I never had her, while others obsess over what could have gone wrong. You're the first to patiently listen. Thank you."

"There's no need to thank me." He smiled with loving sadness etched onto his features. After kissing her again, he pushed himself back off the couch. "Let's get to bed. You've got an early flight in the morning."

Her flight was scheduled to take off at seven. Nodding, she took his offered hand and let him pull her up off the couch. They made their way down the hall arm in arm.

* * *

Morning was there in a flash. She wanted to pull the covers over her head and hide. Instead, she swung her legs to the floor and prepared for travel. The day had a drastically different tone to it than the previous one.

This was almost dispiriting. She couldn't shake the feeling that she would never be coming back here again. She took a shower and got dressed in a trancelike state.

Jackie didn't notice much about the morning. Everything felt like it was happening to someone else, not to her. She couldn't ease the terrible anxiety she was feeling. This despair surely could not last all day. But it would be the first time in weeks she would go somewhere without Darrin.

She wouldn't be alone, Jackie tried to remind herself. But she would not be with the one she needed. Trying to look brave, she plastered a smile on her face when she got to the kitchen. Darrin was waiting with a cup of coffee made up for her.

She took it without making eye contact. Looking at him would pull the stabilizing brick from the wall holding back her tears. Mumbling her thanks, she took her coffee to the bar and sat down. Staring into the depths of the liquid, she thought of backing out. *What will I do if the stalker decides to show up at the airport, the hotel, or anywhere in California?* True, she wouldn't be alone, but something felt off. She wondered if she should have called Tony.

The anxieties building inside her middle were wreaking havoc all over her body. Her hands were clammy and sweaty. Her eyes were stinging with unshed tears. Her mind was spinning with the fears that swam around in its depths. Her breathing was labored. *Is this a panic attack?*

The coffee in her hands almost fell to the counter. The feel of Darrin's hands on her shoulders had almost broken all her composure.

"Jackie, if you don't want to go without me, please don't feel you have to."

His whispered plea made her want to back out even more.

"It's one day. I'll be all right." Her voice made her words ring through the house, and she did not sound all right. Everything about her felt brittle. She cleared her throat. "Margie will be with me. I'm sure I'll be just fine."

"I can get an earlier flight if you need me to." His steely-blue eyes conveyed their concern.

Touched, she laid her hand on the hand still resting on her shoulder. She could feel his strength transferring to her. She needed to do this. She needed to know she could handle being alone. It would be impossible for them to be together every moment.

Taking a deep breath, she slid off her stool. "Ready?"

He took her hand and led her out to the car. Her bag was loaded in the back.

The drive to the airport was quiet. Both knew words would do little to change the tension and stress in the air. Each was afraid that if they moved too fast, the balloon would pop, and neither wanted to risk damaging the delicate balance.

"Why don't you just drop me off at the curb?" she said.

"You don't want me to come in?"

Looking down at her nails, Jackie fidgeted. "I do, but I know it will be harder to leave if you come in with me."

He reached over, took, one of her hands, and gave it a gentle squeeze.

"I love you, Jackie."

"I love you."

After unfastening her seat belt with more care than necessary, she got out and pulled her bag from the back.

* * *

She found Margie waiting at the security check. That was where she'd agreed to meet Jackie. Margie was checking her watch when Jackie caught up to her. She knew flying was Margie's least favorite way to travel. She felt bad putting her in the position of having to do so.

"Jackie, there you are," she said, smiling with relief.

"Sorry to keep you waiting. Shall we?" Jackie asked, tipping her head to indicate the security check-in.

They made it through security without a problem and settled into their seats. It was only going to be a few hours on this plane, and then they would get on their connecting flight in Phoenix. Jackie wished that for Margie's comfort, she'd been able to find a nonstop flight.

"Do you want anything for your nerves?" Jackie hoped her expression conveyed her concern.

Margie shook her head. Her eyes looked far away. Her expression was tenser than Jackie had ever seen, her jaw was firm, and her brows were furrowed.

DARRIN

"Mia, what do you have?" Darrin asked, letting himself into his office.

"Darrin, this is the third time I've tried calling," she nearly shouted.

"Sorry. I didn't know. I was running some errands after I dropped Jackie off."

"Fuck," Mia panted. "Has her flight left?"

The question had bile rising in Darrin's throat as his stomach filled with boulders. "It left almost two hours ago. She should be getting ready to board her connecting flight soon."

"Darrin, I found out who went missing—the person who worked at the garage Jackie took her car to." She was talking so fast Darrin hardly understood what she was saying. "He's in the hospital at the moment, with a gunshot wound."

"Do you know who shot him? Who is he?"

"They tracked the firearm back to a man who is deceased. The last person it was registered to was Dale Kennison. Do you recognize the name?"

"No."

"Well, I looked into him while I was trying to call you. He was severely injured while working as a subcontractor before he died."

"I don't understand why this matters!" Darrin barked. He wanted the important facts now.

"I'm getting there," Mia scolded. "He was working on a building for Jackie's father's company when it first started. It was her father's building he was in when he got hurt. The family tried to sue."

Darrin felt the boulders sink deeper into the depths of his stomach. He remained silent while Mia explained everything she'd found. While talking with her, he messaged Tony, telling him to try to call Jackie and tell her not to board the flight.

He finished his call with Mia and was racing out the door when his phone rang again.

"We've been able to locate and identify the young man who rerouted Ms. Martinez's exhaust. Is she with you? It's imperative we speak to her," Officer Thompson said. "I've tried her cell phone with no answer."

"She's on a flight to California right now." The breath in Darrin's lungs felt insufficient. He could feel a tightening in his chest.

"Is she alone?"

"No. Her assistant went with her."

The officer had made a sound like he was concerned. Darrin didn't feel that was a good thing.

"Lucas Kennison has been working for someone else. I've just left his room at the hospital. He told me everything. Jackie is not safe. I need to know what airport she's flying into and what hotel she's staying at."

Darrin listed off all the information the officer asked for, omitting the fact that he already knew the man's name. He could feel the panic-induced adrenaline coursing through his body. He needed to get to Jackie. He checked his watch. He had ten minutes to meet Tony.

"You can't do anything crazy, Mr. Dominic."

"You just told me the woman I love is in life-threatening danger, and you tell me not to do anything crazy? If anything fucking happens to her, crazy is exactly what I'm going to be. Now, get off the damn phone with me and do something."

After hanging up, Darrin made one more quick phone call and rushed out of his office. Without stopping to speak to anyone, he ran out of the building, got into his car, and started driving. He was amazed he wasn't pulled over. He sped the whole way and had no idea if he'd stopped at any of the traffic stops along the way.

He got himself to the appointed place with only seconds to spare. Everything inside of him was spinning. The dreaded thoughts tangled around one another. His organs felt like they had gotten snarled together. He should have stopped her. Told her to wait for him. What a foolish plan.

The one person he'd never suspected...

JACKIE

"Margie, are you okay?" Jackie asked, concerned.

"I hate flying."

"I remembered that just this morning."

"It's fine. Let's just get to the hotel and get things settled."

Jackie drove to the hotel. It was the same one she and Darrin had stayed in on her first trip to California. The nostalgia sent a pang of sadness through her.

They drove in silence. It was evident Margie needed some time for her own thoughts. "Why don't you stay in the car?" Jackie suggested. "I'll go in and get the room set up, and then we can go get something to eat."

"That would be great," Margie said with a subdued nod.

Jackie made her way to the front desk and noticed the same young girl was working the counter as the first time she'd checked in. After retrieving her room key, she took their bags up to the room. She tried to be vigilant as she went, watching the movements of those around her.

She'd been so absorbed in her own thoughts and feelings that she hadn't taken the time to consider how Margie might feel about going on this trip. Jackie dropped their bags onto the small sofa and returned to the elevator. Checking her pockets, she realized she'd left her phone in the car. She intended to text Darrin to let him know they landed. The time between their flights was so short she hadn't bothered turning her phone on in between landing and getting to the rental car.

Exiting the elevator, she was waved down by the young woman at the front desk. "Ms. Martinez? Were you able to answer the call I just sent up?"

"No, I must have missed it." Jackie furrowed her brows in confusion.

The girl looked concerned. "I don't know if I can pull the call back to the desk. The man sounded very concerned and said he needed to speak with you." She fiddled with the cord to the phone sitting next to her. As she was lifting her hand away, it rang again.

"I'm sorry, sir, you've got a bad connection. She's actually standing right here."

Jackie accepted the extended receiver. "Jackie Martinez." Her eyes narrowed with concentration. The caller was nearly impossible to understand, although she recognized his voice instantly.

The only words she understood were "stay" and "Margie." There was far too much background noise for Jackie to understand him.

"Tony, I can't hear you. I'll stay with Margie. Don't worry. Are you with Darrin?" She paused to listen. "Tony, are you there?"

Not hearing a reply, she handed the phone back to the front-desk clerk. She was torn about what to do next. She'd told Margie she would be right back, but there was something off with her brother. *What was he trying to say?*

Taking a glance at the parking lot, she decided she should go back out to Margie. She said goodbye to the clerk and went out to the parking lot. Settling back into the driver's seat, she asked Margie if she would like to go see the new location first or if she wanted to get something to eat. She would make sure to turn her phone on when she got back out to the car.

"I'd love to see the new building."

"Good. I haven't seen it in a while and can't wait to see what's been done to it." Putting the odd conversation with her brother into the back of her mind, she pulled out onto the busy streets of San Diego. "Margie, do you see my phone in my purse?" Jackie asked as they drove.

"No, I don't. Maybe you put it in your suitcase. I thought I saw you tuck it into the front pocket."

Jackie furrowed her brow, concentrating on her actions of the day. She didn't remember that, but it was certainly possible. Now that she had a replacement, she hated not having her phone but decided she would be okay for a few minutes without it. Before dinner, she would go back to the hotel to find it.

When they arrived, Jackie was surprised to see that the cable company wasn't there. She'd thought they would be setting up the last of the communication equipment that day, but she and Margie would have the building to themselves. It would be a good opportunity for them to talk.

They entered the building, and Jackie gave Margie a full tour. "Oh, I almost forgot—there's a full gym downstairs." She ran down the last two flights of stairs. "The gym was something Darrin was excited about. It will help employees, and the community will have an affordable gym," she said excitedly.

Flipping on the lights, she turned to Margie to remark upon the advantages of having all the exercise equipment available to the employees. The look on Margie's face ended all other thoughts. She looked angry. No, worse than that—she looked deranged. Jackie had only seen someone's face look like that one other time, and that encounter had ended with her getting slapped in the face.

"Margie, are you all right?"

"Just fine." Her voice sounded strange, hollow, crude. "But I do wonder. Do you remember a man named Dale Kennison? He worked for your father many years ago." As she spoke, she was slowly encroaching on Jackie.

A fear flooded through Jackie that she hadn't known she could feel. She backed into the room, trying to be conscious of all the equipment around her. She tried to speak but realized her mouth was too dry. Her heart was beating faster than she'd ever thought possible.

"No? Well, you see, he was my husband."

With a sharp intake of breath, Jackie remembered. Her breathing continued to be short and clipped.

Margie's husband had been one of Jackie's father's electrical subcontractors. *How did I not recognize the name when I hired her?* She thought back to those days. *Dale's wife was not named Margie. But what was it?*

"Catherine." Jackie didn't realize she'd spoken aloud until she heard a hard, cold laugh erupt from Margie's lips. The sound was ominous and had Jackie's hands moistening as she clasped and unclasped them.

Margie's husband had been injured while working on one of her father's buildings more than twenty years ago. They'd known it was going to be a difficult project. The building needed to be completely gutted. In the first few days of construction, they were pulling up the flooring on the first floor, and dark markings on the plywood indicated the damage below the linoleum tiles. Hoping it was only the plywood that was damaged, they began the time-consuming process of removing each piece. Several men were working on this project while Dale was in the basement, checking on the breaker box and the wiring. No one was supposed to be in the basement in the event that something fell.

Everything happened at the exact same time. As Dale was making his way out of the basement, one of the contractors stepped on one of the damaged beams. It gave way, breaking through the tile ceiling in the basement. Dale was immediately below, and the broken beam caught him in the back of the head at the base of the neck. His hard hat did little to protect him.

Dale was knocked to the floor by the inertia of the beam and weight of the other man. He landed face down on the concrete floor, knocked unconscious. The suddenness and seriousness of the situation caught each person off guard. The foreman ran to the basement and, immediately realizing the dangers of the situation, he called emergency services.

The blow to the head resulted in a fractured skull and severe bleeding. Dale was rushed into emergency surgery. All this was done in a matter of hours; however, the damage had been done. Dale was in a coma for weeks, and when he awoke, he had severe brain damage. He was never the same.

"I was forced to get a job to support Dale and our three young children." Margie's hollow tone sent a chill up Jackie's spine. She stepped closer still, nearly backing Jackie up against a weight bench. "I never wanted kids, but Dale did, and I loved him, so I did it. Now I was stuck with three little leaches and a worthless husband."

Jackie felt a pang of sadness for all Margie and her family had endured.

"After Dale died, I returned to my maiden name and started going by my middle name. I didn't want anyone to be able to attach me to the horrid accident. I didn't want anyone's pity," she spat.

Margie's smile was that of a murderer, not the sweet woman Jackie had thought she was working with. Jackie's eyes shifted to a pistol Margie had removed from her handbag while talking. Her heart leapt to her throat; panic raced through her, clouding her thoughts.

"Now, I promised my Dale that I would get revenge for his murder," she said, her voice growing louder at the last word.

"Dale wasn't murdered!" cried Jackie. "That was a terrible, unthinkable accident. Margie, look at me. My father never would have asked any of those men to work in that building had he known about the damage."

The glint in Margie's eyes showed she was not about to change her mind. Those eyes held nothing but hate. Jackie looked from Margie to the stairwell they just descended. The only other possible exit was one of the small windows at the top of the concrete walls or the elevator. There was no way Jackie would have time to wait for the elevator or climb out one of those windows.

Wiping her hands on her pants, Jackie began to inch around the bench behind her.

Ignoring Jackie's response, Margie continued. "At first, I didn't know what I would do, but I kept tabs on you. I watched from a distance. You went to college, got married, and then got pregnant. I waited outside the hospital when you left, but to my astonishment, there was no baby."

Margie's nonchalance while talking about Jackie's lost child caused an ache in Jackie's chest. The woman's complete disregard for the pain associated with the loss was a brutal slap of reality. Of her utter instability.

"I was curious, so I called the hospital and inquired if you were still in the hospital and how the baby was. But all they would tell me was you had just left. So I stayed to see if you would be going back to the hospital—maybe the baby was being kept for monitoring. But you didn't come back."

Jackie stared at her in disbelief, wondering how the woman who had shown her so much care and commitment could be capable of this. Jackie's throat was constricting. Her thoughts raced, but her movements were sluggish as she staggered farther back, maneuvering farther around the bench behind her. Beyond the bench was a rack of weights.

"I began to think maybe this was the punishment your family deserved after what happened to my family, my husband. But how could it be?"

Tears threatened to spill out of her eyes. "You hadn't spent years at that child's side, encouraging it to follow its dreams. You didn't take care of that child when he became mentally incapacitated!" she shouted then continued at a near whisper. "No, there needed to be something more. Something to make your father suffer as I did. I began to make my plans. I kept close watch on you. You got divorced and finished your education shortly thereafter. I waited. Patiently. Until I could get a job right next to you."

"How could you do this, Margie? It's not too late to change your mind. Let's talk this out," Jackie pleaded, her voice cracking. In a moment when she needed strength, she felt like everything was failing her. She couldn't speak—couldn't find a way to get herself out of this. Her best bet was to get to the rack of weights and throw one at Margie.

"It's too late for me. I lost the love of my life, and my children lost a loving father. Maybe your father will think twice about his decisions when he loses his precious baby." She took a few steps closer to Jackie.

Hearing the metallic click of the firearm, Jackie panicked. Sweat was streaming down her face and ribs, and her hands shook uncontrollably. She couldn't move her feet. They felt like they were trapped in concrete. Her brain was screaming at her to move, run, defend herself. But she couldn't.

Chapter Forty-Three
DARRIN

Darrin could hear Jackie pleading with Margie to change her mind. He silently crept down the last few steps. He was afraid if he made too much noise, it would alert Margie to his intrusion.

He'd flown to California with Tony in his father's jet. He'd remembered Tony saying Darrin should let him know if he ever wanted to take a ride in one. They'd cut the travel time by close to an hour and a half thanks to not needing to make any stops along the way. The air on the flight had felt suffocating.

They landed at an airport close to the new office, and Tony tried to call Jackie but had terrible reception. Darrin had a hunch Jackie would want to go to the new building.

Seeing the rental car in the lot sent a mixture of emotions flowing through his body—relief that he'd found her and panic that he might be too late. It was the only car there. Dread filled his soul. He snuck around the first floor until he could hear the voices coming from the gym. He'd motioned to Tony before descending the stairs, and Tony had split off to call the police.

Stepping down onto the floor, he was thankful for the quiet approach the foam covering allowed him. He raised the pistol he'd removed from his closet earlier. He was an excellent marksman, but he didn't like coming up behind Margie with Jackie directly in front of her. He hoped Jackie would see him and control her reactions.

Their eyes connected. He motioned for Jackie to drop at his signal. When he nodded, Jackie dropped to the floor. Startled, Margie shouted as Darrin fired.

The shot hit its target, directly in the back of her calf. She fell, keeping a grip on her own gun. Her deranged eyes shifted angrily between Darrin and Jackie.

"Margie!" Darrin called. "Think about what you're doing. What about Lucas?"

"He was a fucking traitor," she spat. The blood was pooling around her, and the sight was sickening. "He proved to be useful for a while." Margie shrugged, turning back to Jackie.

"He's still alive." Darrin was desperate to keep her attention on him. He strained his ears for sirens, anything. Officer Thompson was supposed to be in contact with someone here.

"No, he's not. I shot him just like I'm going to shoot—"

"He is—that's how we found out it was all you," Darrin rushed to say.

He watched Margie's breathing accelerate. Her arms tensed, and her grip on the firearm increased. Her fingers were turning white. Jackie was crawling to get behind the rack of weights at her back.

With one last look at Darrin, Margie raised her gun, directing it at Jackie.

"Jackie, take cover!" he shouted just as the shots were fired, Darrin getting his shot in before Margie could take proper aim. Margie fell again, the red pool surrounding her growing substantially.

Darrin rushed to Jackie. The blood pouring from her upper arm was shocking. Margie had taken her shot at the same time Darrin had taken his. He tore the shirt from his body and was tying it around her arm as Tony leapt down the stairs. Tony paused as he looked between Darrin and Jackie and then Margie lying motionless. He knelt at Darrin's side.

"Jackie," Tony whispered, pulling her hand into his. "Police are on their way."

Darrin, knowing Jackie was in good hands, rose to his feet. He looked at Margie. The thought of killing someone was a hard pill to swallow, but he needed to know. Feeling for a pulse, he was met with nothing but lukewarm skin. Bile rose in his throat.

He was numb. He'd ended someone's life.

Jackie rested against her brother's chest, her eyes wide. The thought that she could have been killed was going to haunt him for years to come. *Why did I never suspect Margie?* That would also haunt him, but the fact was she'd never given anyone a reason to suspect her.

He was making his way back over to Jackie when he heard the sirens.

"We should get her upstairs," Darrin whispered. He was unblinking, and his breathing was erratic. He'd hoped it wouldn't come to this.

* * *

Jackie was loaded into the ambulance. She hadn't uttered a word since Darrin had arrived—since his initial shot at Margie. While Jackie's wound wasn't life-threatening, it still needed treatment.

Tony drove him to the hospital and, once they were there, spent the first several minutes on the phone with his parents. Numb to everything going on around him, Darrin sat with his head in his hands. He was still partially disoriented when the doctor came into the waiting room to retrieve Tony. After hastily rising to his feet, Darrin followed the men down the hall. There was blood on the arms of his scrubs. Jackie's blood. They entered the room to find Jackie sitting, propped up by pillows and the incline of the bed.

Putting on a brave face, she tried to smile for them. Tony looked as if he might pass out. Ruffling his sister's hair, he said something into her ear and kissed her forehead. Then he sat down in the chair next to her bed. Tony let out a deep breath, pressing his thumb and index finger into his eyes. Darrin wondered if he was struggling with the same what-ifs.

Stepping closer to Jackie's bed, Darrin desperately wanted to pull her into a hug but settled for taking her hand and sitting next to her on the edge of the bed. "Jackie, I am so sorry." This was all his fault. He had figured their ruse would throw the stalker off, not give her direct access.

"You couldn't have known it was her. I had no idea, and I worked next to her for a year." Her voice was low, strained. "How did you know?"

"She was using her son at the auto garage you took your car to. He was the stalker we saw here on the first trip. He was the one that rerouted your exhaust. When he got sick of it and refused to help Margie anymore, she tried to kill him. He awoke in the hospital this morning and told the police everything when they were questioning him about getting shot."

Tears welled up in Jackie's eyes. "That's terrible. That poor boy," she said weakly.

Darrin wasn't surprised by the compassion she easily felt for this man. He nodded. "I guess she began resenting all the kids while they were growing up. The youngest, Lucas, took it the worst. She made it evident every day that she didn't want them. Lucas's older siblings had cut all contact with Margie after they'd grown up, leaving Lucas alone in the lion's den."

Darrin filled her in on all the details he'd learned from Mia. She'd called to pass on all the information on his way to the new office building. She hadn't wanted him to be ill prepared.

He could see the fatigue Jackie was fighting, while he was fighting his own problems. He knew he'd had to kill Margie to save Jackie, but guilt was still wrapping itself around the relief he felt. "Get some rest, my love. I'll be here when you wake."

Giving him one more weak smile, she closed her eyes.

CHAPTER FORTY-FOUR

EPILOGUE—2 MONTHS LATER

"I can't believe you did all this for me." Jackie looked around at all the smiling faces in the conference room. Everyone from the New Mexico office had traveled to California to help with the finishing touches.

She'd initially been worried that people would think she'd slept her way to the top. She'd voiced the concerns to Darrin when he suggested the creation of a new position for them to always work together.

"Jackie, if you don't take this position, I am going to offer you the GM position."

"Really?" She was skeptical of his confidence in her. She'd been a mess since he'd started getting to know her. She wanted to assure him that her life wasn't usually this complicated.

"My father wanted you for that position too. He wanted you for the position before I did. I'll admit I wasn't sure in the beginning. That's why he wanted you to go scope out the locations."

Darrin had laughed at the idea.

Shaking her head, Jackie brought herself back to the moment. She found everyone's concern for her touching. Taking another look around the conference room, she had to do a double take. Her parents were in the back, smiling proudly.

After the incident with Margie, they'd put their thoughts of her future to the side and rushed to California. Tony had called them from the hospital waiting room and told them everything that had happened over the past months. Jackie was shocked to see them be more supportive than ever. When they arrived at the hospital, they'd taken turns apologizing for their last meal together. Her mother was still difficult to talk to, but her father made a point of checking in on her at least once a week. It was strange and hard to get used to, but they clearly wanted to be part of her life.

Everyone had expressed their willingness to help. The months had passed with so many adjustments. Although she was the one behind everything, Jackie still half expected to see Margie at the New Mexico office.

The condolences and congratulations extended to Jackie lasted for several hours. When people finally began to dwindle, she excused herself to have some alone time. Exhausted and still experiencing pain whenever she moved her right arm too much, she needed a break. Which could be highly inconvenient, considering she was right-handed. She would need to rely on the people around her more than she was used to.

Darrin found her as she was gazing out one of the large windows in their office. It was a stunning room, with desks situated on one side and a simple sitting area with four armchairs and a small coffee table on the other.

"This is amazing," Jackie said, tearing up as she self-consciously ran her hand over the concave mark on her arm. The bullet had caused large amounts of bleeding and had required stiches. The mark left behind would forever be a reminder of how close she'd come to losing her life. Looking at Darrin, she could see he was still healing from his own scars. He'd begun seeing a therapist. Jackie was happy to see that there was more life in his eyes.

Dipping his head, Darrin kissed the indentation on her arm. "I love you, Jackie."

"I love you."

"I have one last surprise for you today. I know it's been a long day, but this will be quick." He paused. "I hope." He removed a small deep-blue box from his pocket then got down on one knee and flipped open the lid.

ABOUT THE AUTHOR

E. Lynn has loved reading since her mother read books to her as a child. Something about being able to get lost in a book took hold of her imagination. It was not until the pandemic, spending long days and weeks at home, did she begin writing. She found a release in letting out the ideas that clogged her mind. As one story swam to the surface others would find their way into the pool of possibilities. With many more novel ideas on the horizon, E. Lynn hopes to pull people in with her own stories of love, loss, and suspense.

She has lived in Vermont her entire life but has enjoyed traveling with her husband. They hope to do much more traveling when their children are older. So, until the day she can wake up and walk out to the beach each morning she will live vicariously through her characters.

If you have enjoyed this book, please follow E. Lynn on her various social media accounts for more author content.

Facebook: Author E. Lynn

Instagram: @e.lynn.author

TikTok: E.Lynn

ALSO BY E. LYNN

The Depth Series

    The Depth of Their Scars

    The Depth of Their Regrets (Fall of 2025)

    The Depth of Their History (Fall of 2026)

Holiday/Seasonal Romantic Comedies

Spring In My Step

Bazaar Holiday (Late 2025)

Fall in Love with Paris (TBD)

Crime Drama/Thriller

Roadrunner Motel

Trial of The Roadrunner Motel

Romantic Suspense

If I Had Been There

ACKNOWLEDGEMENTS

A grateful Thank You to all the editors and proofreaders at Red Adept Editing. These patient and understanding editors have helped me to see what I need to do to improve my future novels. The help I received was invaluable. Because this was my first novel, there was a lot to learn—there were more red markups than I think I have ever seen in one document. Perhaps in the future, I will be able to send in manuscripts that receive far less red.

I would also like to give special thanks to my sisters and mother for being my beta readers. I am sure they could feel my anxieties as I asked them multiple times if they were sure they wanted to read my writing. I suppose in a way, it is almost always easier to ask someone you don't know to read your work. Asking people who know you and your personality makes it all the more nerve wracking. At least, for me it was. So to my mother and sisters, thank you for being open-minded and making me feel comfortable enough to share my work with you. I will never be able to thank you enough for your feedback, support, and patience with me throughout this process.

So, again, I say thank you to you all for all your encouragement, critical eyes, and feedback. Fingers crossed that there will be fewer "oopsies" in the next one.